STRANGELY
FUNNY VII

MYSTERY AND HORROR, LLC
CLEARWATER, FL

STRANGELY FUNNY VII
COPYRIGHT© 2020 MYSTERY AND HORROR, LLC
CLEARWATER, FL

EDITED BY SARAH E GLENN

ISBN-13: 978-1-949281-13-2

ACKNOWLEDGEMENTS

There are a number of people without whom this book would not have been possible. First and foremost, we want to thank the loyal readers who love and buy these stories. Anthologies are one of the few sources left for short fiction. Mystery and Horror, LLC is very proud of being able to provide an outlet for the short stories we enjoy. The fact that those stories have found a home on your bookshelf is humbling. We could not have kept the series going without your support.

Sarah and I also want to thank all our authors. Some of you are regular contributors to the series. After eight volumes of *Strangely Funny*, you're old friends whose stories we look forward to seeing each year. Others are making their first appearance in these humorous tales of the paranormal. Welcome to the club. Whether a first-time visitor or a regular contributor, your stories are appreciated. While nobody is getting rich off writing these strange little tales, readership is growing. We have reached the point of sending royalties to some of our authors. That milestone means we can keep the series going as we work toward the day when we can offer a better advance.

As always, a special thank you goes out to Kathy Glenn. Her love and support mean the world to us.

TABLE OF CONTENTS

The Arrogance of Angels
by Jonathan Shipley

"So, what did you see when you died?" I asked Rhonda as I faced ten-dollar bills in the cash drawer.

In the teller station beside me, Rhonda gave a shrug. "Hard to explain. It doesn't really translate into words. I don't even try anymore."

She made it sound as though her near-death experience was long-distance, but it had only been last month. In an era of media frenzy, however, a month could be a lifetime. I'm sure she had been badgered relentlessly when released from the hospital after her successful/unsuccessful surgery. Hard to call it successful when the patient died; hard to call it unsuccessful when the patient was back living her life. I'd read about it and promptly journeyed to Chicago to follow up at a branch of BankUSA. It wasn't hard to land a teller position and insinuate myself into the station next to her. After a week of small talk, we were at the point where she felt comfortable talking to me, and I could ask about the near-death event. Call it professional curiosity.

"So, no bright white light or streets of gold?" I prompted. I knew what happened to people when they died, but dying and coming back was something different. Especially interesting were those who came back with healing powers or prophetic visions—as though the Celestial Court wanted to communicate with the Earth below. But it was just as likely all near-death incidents were mistakes that no one wanted to 'fess up to.

Rhonda shook her head. "Definitely no streets. There was a light, but it could have been the overhead lighting in the operating room. I seemed to be floating on the ceiling. At the same time, I was sensing odd things, like a door open to somewhere else with stuff leaking through.

And suddenly there was this overpowering smell of rainwater-peach and a voice spoke, though I can't recall the words."

That sounded as if she had accidentally died—that is to say, died without being on The List and so got popped back into her body as soon as somebody noticed. But that was unusually sloppy for Death, who ran a lean, efficient operation. But no healing, no prophesying. Just a middle-aged woman with bleached hair returning to work after a blood clot removal and carrying on as if nothing had happened. But she remembered specific details, which piqued my interest.

You would think that if her death were a mistake—yes, Death made so many mistakes—that she would have been wiped of memories. But that hadn't happened. So, there had to be a paranormal plan in the works. If she could just describe more of the experience, I might be able to piece together the clues, figure out which entity was behind it.

"Strap of twenties?" Blitz, the teller on the other side of me, asked.

I sighed at the non sequitur and dug a bundle out of my cash drawer in exchange for the twenty hundred-dollar bills he was offering me. Blitz was a little odd himself, over and above the name. He was youngish; Nordic blonde hair with a deep olive complexion; and big-boned for an overall height of at least six-four. And a strange vibe, though deciphering Rhonda's near-death was more interesting. There is so much strangeness in the world that you must pick and choose—or ignore all of it entirely, which is smarter but boring. There are lots of unusual beings in circulation trying to quietly pass as human. If you want deep-muscle massages and chocolate strawberries and Internet shopping, the modern world requires it. All of which is the long way of saying Blitz probably wasn't quite human, but I didn't care.

I turned back to Rhonda. "How long did it last? Did one moment feel like eternity?"

She nodded. "I hadn't thought about that before, but—"

At first I assumed she was pausing for dramatic effect, but when nothing issued from her half-open mouth for long seconds, I knew it was something more. Glancing around the lobby, I saw patrons frozen in the act of walking, bankers frozen in the act of greeting clients, doors frozen in the act of closing. Someone had stopped time locally, which implied a very short list of possibilities.

Keeping my body rigid, I panned my eyes right to left, searching for anomalies. And right beside me, Blitz continued to count the twenties I had just handed him. He was even odder than I had guessed.

I subtly snagged notepaper, scribbled, "Pretend you are frozen" in quick letters, and shoved it along the counter. He glanced at it, then around the room, eyes widening as he realized what was happening. I tapped the note impatiently. He wasn't pretending well. He got the message and stopped moving. Only his eyes remained animated.

It was a waiting game. Fortunately, it was also a game of patience, and entities that employ time manipulation are seldom very patient. But Blitz didn't know that, and the pretense of being frozen wore on him. I gave an encouraging flick of the finger a few times. Finally, I noticed a flicker of movement. A moment later, three of them stepped from elsewhere into the lobby. Angels. Robes and wings and all. Well, damn.

One of them took a position in the corner with head bowed and fingertips touching. Maintaining the little time bubble, I guessed, and it didn't improve my mood. If it took three of them for a simple intervention, then these were very low-level angels. The kind that meddled when they shouldn't because they didn't know any better.

The other two started noiselessly prowling, inspecting each frozen person by sniffing at them. So, it was a smell that had attracted them here. Who did that point to? Rhonda? Death left a bit of scent, but why would angels be tracking her … unless her return was a mistake to be set aright. But that felt peculiar. Rhonda was only interesting in a small way, not at the celestial level. That left Blitz.

I gave my right-hand neighbor a quick glance and saw he was having a hard time. His hands had started trembling, and a bead of sweat was making its way down his cheek. I indulged myself in a little sniff and did detect a scent I'd smelled a long time ago. Good scent, bad scent? I couldn't be sure. It was hard to keep track over long reaches of time.

These angels were going to sniff Blitz out in the very near future … unless I did something. That was a bigger "unless" than you might think, because I am basically non-interventionist. The world turns, people live and die, and entities like me need to stay out of petty, century-to-century issues. The alternative is the biggest mess imaginable. But in this case, I was waffling. It wasn't that I was fond of Blitz—barely knew him—but I was particularly unfound of meddlesome angels. So, I waffled as the two angels sniffed around the bank lobby. Smarter to stay out of things, I kept telling myself.

Then I heard one of the hunters murmur, "That Nephilim has to be close."

Nephilim? No wonder I couldn't place the scent. The last Nephilim I had encountered had been in ancient Egypt before the pyramids. Supposedly they had all been hunted down and destroyed, but apparently not. And to top it off, I would have bet money that Blitz was not at all old as I reckoned time. If he was young, it meant that very recently some angel had procreated a child through a forbidden union with a human woman. The Celestial Court must be going wild to fix the abomination right under its nose.

This was interesting on several levels. I decided to intervene. I began typing on my computer keyboard. In that frozen, soundless lobby, the little clicks were deafening. I had both prowling angels at my stretch of counter within half a second. They sniffed at me, then frowned.

"Too much cologne?" I asked with feigned innocence. "Deposit or withdrawal?"

"What?" one of them responded in confusion. "Neither."

"A new account, then. Can I assume the two of you are partners in an LGBT sense?"

They blinked at each other. "Do you not see the wings?" one demanded.

"LGBTW, then," I shot back. Oh, I was being wicked, but low-level angels deserve it.

One of them whipped his hand through the air and a flaming sword appeared in his palm. "Do you know what this is?" he demanded smugly.

What was this—the Garden of Eden all over again in a bank lobby? "A phallic substitute?" I suggested archly.

The angel's smugness faded. "You play a dangerous game, creature. You should hold your tongue with your betters."

My betters? No low-level angel was my better in any reality I was familiar with. But I managed to keep my mouth shut.

"And unless you want a taste of the sword in your flesh," the angel continued, "you will tell us what we require."

Hard to do when holding my tongue, I thought impishly, but didn't say it. Low-levels had no sense of humor and were always full of themselves. Sooner or later that would piss me off, and those moments never ended well. I needed to get these fools out of my face.

"My flesh will not have a taste of your sword," I said coolly, "because that is not within your mandate. Low-ranking angels cannot kill at will ... unless of course you're going rogue."

Both angels stiffened as if goosed. "Rogue" was a trigger word in the angelic vocabulary. Going rogue implied gross disobedience worthy of being hunted down and destroyed by the celestial hosts. It was a word that slapped independent thinkers back into line, made everyone into company clones.

"Hardly the case," he said tightly and withdrew the sword. With another air snap, it disappeared. "We have no mandate concerning you, merely for the Nephilim. But you would be wise to keep from coming to our attention."

With a rushing of wind, the three of them disappeared. Time clicked in and people continued their business. Blitz gave a great sigh of relief and collapsed onto the counter. Well, this was a pickle.

Nephilim had supposedly been hunted out of existence, though some clever ones might have survived. But their scent was usually their undoing. In very ancient days, there had been great Nephilim kingdoms in ancient Africa. Interesting times, those ancient days. That was before the Celestial Court had decided on abomination status for their inconvenient offspring.

A hand tapped mine. Blitz was staring at me with mad eyes. "What the hell?" he asked in a low voice. "Angels? Time stopping? Flaming swords?"

"Not here," I murmured back. Maybe not anywhere. Maybe it was time to forget the recently dead Rhonda and move on to another life. I didn't need to get involved in a Nephilim hunt.

"So much in my life has never made any sense. And now angels?"

My eyes narrowed. "You sound naïve. How old are you really?"

"Twenty-eight," he shrugged.

"Is that truly twenty-eight, or the appearance of twenty-eight but actually much older?"

"Twenty-eight," he repeated.

Blitz sounded so lost, I felt sorry for him. "All right, here's a survival tip. You know that you're the Nephilim the angels are hunting, right?"

He nodded. "I've had clues all my life that I was something weird like that. But I don't understand what's happening."

"Well, understand this—low-level angels cannot land the first blow in any confrontation. If you don't fight, they are stymied."

"Okay, so they can't attack, but I'm still screwed if I'm frozen in time," he pointed out. Then he said the words: "Will you help me?"

I grimaced because he had no idea what he was asking. "My help is a dangerous commodity. Better to find your answers without me."

"Then help me do that," he persisted. "Please. You have no idea how confusing this is." When I looked unconvinced, he added, "At least help me find my own kind—other Nephilim."

Not an easy ask with a supposedly extinct subspecies. "I'll give it some thought," I said and went back to counting bills.

"Dragon's blood," someone said.

Startled, I looked up from the money and realized it was Rhonda. I'd all but forgotten we'd been in the middle of a conversation when time froze. "Pardon?"

"When things started smelling rainwater-peachy, the voice said, 'dragon's blood be thy aid and succor'—those exact words." Rhonda gave an emphatic tap on the counter. "I remember thinking it was an odd phrase, then forgot all about it."

I gave a nod. "Very odd phrase. And the voice—did it have an echo, like someone speaking with reverb on."

"It did—I'd forgotten that, too. How did you guess?"

"Oh, I've read about these things," I said casually, but my mind was awhirl with this new information. "Could you hold down the fort while Blitz and I take a quick break?" I put a little effort into the question so that it would be impossible to say no to. One of my minor talents that was incredibly useful.

As Rhonda nodded, I snagged Blitz by the arm to pull him toward the exit. "I have your answer. We need to talk fast, and then you need to move fast. No more BankUSA for you."

As soon as we were outside, I took a sniff of him to confirm his scent was rainwater-peachy, then plowed into it. "Rhonda got a message when she had her near-death experience—a message directed toward you. Someone upstairs knew you two worked together."

Blitz looked amazed. "Someone sent me a message? Who?"

"She described an angelic voice effect. The Celestial Court as a whole wants you destroyed, but with one obvious exception—the angel who couldn't keep his flaming sword in his pants."

"My father?" Blitz whispered, wide-eyed.

"My guess exactly. Rhonda's whole experience felt off. I don't think she was supposed to have a near-death experience, but your father was improvising when he realized the hunt was on. The message was 'dragon's blood be thy aid and succor'. That had to be directed at you."

Blitz shook his head. "Never even heard of dragon's blood."

"Then listen. Mostly 'dragon's blood' is a term for crocodile blood as used in the Egyptian Old Kingdom. That's where this gets interesting. Ancient Egypt had Nephilim aplenty. They had a hand in designing the pyramids and included all those secret chambers for their own use. They were still hunted back then but were able to hide in hide in plain sight by masking their scent with ...”

“Crocodile blood?” Blitz supplied uncertainly.

I nodded. “If you had to wrestle a Nile crocodile for its blood, you would call them dragons, too. But these days it should be easy.”

“I doubt that wrestling crocodiles has gotten any easier.”

“No, but now there are zoos. Slip into the reptile house after hours, trank your target, and extract a few vials of blood. The ancients would be green with envy.”

“And then?”

“Boil the blood in a pot of vinegar, let it cool, and baste your whole body. Done right, it can last a whole year. That’s a whole year out of the crosshairs of the angelic kill squads. Do it now and grab the next flight out of town.”

“If I’m safe, why do I need to go?” Blitz asked.

“One, because this branch of BankUSA is going to be crawling with hunters, and two, Egypt is your best bet of finding your own kind. You could fly directly to Cairo and start looking, or take a slower route. Go back to school, get a degree in tomb-raiding or whatever, then join a dig. It would take years, but quite frankly, you have a great deal of time to play with.”

He looked up suspiciously. “How long do Nephilim live?”

I gave a shrug. “If you run into an angelic kill squad, not long at all. But assuming you’re fast on your feet, you could live until the end of time.”

Blitz gave it some thought, then nodded. “So, Egypt it is. And don’t strike first with angels.” He hesitated, then added, “Thank you. I don’t know who or what you are, but I know you’re a friend—”

I shivered at the mega-awkward word. “I can’t really afford to have friends, just—”

“—and I think you should come with me because helping me has put you in danger, too.”

I gave him a sad little smile. “I’m not in danger ... from anything or anyone. Eventually my three brothers and I will have a job to do, but not until the End of Days. Until then, I follow my areas if interest, so eternity isn’t quite so boring. If you live out your full life, you’ll be seeing me in an official capacity at the End of Days—whether that be tomorrow or ten-thousand years in the future. Even I don't know when."

Blitz absorbed that with a thoughtful frown. "I see." Then, "Come to Cairo with me anyway. I'm okay with the End of Days, whenever that comes up, and it'll be the opposite of boring."

It was already the opposite of boring. "Maybe," I said tentatively, even though it would be smarter to walk away. "Let's see how you handle the crocodile blood." I didn't want to deal with more angelic kill squads—with those morons, it was hard to keep my finger off the trigger.

But a jaunt to Egypt had its appeal. And why not? I had all the time in the world.

Jonathan Shipley, a member of Science Fiction Writers of America, writes short stories and novels in the genres of fantasy, science fiction, and horror. In the writing profession, there are two huge challenges. One is the writing itself, and the second is getting the works published. In terms of output, he has written nine novels and over a hundred short stories. On the publication front, he has sold over a hundred short stories, most of which are currently in print but several are still pending. A listing of his short stories can be found at:

www.amazon.com/author/shipley or www.shipleyscifi.com .

When not writing, Shipley teaches high school where his classes include—not unexpectedly—creative writing. And when not writing or teaching, he works on the restoration of his 1914 historic home and collects antiques to go in the home. And when you add all those things together, it always seems to come out to more than twenty-four hours in the day.

Number Four Took My Clothes
By N.L. Dalton

It had been a long, brutal night. Burrows had spent the first half hour of his shift getting reamed by his boss for being late, and another fifteen minutes listening to the "taking pride in your job" speech. Like being a morgue assistant on the graveyard shift was something to be proud of. He'd been here for a year, and he'd spent the vast majority of it mopping up blood and washing bodies.

This night had gone from bad to worse in a hurry. There had been a massive pileup on Route 93, and he was up to his knees in his work—literally. He'd had to change his lab coat twice, and his shift was only half over. At about three in the morning, just as he was finishing the last of the mess from the accident victims, more bodies were brought in. The victims of various crimes and tragedies, they were nearly as messed up as those from the earlier pileup. The eight tables in Exam A were filled in less than a minute. The medical examiner entered the room as he began washing the body on Table One.

"I heard the old man chewed you out again. Late?"

"Yeah, by thirty seconds. Doesn't that guy have a job to do?"

"You mean aside from screwing with you? Not really."

"I wish that cracker would get himself a new hobby."

"That's not too likely. You do know you forgot to put the drain tray on that table, right? It's spilling all over the floor."

"Oh, what the f ... Jesus, Harv, don't mess with me like that. I've had a bad night." Burrows said angrily, looking down at his wet trousers. "And now my pants are wet, dammit!"

"My night just got a bit better," said Harv.

The medical examiner stopped in front of Table Four and took a closer look at the body. The skin that wasn't covered in blood or shredded clothing was sickeningly pale, almost white. Lacerations covered his face, neck, and shoulders. The most revealing of these scars was a deep ragged tear on the left side of the throat just under the ear. Burrows was removing the clothing from Number Two when Harv called him.

"I'm thinking natural causes on this one. What do you think?"

"I think you might need glasses."

"This dude is fucked up pretty good. I can't even guess at the animal that did this."

"Stray dog, maybe?"

"Doesn't look like a dog to me."

"These other folks don't look too good either. So, where'd they find the guy?"

"Central Park. You be real careful with the clothes on him. Trace wants them."

"Why don't the forensic boys take the clothes when they finish the crime scene preliminary? It would sure save us some time, Harv."

"Maybe they don't want to send you to the unemployment line. Just be careful with them."

"Will do; anything else?"

"Nope. Just let me know when they're prepped, I got some reports to fill out."

Burrows went about his job mechanically, carefully folding and bundling the clothing of each cadaver and bagging it, then putting the personal information of each victim on the appropriate bag. He did this every day, and at this point could probably do it in his sleep. He took extra care with Number Four. He gathered up anything that fell from an article of clothing, placed it in a small baggie, and pinned it to whatever garment it fell from. Every loose thread, drop of blood, and unidentified particle was packaged, labeled, and placed on the rack. Except for 'cause unknowns' like the man on Table Four, one Albert Wallace, the job had little day-to-day variance. Strip them, wash them, tag them and call Harv.

He was finishing up Number Six when he caught a flash of movement out of the corner of his eye that seemed to come from Table Four. When he turned his head, however, the body was as it had been. No sign of movement whatsoever. "Great, now I'm seeing things" he mused. "Must be the formaldehyde."

He was just finishing Number Eight when one of the tables creaked. Burrows looked down the row of tables again, mentally slapping himself for being such a pussy. Unlocking the wheels on Number Eight, he rolled the table down to Bowman in storage, another special case. He spent the entire trip looking over his shoulder, trying to convince himself that things were the same as always. It wasn't working very well.

By the time he got back, he was fighting a rapidly building shiver running up and down his spine. For some reason, he was terrified. He could barely keep the tray in his hands from shaking when he returned to an exam room that had suddenly become stifling. What happened next should not have scared him; this sort of thing happened a lot with corpses, but for some reason it nearly gave him a coronary this time. He was nearly to the table with the tray of instruments when one of the corpses decided to pass gas, loud and foul. He nearly jumped out of his pants.

Harv ran into the room when he heard the screaming only to wind up laughing hysterically when he saw Burrows. The man was on his rear, back to the wall and panting. The contents of the instrument tray were all over the floor.

"What's with you, Burrows; why so squirrelly?"

"I guess I'm just really jumpy tonight. That sort of thing usually doesn't bug me."

Harv didn't have to guess. By now he could smell it. "You damn near jumped outta your skin for a corpse fart? Holy shit. Umm, no pun intended."

"Gee, boss, you are one funny motherfucker," he said, his voice dripping with sarcasm. He regained his feet and some of his composure. "Guess I'd better clean this up."

"You'll need a stepstool," said Harv, pointing at the ceiling in response to Burrows' questioning glance. "Look up, man."

There were two syringes stuck in one of the ceiling tiles. Sighing, Burrows went to get the stool while Harv went back to the office, still laughing softly to himself.

As Harv opened the door to his office, there was a rush of air in the dimly lit hallway and he was yanked from his feet and into the office. Harv was pinned against the wall, held effortlessly by the formerly deceased Albert Wallace.

Burrows had finished cleaning up the mess and was about to go for another tray when he noticed that Table Four was empty. He immediately went to see Harv. When he opened the door to Harv's office, he found himself grabbed by the throat and pinned behind the door. Wallace stared at him and put a finger to his lips, shushing him.

The gesture might have seemed comical were it not for the person doing it.

"Your pal is fine. You keep your cool and you'll both stay fine." The first thing Burrows noticed, aside from the obvious red, slit-pupiled eyes, was the wound in his throat. It hadn't healed completely, but it was well on its way. His skin had a pale mottled look to it, like a man with a really bad flu, and he was cool to the touch. Not clammy or anything, just cool and dry.

"So, are you going to stay calm?"

Burrows nodded.

Wallace let go of his throat and motioned for him to sit in the chair across the desk from Harv's.

The man's demeanor changed almost immediately. He relaxed and sat on the edge of the desk, his expression quite friendly despite the fangs.

"So, do you guys ever take a pulse?"

"What?"

"A pulse, dude. You think I enjoyed waking up on a slab?"

Burrows didn't know what to say, really. So, he just winged it in the hope his captor wouldn't tear him up. "The paramedics always check vitals, even when death is obvious. You're dead, or you were dead anyhow. You've been on that table for hours."

Wallace looked confused for a moment, then placed his fingers to the healing wound on his throat. Then he smiled and, looking a bit embarrassed, he continued. "I guess you're right at that. You'd think a guy would notice that sort of thing, wouldn't you?" Then he looked down and laughed. He reached down to his right foot and pulled off the toe-tag. "'Albert Wallace, age: 34 yrs. Sex: M, Cause of death unknown.' Well, color me stupid."

"What now?

"Well," mused Al, "you need to help me get out of here."

"Your effects are down in Trace, so getting them back won't be easy."

"So ..." He thought a moment before finishing his question. "Did I have my wallet with me?"

"No, actually. You had an employee ID and a cellphone, but nothing else; we got some of your info off your cell phone. Wait a sec, there were a couple of twenties in your pocket. They'll be in an envelope with your clothes."

"Then my wallet is still at home. Excellent. All I have to do is report my ID stolen when I get back to the house." Then he touched the healing wound on his throat again and paused, obviously worried about something. "So, my clothes are in Trace?"

"They're in Trace, yeah. They're completely trashed, though." Burrows furrowed his brow, obviously worried about something. "Damn."

"What's the matter?" asked the vampire.

"I realized this is a weird time to think of it, but how the hell am I ..." he paused,   "Are we going to explain a missing body to the boss?" He motioned to the unconscious Harv in the next chair. "It's not like Harv and I can tell him you went for coffee."

Wallace woke Harv then, and the two of them brought him up to speed. After a few minutes it was decided that Burrows had a point. The biggest issue, other than finding clothes for Al, would be Dr. Martin. Getting him to play along would take a little finesse.

They couldn't think of a practical way to rope Martin in, and Wallace was getting a little bit flummoxed at the lack of a solution. Then he smiled, a wicked little smile, and put his hands on Burrows' shoulder. "I think I have an idea, but I need to know something. About how big is this boss of yours, and where is he now?"

"He's about your size ... oh, nice. He's right down the hall, fourth door on the left just before the Trace lab."

"Now let's find some suitable clothes for your boss from one of your other guests, and get to work."

It was around 11:15 the following evening that Harv sat down in the cafeteria to have a quick cup of coffee and read the paper before his shift started at midnight. Of course he'd have to make the coffee himself; he always had to. After all, how could the other eight people on shift in the adjacent labs be expected to make a damned pot of coffee when they come in? That would be considerate. Standing again, he walked over to the coffee machine.

He was at the counter setting up the machine when Burrows entered the break room that all the labs shared. "Here you go, Boss," he said, offering him a full carton of creamer.

"Put it in the fridge, Burrows. I'm kinda busy here, you know?"

"Sure, sure, just trying to be helpful." He put the carton in the fridge and took a seat across the table from where Harv had placed his newspaper.

Harv took a seat at the table and opened his paper to the sports section and began to read, but he couldn't concentrate on it; the elephant in the room was just a little bit too big. Frustrated at his inability to relax, and making sure he and Burrows were the only two in the breakroom, he folded the paper and placed it on the table. Burrows was waiting for him to speak, the intuitive little bastard. "Will you stop looking at me like that?" he asked, a touch of irritation creeping into his voice. "You look like a ten-year-old waiting for ice cream."

"I want to know what happened after I left this morning, Boss. I heard you and Martin were talking to the higher ups for two hours after they were done with me, so what's the skinny?"

"Fine, fine," said Harv. "Martin backed us up just like Wallace said he would. It's not like he had much choice after what we did. He told them that after we searched the other labs for the body he made his report, and he vouched for both of us, too. He claimed we were both in his office at the time the body was stolen. Remember to say we were in the office with him at 5:30 a.m. for an hour or so if they ask you again." Harv chuckled at that. "There wasn't much else he could say about it without implicating himself. Now that I think of it, did you make copies of those photos we took?"

"Sure did" said Burrows, taking an envelope out of a jacket pocket. "He looks adorable, doesn't he?"

"Yep, it's a good thing we had that drag queen on Table Seven. I still can't believe that her
clothing fit Martin so well, right down to the underwear."

N.L. Dalton is best known for writing horror and science fiction, speculative fiction, and dark-humored tales of various stripe. While working as an editor for Daverana Enterprises, it became apparent that she did her best work when she allowed a bit of her admittedly morbid humor to seep into her writing. Coincidentally, that's also how she managed to end a few of her relationships, but that's neither here nor there. Some folks just can't take a joke.

She has been a paralegal, legal assistant, laboratory technician, construction worker, electronics inspector/programmer, and, funnily enough, a cosmetologist.

Dalton draws many of the settings and characters in her stories from the working class and working poor neighborhoods she's lived in most her adult life.

Pixiedelphia Freedom
by Robert Allen Lupton

Ben Franklin was drunk. John Adams had been unbearable the entire day. That wasn't news; John was always unbearable, but today he'd outdone himself. Independence from England was a dream vanishing into the mist because John's obstinacy and sense of self-importance alienated everyone he came in contact with.

Jefferson poured another tankard of rum. "I don't know how Abigail stands the man. She must be a saint."

"Well, she did send him to Philadelphia for six months, didn't she?"

"You've got me there."

"He's always been an uncompromising little shit, but he's been worse this week. It's like he wants to sabotage our plans for independence."

Jefferson ordered a plate of sausages. "Ben, he's your friend. Talk to him."

"It's hard to talk to a man like John. He doesn't drink or smoke. He stays away from bawdy houses. I suspect he'd have become a priest except he couldn't stand Almighty God telling him what to do."

"Talk to him. We present the Declaration of Independence for final comments and a vote on Monday. You have to make him behave."

A short, impeccably dressed man stepped up to the rude wooden tavern table. He wore a tight leather cap strapped under his chin, and leather-bound goggles covered both eyes. He shoved the goggles onto his forehead. "Excuse me, gentlemen. I don't wish to intrude, but it's possible I could be of service. I know John rather well."

Jefferson stood up. He was over six feet tall and twice the height of the little man. "I don't believe I've had the pleasure. Thomas Jefferson of Virginia, and this is Benjamin Franklin of Pennsylvania."

The little man climbed into a chair and helped himself to a pewter mug of rum. "Marvin, my name's Marvin."

Franklin snorted, "Why don't you help yourself? Have some sausage while you're at it? I didn't catch where you're from."

Marvin ate three sausages in as many bites. "I didn't throw it. I'm not really from anywhere or anywhen, so to speak. I'm more like a citizen of the world."

Jefferson said, "Now that you've eaten our food and drunk our rum, explain yourself or move on. Little man, we have important things to discuss."

"Indeed you do, and poor John Adams' behavior is the least of your problems. Please start by not calling me 'little man.' I'm plenty tall enough. Same as you, both my feet reach the floor. My hands reach plenty high enough. Watch."

Marvin waved three fingers in the air and the barmaid brought another round of rum, scooped up the empty trenchers from the table, and stepped away. Franklin picked up his rum and Marvin jumped on the table and knocked the mug out of his hands. He kicked the other two mugs off the table.

Jefferson grabbed Marvin by the silk scarf around his neck. "Explain yourself."

Marvin wiped his nose and slathered Jefferson's arm with a healthy dollop of snot.

Jefferson shoved Marvin to the filth-covered tavern floor. "I'm not a man to challenge another, but no one does that to me. If you weren't half a man, I'd kill you now. Be gone."

Marvin said, "The rum contained a sleeping draught. Look around the tavern."

The patrons and staff appeared differently than before, at least to Jefferson's eyes. The barmaid had pointed ears and her skin was a red as an apple, and the men at the next table were short with strong forearms, broken teeth, and extremely large heads. The men standing at the bar were immense and their arms dangled almost to the floor. Jefferson looked closer at the barmaid and it was clear that whatever she was, she wasn't female or human.

The barmaid took the cigar out of his mouth. "Marvin, is that you? It is, isn't it? I'm just trying to make a living here."

Marvin tapped Jefferson's wrist and the Virginian released the little man. "Hello, Grandma, the second I saw the sign, Grootmoeder's Huis, I knew this was your place."

"I didn't know pixies spoke Dutch."

"Pixies can speak anything. You should hear me speak Yiddish with a Portuguese accent."

Jefferson was speechless, but Franklin spoke up. "What is happening? I don't understand, little man."

"I told you to stop with that little man crap," said Marvin and he splattered Franklin with a dollop of snot. Ben flinched and dabbed his arm with a handkerchief. He gasped when he noticed the variety of creatures in the room. "Jefferson, these people look quite strange and they're staring at us. I hope they don't mean us harm; I'm not good at defending myself."

Marvin stood on his chair. "Grandma, perhaps you'd be kind enough to bring us some untainted rum. Join us. I'd like to hear why you're in Philadelphia. Cigars would be nice."

He dropped into the seat and whispered. "I'm a pixie, and pixie snot is magic. It destroys spells, enchantments, and bewitchings. It deglamorizes glamors. As long as it's moist, you can see all creatures as they really are. The barmaid is the owner, my old friend, Grandma, and a red fairy. They cast the best glamor spells. Sometimes we're on the same side and sometimes we're not."

Jefferson took an untainted mug of rum from Grandma. "I don't understand."

Marvin said, "One thing at a time. I'm here to help you. I'll explain later. I'll speak slowly. Try to pay attention. For now, let's figure out what this ugly red fairy wants."

Grandma pulled up a wooden bench. "Marvin, these are dangerous times. The consortium of red, blue, and yellow fairies wants this independence thing to work. Most trolls, orcs, goblins, dwarves, gnomes, and even the leprechauns are with us. We believe we'll be safe in this country because these colonists are a stubborn people and they don't believe in fairies or any of the Fae.

Marvin snickered. "You want them to clap their hands and chant?"

Grandma put out his cigar. "This is a huge continent and we can blend in here. The leprechauns can go about their business without a hundred Irishmen looking for their gold. There are beautiful forests for the dryads, rivers aplenty for naiads, and mountains waiting for gnomes, goblins, and dwarves. Non-believers will leave us alone. In a couple of hundred years, humans won't believe we ever existed."

"And you'll have an unending market to sell your glamor spells."

"That too, but after two or three centuries of cross breeding, the differences won't matter. We'll all be a little human and all the humans will be a little Fae. Marvin, are you here to stop this?"

"No, we're on the same side, but not for the same reasons. Let me explain things to these two humans. They've got a real problem. Once they figure out what to do, I'll let you know if we need help."

Franklin was asleep. Marvin said, "Jefferson, take your friend home. I'll meet you at breakfast."

"Aren't you coming with us?"

"No, Grandma and I have some serious drinking to do."

Jefferson's head pounded louder than the fist hammering the front door. "Wake up, Jefferson. Early to bed and early to rise, and you don't get caught with other men's wives."

Jefferson answered the door and held it open for Ben Franklin and Marvin. "Damn, Franklin, how can you drink that much and be so chipper the morning after? And Marvin, I was sure you were a product of too much rum and tobacco. I expected you to vanish at the dawn's early light."

Marvin sneezed and flipped a drop onto Jefferson's wrist. "Happy to see you too. Can you make coffee?"

"I'll send a servant for a bucketful. I don't keep it in the house. I prefer tea."

Franklin snorted, "How unpatriotic, Tom. You mustn't let John know. You'll never hear the end of it."

Marvin and Franklin sat at the table and drank coffee while Jefferson dressed. Franklin poured Jefferson a mug and said, "I took the liberty of soaking willow bark in your coffee. I find it helps alleviate the aftereffects of rum. Pay attention now. Our new friend, Marvin, has things to tell you."

Marvin filled his pewter tankard with rum and coffee and fired up a cigar. "I'm a pixie. I've been ordered to help you by POOPHEADS, the Pixie Order Of Pixilated Helpfulness And Direct Succor. They want your plan for independence to succeed."

Jefferson held his head. "Franklin, it's too early Sunday morning for me to believe in pixies or fairies or any other such impossible things."

"Nonsense, that's just your provincial Virginian upbringing talking. I make a point of believing in two or three impossible things every Sunday morning. I find it hard to accept that you believe in an invisible, benevolent, and omnipotent god who'll burn you in hell for not tithing, but you deny the existence of the pixie sitting at your table. Last Sunday, I decided to believe in freedom of the press, open marriage, and the right of all men to pursue happiness. Today, I believe in pixies."

Marvin snorted, "Believe or don't believe, that's not the question. I don't care. I'm here because it's my job. Next week, I'll have another assignment. POOPHEADS wants your new country to succeed. Your stubborn attitude will make it easy for all Fae, especially pixies, to blend in. Several of our future generations will live on this continent. A couple will even become future presidents."

Franklin spit out a mouthful of coffee. "You can see the future? That's three impossible things. I can only believe two at a time."

"Time is flexible for POOPHEAD agents. I go when and where I'm told. If you guys figure this out, you'll be famous. Jefferson gets to be president and Ben will be postmaster general. You'll both be on the money."

Jefferson asked, "And Adams?"

"He'll be president, too, but he won't be on the money. Never mind that. You need to find John and pass your independence resolution. Time is short."

"John will be at the Pennsylvania State House in less than an hour. He'll be easy to find. He'll be the one screaming at the other representatives."

"No, he won't. The real John is being held captive about a mile from here. The John Adams at the Continental Congress is a Rage Boggart glamorized to look exactly like John Adams. The boggart's job is to keep the other representatives so angry and offended that they'll vote down your resolution of independence."

Franklin drained his coffee. "A rage boggart. No wonder we can't tell the difference. Why do your POOPHEADERS care what we do?"

"The countries in Europe are ruled by kings and queens who are all related to each other. None of them are humans, or even pixies for that matter. Some are Sluagh. The Sluagh are the darkest Fae. Rumpelstiltskin was a Sluagh. Years ago, Underbreath, a Sluagh prince, changed his name to Charming and married a mortal woman. Their son was a mighty warrior and eventually became a king. The charming king married the princess, Madreen, a full blooded Sluagh, and she bore many children. She was clever and arranged marriages for her offspring and now, the Sluagh rule every country in Europe."

Tom lifted his head from the tabletop. "What's this about Sloo-ee ruling Europe? Sounds like a farmer calling hogs. Tell me why I care. Why do you care?"

"Are you being deliberately slow? May the gods have mercy on your new country if you're one of its leaders. Listen to me. The Sluagh are outcast Fae, the results of bad interbreeding, misshapen of form, and evil in their hearts. They torment humans and other Fae for no reason other than to amuse themselves. Most Fae, including pixies and red fairies like Grandma, want to prevent the Sluagh from ruling this continent. Later, we'll figure out how to deal with them in Europe."

Franklin said, "Do you have any proof to offer us?"

"Mr. Jefferson, himself, penned the proof you request. 'He has plundered our seas, ravaged our coast, burned our towns, and destroyed the lives of our people. He has denied us his protection and waged cruel war against us.'"

Jefferson smashed his fist on the table. "Don't turn my words against me."

"Get used to it. You plan to be a politician, grow thicker skin. You think I'm using your words against you, wait until Alexander Hamilton gets his turn at bat."

"Turn at bat?"

"Never mind. I get confused about idioms and centuries sometimes. The important thing is for you to free the real John Adams and evict the rage boggart from your congress."

"What's your plan?" asked Franklin.

"Plan? I'm not in charge of plans. My role here is to be more of a helper, not a planner. I'll slap some snot on you from time to time. That way, you'll know who's human, who's a boggart, a fairy, or a troll. Pixie snot disenchants, deglamorizes, and dispels all forms of magic."

"I know, you told me about your magic snot. If you aren't going to help, why are you here?"

"Orders. I was conscripted. I didn't volunteer. Years back, I had a brief relationship with a pixie princess. It ended badly and I turned her into a beautiful poodle. Her father, the king, was beside himself, and when she ran away and took up with a Shetland pony, he locked me up. Their marriage was a real dog and pony show, but the puppies were adorable. Shetdoodles are hooved, smart, and their snot works like mine.

The king gave me the choice of becoming a POOPHEAD agent or becoming a head shorter. Easy choice. I get paid the same, no matter what happens. I'm out of here on July fifth. So again, what's your plan?"

Jefferson stood. "Enough talk. Let's hie to the State House. I want to see this rage booger with my own eyes."

Franklin shook his head. "Rage boggart. A booger is snot. Pixie snot is magic. How's this going to work if you can't keep things straight?"

Jefferson threw his pewter mug at the wall. "Get in the damn carriage."

John Adams was lecturing the congress when Franklin and Jefferson arrived. He pointed at them. "Gentlemen, good of you to join us. Does eight o'clock arrive later in Virginia and Pennsylvania than it does in Boston? Who's that dwarf with you?"

Marvin slopped a fistful of fresh snot on his companions and Adams was no longer Adams. He was even shorter than the real John and mostly bald. His nose was quite long, and his skin was brown with a greenish tinge. Gnarled fingers ended in nails long enough to be talons.

Franklin stared at the living evidence of Marvin's claims. "Good morning, John. Say hello to my little friend. Marvin is our new consultant."

Ben rubbed one finger under Marvin's nose and applied the mucus to John Hancock's face. "Marvin is quite clever. He knows what's true and what's not."

The rage boggart turned a brighter shade of green. "Sit down and shut up. I haven't yielded the floor."

Jefferson glanced around the room and counted the representatives in attendance. At least a dozen weren't human. "Mr. Chairman, I move we adjourn."

The boggart shouted, "I have the floor. Jefferson is out of order."

John Hancock, the chairman, pounded the gavel. "John, for God's sake behave yourself. A motion to adjourn is always in order. Is there a second?"

"I second the motion," said Franklin. "And what's more, I move we adjourn to Grootmoeder's Huis. Drinks are on me."

The resolution passed fifteen to twelve.

Jefferson, Franklin, and Marvin climbed into the carriage. The Adams doppelganger boggart turned off the path to the tavern. Tom

21

tapped the driver on the shoulder and inadvertently transferred a bit of pixie snot. "Follow Mr. Adams."

The driver pointed. "Ain't Mr. Adams. Looks more like my mother-in-law."

"I don't care if he looks like the devil himself, follow him."

The rage boggart wended his way along dirt streets, narrow alleyways, and through a courtyard or two. He entered the King's Tavern and hurried upstairs. Franklin paid the driver. "Wait here. We'll be back."

The three rushed into the tavern and caught a glimpse of the boggart disappearing into the hallway at the top of the stairs. Franklin said, "Tom, we're the only humans in the place."

Jefferson hesitated on the stairs. The seedy tavern was filled with inhuman people large and small. He sniffed and the disenchanted stench was overwhelming. He gagged and held a perfumed handkerchief to his nose.

Marvin snickered. "Filth trolls. Lovely odor, isn't it? The smell would make a man homesick if he'd been raised in a pigsty."

Franklin peeked down the hallway. The passage was filled with armed ogres, giant trolls, and nasty little goblins with sharp swords. Franklin turned and rushed Tom and Marvin down the stairs. "We're going to need a little help. Trust me on that. Let's adjourn to Grandma's and see if we can recruit a congressman or two."

Eighteen congressmen were in the tavern and a quick snot-fueled inspection verified that all eighteen were human. Drunk, but human.

"Marvin, sneeze in the rum. I want them to see what I see."

"Franklin," said Tom. "That's disgusting. Do you think it'll work?"

Marvin snickered. "Of course it'll work. Toss in some coconut and pineapple and call it mucus colada."

Once Grandma served the snot-spiked rum to the house, Franklin said, "Monsters far worse than Hessians have captured John Adams. Look for yourself; these strange looking people in this tavern are our friends. Evil ones called the Sluagh have captured John."

Roger Sherman raised his mug. "Here's to me not being the ugliest man in the room. As for John, they took him; let them keep him."

"Roger, you don't mean that," said Franklin. "I have to help him. Abigail knows where I live. She'd never forgive me, and she's more relentless than he is. Help us save John and our as yet unborn country. I'll buy the drinks until we finish in Philadelphia."

Stephen Hopkins drained his tankard. "That's a cause I can fight for. Let's recruit some local militia and go get John. If we don't hurry, like as not, he'll talk his captors to death."

Marvin lit a cigar and said, "As I said, I'm more of an observer than a planner. I think of myself as a consultant. I'm not much of a fighter either. I'm more of a lover. It would be so unfair to Fae women everywhere if this magnificent face was damaged."

Tom asked, "Is there a point in there somewhere?"

"Look at yourself and look at the rest of your friends. None of you are exactly what I'd call warriors. John Adams is guarded by orcs, ogres, and trolls. Creatures larger than you, meaner than you, and stronger than you. I suggest battling the Sluagh with a bunch of out-of-shape lawyers, farmers, and businessmen will work out very badly. It will give the Sluagh exactly what they want. Dead men can't sign a declaration."

Franklin sniffed a pinch of snuff, coughed, and said, "Agreed. The pen is mightier than the sword, at least in my case. What do you suggest?"

"Make a deal."

"A deal. What kind of deal?"

"You're supposed to be a great negotiator. You tell me."

Franklin thought for moment. He and Roger Sherman whispered to each other. Roger nodded his head and smiled. Franklin took a sip of rum and cleared his throat. "Deception is the better part of valor. I must remember to write that down. The rage boggart doesn't know that we know he's an imposter. Tomorrow, we'll overpower him as soon as Hancock calls congress to order. We'll offer to trade him for the real Adams. If necessary, we can offer the Sluagh a county or two somewhere west of the Cumberland Gap."

Stephen Hopkins placed two single-shot pistols on the table. "Worth a try. Diplomacy first. Fight later."

The boggart Adams was one of the last to arrive the next morning. He pranced into the chamber. "Hancock, start the meeting. I know you people didn't accomplish anything before my arrival. I'm the shepherd, and you're the sheep. It's a wonder you men can find your way here every morning without me guiding each and every one of you. It never ceases to amaze me that you can even dress yourselves."

Hancock pounded his gavel. "Be quiet, John. You don't have the floor. I haven't recognized you."

"Recognized me? Are you so rum-addled that you can't see who's right in front of you? I move to close debate and vote on the declaration immediately. God knows I can't stand another day of listening to you people whine and complain. Vote. Vote now."

Marvin crept from behind Jefferson's desk. He crawled on his hands and knees and positioned himself behind the fake John Adams. Hancock confronted the boggart and held the gravel inches from the Fae's long nose. "I said I didn't recognize you, but that was a lie. I know you're not Mr. Adams."

Hancock shoved the boggart, and it fell backwards over Marvin. Hopkins, Sherman, and Jefferson scrambled and held it on the floor. Even John Dickinson helped restrain the squealing and writhing little beast.

Franklin said, "Hold him down and tie him up. I'll take the pixie and Mr. Hancock with me to negotiate John's release."

Jefferson tied the boggart to a strong chair. "Franklin, I'd like to come with you."

Before Benjamin answered, the front door opened and three short men and one woman walked into the hall. They weren't human. The woman spoke, "My name is Abtonia. I am Queen of the Sluagh. One of my powers is that I'm in mental communications with my minions at all times. I know you have my boggart, and you think you can negotiate with me."

"Good morning, Abtonia. You look quite fetching this morning."

Queen Abtonia smiled. "Marvin, is that you? Come out where I can see you or I'll turn your little pixie body into a frog."

Marvin said, "Now Queen, you aren't still mad about Paris, are you?"

"Why would you think that? I woke alone in our room. You drank all the wine, left like a thief in the night, and stuck me with the entire bill. Abandonment is hard on a girl's self-esteem."

"Alas my dear, I was called away on business, but I remember our time together fondly. Perhaps once our business here is concluded, we could engage in a rematch. If not, well, we'll always have Paris."

The Queen's eyes twinkled. "Business first. I can make this quite simple. You have my boggart and I have Mr. Adams. I propose an immediate exchange."

Franklin replied, "I trust John is well and unharmed."

"For now, but I can't speak for his safety if you don't take him back this instant."

Jefferson stood taller than anyone in the room and said, "Madame, whatever do you mean?"

"Adams oozes discontent, he breathes dissatisfaction, and revolt and revolution spontaneously combust in his presence. His demeanor screams for insurrection. My orcs and ogres are fighting each other. The trolls are on strike, and half my court signed a document demanding I allow them to form something called a constitutional monarchy. Take him back and keep him away from my people and my court."

Franklin seized the moment. "Will you agree to leave America?"

"You have to agree to keep your Mr. Adams in America."

"Queen Abtonia, we'll do our best, but you realize Mr. Adams is a willful man."

"I do. Keep him away from my court. Live and let live. Release my boggart. I'll give you Mr. Adams this very moment. If I keep him any longer, he'll convince my guards to assassinate me."

She waved her arms and her guards escorted John Adams into the hall and released him. The Queen stepped to the door. "Mr. Adams, I trust we'll not meet again. Marvin, I'll be in Switzerland. I've booked a suite of rooms at the Edelweiss Inn in your name. Don't make me come after you."

Marvin winked at Franklin. "As you command, once my business here is finished."

The Adams boggart ran after the rest of the Sluagh. The men of the Second Continental Congress stood quietly. Adams straighten his coat pulled his shirtsleeves into place. He said, "Gentlemen."

Franklin said, "John, what have you done?"

"Those are terrible people. She's a worse tyrant than King George. Someone had to make her people understand how badly they're being treated. They don't even have lawyers. Can you imagine a society without lawyers? That's not all, they ..."

"Welcome back, John. Sit down and be quiet."

"I suppose you haven't voted, have you? I knew you'd never accomplish anything if I wasn't here. Unforgivable. I've been gone less than a week, and you've reverted to a society of washerwomen and bootblacks. Step it up, boys. King George isn't behaving any better while you shillyshally around."

Hancock pounded the gavel. "Shut up, John. I haven't recognized you. You don't have the floor."

25

"Floor be damned. Delay, delay, delay. I want to talk about conditions in South Carolina. New York is filled with spies. And John Dickinson. I see you, John Dickinson. I know you for the British sympathizer you are."

Hancock broke his gavel on the desk. "John, I promise we'll vote if you only shut up and take your seat."

Adams said, "Franklin, is this a trick?"

"No, John let us vote."

"Who's that little man the Queen was talking to? Marvin, was it? God, man, you're shorter than I am. Why are you here?"

"You're a fine one to be calling anyone a little man. I came to sell one of my dogs to Mr. Franklin. I have a litter of six Shetdoodles. Wonderful guard dogs, although they do drool a bit. Perhaps Abigail would like one."

"We raise our own dogs in Braintree. Hancock, evict this dog breeder immediately. It's time to vote."

Franklin smiled, "Marvin, I'll take two and see that one is delivered to Mrs. Adams."

Marvin downed a mug of rum, lit a cigar, and pulled his goggles over his eyes. "I'll deliver the pups in a week or two, but first I have an assignation to keep."

Jefferson bowed toward Marvin. "I hear the Alps are beautiful in the summer."

Robert Allen Lupton is retired and lives in New Mexico, where he is a commercial hot air balloon pilot. Robert runs and writes every day, but not necessarily in that order. This is his fourth appearance in the *Strangely Funny* series. More than a hundred of his short stories have been published in several print and online anthologies including the *New York Times* bestseller, *Chicken Soup For the Soul—Running For Good*. His novel, *Foxborn*, was published in April 2017 and the sequel, *Dragonborn*, in June 2018. His first collection, *Running Into Trouble*, was published in October 2017. His latest collection, *Through a Wine Glass Darkly*, was released in June 2019.

https://robertallenlupton.blogspot.com/
https://twitter.com/robert_lupton
https://www.facebook.com/profile.php?id=100022680383572
https://www.amazon.com/-/e/B01GW77JY4

Not Like Other Ghouls
by Jennifer Lee Rossman

There was something wrong with me.

All right, I should be more specific because there were a lot of things wrong with me, not the least of which was my being an autistic zombie with attention deficit disorder.

Which is not to suggest that autism or ADD were necessarily problematic—on the contrary, both are perfectly fine and wonderful variations on the human brain. But that's just it: I was not human, and being a zombie came with a whole new slew of sensory irritants that made it more difficult to be autistic, and the whole lack of a metabolism thing meant my ADD pills were basically useless. But otherwise, yes. Hooray for neurodiversity.

And hooray for being a zombie. It may not have been a choice, and it may have impacted my life in a significantly negative way, but I was proud to be a ghoul. In theory, anyway. Which brings me back to my original point:

There was something wrong with me.

I stood in the shadows, watching the man fumble with his keys, his arms full of groceries. It would be so easy to sneak up onto the porch, sink my teeth into his meaty shoulder, and then run for my life (or lack thereof) with my supernatural speed. He would never catch me, would not seek medical attention until it was too late.

I could create a new zombie.

And yet, I had absolutely no desire to do so. None.

I knew I should have that instinct, knew that zombies existed only to spread the virus, but I just … didn't want to.

Oh sure, if I met someone years down the line, fell in love, and they asked me to turn them, I would be okay with that. But there was no desire.

I emerged from the shadows—slowly, so as not to frighten him. I walked soundlessly up the porch steps. He smelled of sweat and blood and Old Spice and all those other things that were supposed to ignite my instincts.

I was so close. If I had needed to breathe, he undoubtedly would have heard my breath in his ear. Personal space, I reminded myself, and took a step back.

"Excuse me," I said, startling him into dropping his keys. "Let me help you with your groceries."

Now that the can of worms had been opened, so to speak, more worms just kept slithering out. It was a clown car of worms. A pocket universe hidden in a hypercube, just oozing worms nonstop.

I briefly wondered why cans of worms were so bad to open, when worms had many uses—fishing, turning dirt into slightly different dirt, and my favorite: squirming around inside decaying bodies—but "being bad at idioms" was just one more worm in the can. Or maybe out of the can. It was definitely another worm, in any case.

Admittedly, I didn't have much experience with other zombies, since we tend to hide away like monsters in the closet, so I was probably basing most of my assumptions about how I was "supposed" to act from the media. But most zombie movies and shows had the basics of my physiology correct.

(Got bit by a zombie, died a little, have no or considerably slowed vital signs, must eat the living in order to survive, have a natural affinity for white and red striped umbrellas. All right, maybe that last one is just me. I like umbrellas. They're twirly.)

So I had to assume they were mostly correct about what it was like to be a zombie. You know, the insatiable craving for human flesh, being either slow and sluggish or fast and vicious, wearing a lot of makeup to hide your deathly complexion from the living.

I wasn't like that at all. I ate people to survive, not because I wanted to. I was awkward and clumsy, but then I was awkward and clumsy before I was bitten, and I alternated between laziness and hyperactivity, like I couldn't be wedged into one stereotype or something. And as for makeup ...

28

I don't know about this whole deathly complexion thing. Maybe that's just for white people who become zombies. My skin has seen better days, but I didn't need to slather on concealer just to hide my identity. Never really saw the point, since I never looked in the mirror much and I didn't care what other people thought of me. Plus, most makeup has a smell and texture and I don't do smells and textures.

And yet there I was, putting on lipstick.

Because I had a date.

I sincerely do not know how it happened. Between my autistic tendency to dissociate in stressful situations and my zombified tendency to zone out in order to conserve energy, I think I just kind of ... went on auto pilot. I could see me talking to the guy on the porch, could hear our conversation, but it didn't feel like I was controlling myself. I was powerless to do anything but yell, "Adele, stop acting the way you're acting! He thinks you're flirting with him!"

But did I listen? No. And when he asked me on a date, for some reason I said "Yes."

And then for some other reason, I decided that would be the day I learned how to do makeup.

Which, naturally, involved learning the history of cosmetics. I spent a good five hours lost in the Wikipedia rabbit hole, thanks to my hyperfocus and inability to feel hunger or any of those other pesky human bodily functions that used to interrupt me. But eventually, I got onto YouTube

... where I spent probably way too long watching videos of machines pouring lipstick into tubes.

Then eventually, eventually, I got to the coup de grace (I am not sure I'm using that phrase correctly, but if I go Google it, I'm gonna lose the whole day so just, like, pretend I used a phrase that means "The thing I was looking for" in French): makeup tutorials!

I followed the instructions as closely as I could, but the face looking back in the mirror didn't look nearly as pretty as the ones in the videos. Maybe I should have gone for the Halloween tutorials, made myself look like a proper zombie.

Maybe if I just got to know him, I would want to turn him.

I liked him well enough. Nice, pretty hair, the kind of personality where someone is nice but they pretend to be a jerk because it's funny and you aren't sure if it's real right away, but then he smiles that goofy smile and your heart kind of blushes.

And he didn't even try to take me to dinner. A most fortunate occurrence, because I would not have been able to eat anything other than human flesh, and I was quite certain no restaurant in town served that. So we went for a walk instead, Sam and I, and he did not try to hold my hand. Also a fortunate occurrence, since I am autistic and my skin was extremely cold because my heart only pumped like ten times a minute.

He kept looking at me. Not in a bad way, just ... We were walking side-by-side; why would he look at me when he should have been looking at the ground so he didn't trip over things?

And why was I looking at him, anyway? I should have been looking at the ground so I didn't trip over things.

It had been a while since either of us said anything. That was a bad sign on a date, wasn't it?

I searched our surroundings for anything of interest to comment on. Trees. Houses. Dog. Squirrel. I could regale him with the fascinating etymology of the word "squirrel," which was my go-to fun fact during lulls in conversation, but somehow that didn't seem ... romancey enough.

Why did his being pretty have to short circuit what few social skills I had?

I opened my mouth, but before I could say anything, Sam said, "I keep trying to find something to talk about, but nothing seems interesting enough and I kind of want to tell you about some really obscure historical event, but I'm not sure it's first date material." Then he made his eyes wide and gave an uncomfortable grin, like maybe he regretted saying all that.

If my body was physiologically capable of it, I would have felt butterflies in my chest.

It was only a matter of time until Sam saw me for who I really was.

Oh sure, I could pretend to be normal. I could put on red lipstick (and not just red, but a very specific color called "Crimson Fever," which kind of sounded like a disease from the eighteenth century, but researching cosmetic naming traditions would probably lead to an entire lost afternoon), and I could fumble through awkward flirting the way I fumbled through most social interactions. But at some point, he would realize that he had never seen me eat, that I didn't experience pain, that I was counting every fake breath so I could increase my respiration rate when he came near me and seem like I was just like other human girls.

And why did it matter if he noticed these things? Wasn't I just hanging out with him in the hopes that someday I would feel the urge to bite him?

I think I must have disassociated again, because I thought I was in control but all of a sudden I found my spare moments filled with intrusive thoughts about Sam. Moonlit walks through cemeteries, hand-in-hand with no gloves to obscure my body temperature. Having inexplicable inside jokes like calling coffee filters "duckling tutus." Maybe even being together long enough for him to notice me never growing older, and for him to be okay with that because it would mean I was always going to be as beautiful as the first day we met.

If this were a romantic comedy, this would have been the realization that began to magically reverse my disease. Get my heart pumping faster, dilate my pupils like an ophthalmologist in a Disney cartoon, make me remember how to breathe again.

But that would be the easy way out. And I didn't really want to change back, anyway. I was a zombie. Maybe I hadn't always been that way, and maybe it hurt sometimes, but that was what I was. Who I was.

I didn't need him to fix me. I just needed to tell him the truth.

Sam must have noticed my silence during our chess date. He kept making inappropriate jokes, trying to get me to laugh. Innuendo had never been my favorite form of humor, since my brain just didn't think that way, but if I had been in a better frame of mind, I would have found great amusement in the way he talked about my great opening and raised his eyebrows in that sort of suggestive way of his.

But I could hardly concentrate at all.

I had to tell him, but I couldn't just come out and say, "I am a zombie, but don't worry because I apparently don't love you enough to want to turn you into a zombie."

I mean, I could. But that seemed rude, even to me.

This was one of those times when being autistic was a detriment. I didn't understand the rules of society enough as a human; how could I possibly apply them to my current situation?

I could invite him over to my apartment, ask him to get me an ice cream treat from my freezer, and see if he noticed the cadaver hand I was saving for a snack. Or I could just stop talking to him and never see him again and just avoid the situation altogether. That seemed like a good idea.

Except no, it didn't. That seemed like a terrible idea because even though it solved my "Sam didn't know I was a zombie" problem, it created a new "I wouldn't ever get to hold his hand" problem.

Oh. Handholding. That was a more subtle way to broach the subject, wasn't it? Just casually hold his hand and let him notice that I was as cold as someone who had been dead for approximately fifteen and a half hours.

(My body did regulate its temperature slightly; I was always a little bit above room temperature, and since the body loses approximately one and a half degrees Fahrenheit per hour after death and Sam's thermostat was set at 73, so yeah, approximately fifteen and a half hours to reach my temperature.)

I reached across the table to take his queen with my pawn, intending to fumble with the piece and accidentally grab his hand as I was stopping it from falling off the table. But then I stopped.

I was taking his queen with a pawn. Frowning, I took a quick survey of the board. He was losing. Terribly.

"What's wrong?" I asked. Because something was clearly wrong.

He ran his hands through his hair, messing it all up. "I don't know. I've got a lot on my mind."

"Not as much as I have on mine," I said. And then I realized that sounded like a challenge, so I raised my eyebrows like he always did.

He smiled. "Really? Because I am a zombie hunter trying to figure out a way to tell the zombie that I originally wanted to kill that I may have fallen for her."

I just stared at him. Not quite in his eyes, but close. "What did you say?"

He leaned back in his chair, shaking his head with a grin on his face that I had come to learn was a sign of being overwhelmed, not amused. "You're not like other ghouls, Adele."

"You knew." The shock of my secret not being a secret made it take an extra moment for me to process the rest of what he said. "And you wanted to kill me?"

"You're not good at hiding it, Adele," he said gently. "The first night you offered to help me with my groceries, I noticed you weren't breathing. Or wearing a jacket in the cold. I asked you out because you didn't try to bite me, and I thought it would be an enlightening insight into the mind of a zombie. But you ..." He gestured helplessly to me and gave a sad chuckle. "You're amazing. Not just for a zombie. Just amazing, full stop."

I have never been good at telling when people were lying, but I trusted him. In this moment and in general, I trusted Sam. "There's something wrong with me, though. A lot of things, actually, but mostly I'm talking about the fact that I don't want to turn anyone into a zombie."

I don't know what he expected me to say, but it wasn't that. He gave a nervous laugh. "Well, I don't think there's anything wrong with you, but I know better than to argue with you because you have never been wrong before. But I don't think not wanting to create more zombies is a bad thing, especially because I don't have a particular desire to become a zombie at the moment. I do kind of want to kiss you, though. If you're okay with that."

For a second, I almost felt myself blush. My body temperature must have gone up a full half degree Fahrenheit before my usual, comfortable chilliness took over again. I nodded. "But let me go brush my teeth first. I have cadaver breath."

Jennifer Lee Rossman is not like other ghouls. She is the autistic, queer, and disabled author of too many short stories, one novella, and one novel, most of which are science fiction. Jennifer lives in Binghamton, New York, with several housemates and three fish.

She is also the co-editor of *Love & Bubbles*, an anthology of queer underwater romances. Look it up at:
https://amzn.to/2CWSd22

The Good Girl
by David Bernard

I really planned on retiring. In fact, I did retire. At least until last year, when the idiots in the graduating class of Quaker Grove High School decided that there would be too much adult supervision for the type of prom they wanted. So, the Friday before the senior prom, they decided to have a secret pre-party where they could get as drunk, stoned, and/or deflowered as they desired, without anyone being the wiser.

Having a secret party in Deadman's Woods outside of town was begging for trouble. Having the party on Friday the 13th was not going to help. Confiscating all cell phones so no one could post incriminating photos on social media? Smart—under any other circumstances. Thirty kids throwing a party in the abandoned insane asylum in the middle of Deadman's Woods on Friday the 13th? It was the perfect storm of really bad ideas. What's a retired homicidal maniac to do? I mean, I lived in the asylum basement—they practically invited me to slaughter them all. Not that I needed an invitation with the noise they called music. The last couple of seniors found meeting their maker particularly unpleasant. I had discovered that someone had put ice cream in the ice chest and it had melted before I could have any, and wasting perfectly good ice cream just drives me crazy.

By morning, I had thirty, quickly cooling reasons to pack up my stuff and head somewhere that was not Quaker Grove, Rhode Island. One large grave would have to do, but there was no way even I could hide a grave that big for long. It's really not my style—burying the bodies over a wider area slows down the search parties. But frankly, I'm not as young as I used to be, so I improvised and then hopped the next train. I decided to stick with the Quaker theme and headed to Pennsylvania.

I had no specific destination in mind. That's what the voices in my head are for. And yes, I know the voices aren't real, but they can be very persuasive. I switched trains a couple of times before ending up riding a coal train somewhere between Pittsburgh and the middle of nowhere. That's when I saw it, in the woods just beyond the tracks. A sprawling Victorian mansion left to rot away. I hopped off the train.

Up close, it looked worse. There were more shingles on the ground than the roof, and the clapboards had weathered to a delightfully ghastly shade of gray with splotches of red showing through; the shade of clotted blood. The wraparound porch had collapsed on itself and based on the amount of light shining through the holes in the tower, I knew a kindred spirit when I saw one. It too had bats in its belfry.

I carefully stepped across the threshold. The door was wide open and appeared to have been so since Truman was president. Not a lot of graffiti on the walls, and no campfires. That meant no tramps and no kids. Not that I couldn't resolve either problem quickly and with extreme prejudice.

I was traveling light—all I had with me was my duffel bag of machetes, cleavers, axes, hatchets, meat hooks, scalpels, chains, bone saws, an antique trephine, and the chainsaw I called Meredith. However, the recently deceased prom queen back in Quaker Grove had carried a lot of cash. Odd, since most of her buddies had only carried plastic. Makes one wonder what she felt a need to purchase without a paper trail. Of course, it's none of my business—I have my shortcomings, but gossip-mongering isn't one of them.

I decided to follow the tracks to the nearest town and spend some of the prom queen's cash on essentials. It turned out to be a pleasant walk, maybe eight miles through the woods. Ferrisport was a small town, probably an old railroad mail stop, but the train station was now a dry-cleaning store. The local market was the only one in town. I noticed a lack of hunting supplies, a good sign—no hunters wandering the woods either. I was liking this house more and more.

I didn't need a lot, just some canned goods and a mint chocolate chip ice cream cone. That would be enough to hold me until I could set up a few traps for meat. I also grabbed a can of WD40. I needed to get the front door working before the winter.

Over the next few months, I settled in. The house was full of surprises. The basement had an impressive collection of old-fashioned animal traps, and I discovered a hidden room behind what was probably the original library. It was a private library, filled with shelves of mildewed pulp mystery magazines and the owner's journals. According to the journals, the house was owned by a Pittsburgh steel baron named McBrother, who fancied himself a mystery writer. The house was a combination of his love of mystery stories and having more money than he knew what to do with. More importantly, it showed me all the other hidden rooms and passageways.

Besides the hidden places to play, I discovered the house was built almost entirely of iron and steel—doors, walls, floors, beams, even the window frames and molding—they all looked like wood, but they were actually all steel. It explained why the house was still standing. The decaying shingles and clapboards were cosmetic features, designed to make his metal house look like a wooden Victorian mansion. The only clue was if you looked closely at the red splotches, which were rust. I didn't recall a hardware store in Ferrisport, so treating that rust was going to mean a longer trip.

A metal house seemed a little dangerous to me. If there was a fire and the doors were locked, you couldn't get out of the house. One of the voices pointed out that this was also a disadvantage if you were trapped in the house by a serial killer. That gave the voices in my head all sorts of new ideas. And like I said, they can be persuasive.

The first hobo who came in for shelter from the rain was the test. He set up camp in the parlor and went exploring. He missed most of the traps on the ground floor through dumb luck. If the tripwire guillotine on the stairway didn't work, I would have been very disappointed.

I was not disappointed. He seemed a little divided on the matter, which meant I needed to adjust the tension on the blade—he should have been very divided, as in half. At least it gave me a chance to test the cremation oven I built in a gravel pit a mile or so from the house.

The front door had developed an annoying squeal when it opened, and it was starting to drive me crazy. And let's face it, crazy wasn't much of a drive for me—practically a quick stroll. I had used up the rest of the WD40 getting the steel traps operational, so I was trying to decide whether to risk heading back into town. It had been months, but it was a small town and I ran the risk of someone remembering me. I had run across annoying cold case investigators before, and being remembered usually got complicated, usually right before it got messy.

I could break into the store at night, but then I risked getting caught by the owner, who I suspected lived upstairs. Yes, I could kill him, but then I had to fake a robbery or make it look like a fire. That would bring the state cops and dammit, I was retired from killing (more or less) and it was too much hassle just for a squeaky door. I decided I'd live with it for now. If only the squeak had started before I cremated the hobo. The next best thing to WD40 is a little fat rendered off a corpse. Oh well, if nothing else, the squeal would warn me if someone else opened the door.

The first winter was uneventful for me. Not so for the poacher who stopped by on a ski mobile. Turns out the tough guy didn't like it when you did to him what he was doing to the wildlife. I hunted for food, but this clown thought hunting was recreational. At least until I showed him a choice selection of animal traps from the basement up close and real personal. He lasted almost two weeks. To add insult to injury, I refused to use his fat to fix the door. I assume he caught the insult, but admittedly, he was distracted by more pressing matters. He did make some lovely candles, however.

His nasty, noisy piece of machinery ended up about 15 miles down the railroad track in a pond. I had drained most of the gas tank for Meredith and then ran it through the woods until the gas tank was dry, ditched it in a pond, and walked home. Not only did that minimize any oil slicks that could be spotted by the air, but it was also more eco-friendly. After all, even psychotic murderers need to minimize their carbon footprint whenever possible.

As I watched the sunrise from the tower, I reflected that life was good, although I admit I was getting tired of rabbit stew. It had been close to a year since my last visit to town, and I was thinking I might risk another trip, if only for another can of WD40 and an ice cream cone. One of the voices was against the trip, reminding the other voices that it also meant that it was the first anniversary of the little incident up in Rhode Island, and if the dullards had figured out which escaped lunatic was responsible, my photo would be all over the news. The other voices made fun of that voice, if only for using the word "dullard." I just waited until they figured it out. I'm kind of easy-going when the voices are concerned.

Then we all heard the noise. The meeting was adjourned, and I peeked out of a hole in the tower wall. Sure enough, coming through the woods were a half dozen ATVs. And they stopped in front of my house. Eight teenagers—four girls and four boys—started unloading boxes. It was Quaker Grove High School all over again. I groaned to myself. Getting rid of all those infernal machines meant I was going to be doing a lot of walking. On the other hand, Meredith was going to have more than enough fuel for eight future dismemberments in the cremation pit.

I ducked down a hidden passage and headed out behind the house, trying to calculate whether my cremation pit could handle that many bodies at once. I watched until they finished unloading their stuff into the house. As soon as the door slammed shut, I removed all the spark plugs. I didn't expect anyone was leaving the house alive, but it never hurts to be careful. Next, I quietly locked the front door. I went to the back and secured that door and the cellar bulkhead. Then I went in through a hidden basement crawlway. I went to a peephole to assess my new playmates.

The tall guy had an athletic build and was wearing a high school letter jacket, and it was not an F as in Ferrisport. That meant they weren't locals. What was it with teens and their need to find a party location so far away from home the search parties couldn't find them? Not that I was complaining—things had been a little dull lately. Mr. Jock was getting a little handsy with a girl with unnaturally red hair who could have used a better dye job and about two more buttons done up on her top. Of course, that's probably why he was interested in the first place.

Two brunettes who incorrectly thought it was cute to dress in matching yoga pants and "Hello Kitty" sweatshirts were standing by the fireplace. One had a Ouija board, and another had a black candle. That's when I realized this wasn't a graduation beer party—this was a bunch of wannabe ghost hunters. I think I hurt myself grinning.

A nerdy-looking kid was fiddling with some sort of electronic doodad while a couple in matching flannel shirts and wool hats were untangling cords. A petite blonde just sat in the corner on a pile of logs I had brought in. That was a mistake on my part. Sooner or later, someone would figure out that the wood by the fireplace meant that someone else had been in the house recently.

That was seven people. I distinctly remembered eight. Someone had already wandered off. I heard a faint twang, which the ghost hunters couldn't hear on their side of the wall with all the inane chatter. It meant Number Eight had found one of the piano wire garrote traps in the basement. I ducked down to the basement and sure enough, there was Number Eight. I had never tested this trap, but damn, it was efficient. Number Eight was now Number Seven and Half. His head was on the far side of the room.

I could hear a commotion upstairs. I went upstairs and the jock was slamming his shoulder against the door. Others were pounding on window frames and punching walls. Apparently, someone had figured out they were locked in. Now everyone was discovering the house was really a giant metal cage.

The blonde was still sitting on the log pile. "Barry, that door isn't going to budge. All you're going to do is" —loud pop echoed across the room and Barry the jock dropped to his knees clutching his shoulder— "dislocate your shoulder."

"Okay, that was a bad idea. Let's not panic." Barry seemed to think he was in charge, which might have worked if he wasn't on his knees, clutching his shoulder with tears in his eyes. Based on the twins clinging to each other and crying, he was a little late on the whole "don't panic" thing. I decided he would last long enough to realize he never was in charge.

"I got a better idea, Barry," said the brainy one. "Let's panic. We're locked in a haunted house. Look at us. We're practically a trope from a horror movie—you're the jock. Amanda and Brittney are the cheerleaders. I'm the brain, Lou and Betty are the stoners. Lisa is the slut."

The one he called Lisa shot Brainy Guy a look that could kill and fastened another button on her blouse. Brainy didn't notice. He was already bordering on hysterical. The high-strung ones always made it fun for me.

"It's already started—we're trapped in the house. There's no phone signal in here, and now the token minority is missing."

Barry looked at him. "Minority?"

Brainy looked at him. "Peter's grandmother was from Puerto Rico—has anyone seen him lately?"

I took that to mean Number Eight, currently relaxing in the basement, was named Peter. Calling him a "token minority" seemed a little extreme. I suppose in the middle of Nowhere, Pennsylvania, a little Latino blood could make you a minority. Now I felt bad that he went first.

Brainy blinked. "The only thing missing is the virgin. The good girl is always the only survivor."

They all turned and looked at the little blonde who was still sitting quietly in the corner, ignoring the conversation.

Blondie looked up. "What are you looking at?"

I slipped into another corridor and started disabling the traps. This was going to be fun, and I wanted to stretch out the merriment. I slipped into the basement. I needed to decide what to do next, but if they were going to search for my new buddy Peter, I wasn't quite ready to play show and tell. I dragged him into a hidden room and checked for unsightly blood pools. The dirt floor had soaked up most of it, so a quick sweep to cover wet spots with more dirt meant now no one would know my buddy Pete had met his maker down here. And I remembered to grab his head, too. That gave the voices several ideas.

Brainy seemed to have watched a lot of horror movies, so he might provide some clever ideas, but then again, they seemed to think they were in a haunted house. If he figured out he had the wrong type of horror movie and there was a killer in the house, he might try to outsmart me. I decided to see what he thought was next. If he started second-guessing me, then he'd be next. Otherwise, maybe I'd go for a twofer and take out the stoners together. They made a nice couple, so it seemed appropriate. Just for laughs, I put a fox trap in the shadows of the last cellar stair. It was too easy to bleed out with a bear trap. I had doctored this trap. It would cripple, without killing. Of course, I'd never use it on an animal. That would be cruel.

Once the initial panic subsided, they'd start looking for tools to use to escape. I knew the closest thing to a tool or weapon in the house (that they could find) were the logs Blondie was sitting on. Maybe her sitting on them was distracting the rest of the idiots because no one had considered them as a club. To be honest, steel or not, I'm not sure if the house's seams could take a sustained pounding by a blunt wooden object. One popped rivet and that would give them a weak spot to attack. Of course, the only one who looked sturdy enough to do any damage just dislocated his shoulder, so that was helpful.

The trick was to turn up the fear. I decided to stick with the traditional "put the head in a kitchen cabinet where it would be found later." When they went looking for tools or weapons, Pete would make a special postmortem guest appearance. I tucked Pete in a cabinet and made sure he was comfortable.

I went back to the other group. Barry's fancy letterman jacket was now a bulky sling. Stoner Boy kept offering to pop it back into place, which Stoner Girl insisted he was qualified to do since they had just binge-watched the entire *Marcus Welby, MD* series. Barry kept turning them down, meaning he was slightly smarter than I gave him credit for. Brainy was trying to do something to the electronics which he told the cheerleader twins might get a signal out. I think Brainy was trying to calm down the girls since even radios didn't work in the house, but just in

41

case, I'd have to remove that possibility. Plus, I might bruise if he threw it at me.

Blondie and Bad Dye Job were talking in the corner. They went to the middle of the floor. Everyone stopped to look at them.

The blonde started. "We're doing this wrong. It's a three-story house. There must be another way out. We need to split up, find Pete, then check the cellar and upstairs for a way out."

Brainy looked up from the electronics looking horrified, but not in a good way. The dye job saw him and nodded. "Yes, we know, Walt. The first rule in a horror movie is don't split up, but this isn't a horror movie—this is reality. Plus, we've already wasted the morning. We need to figure this out and escape from here before it gets too dark to get home. This was a day trip. The only lights we have are Brittney's black candle, a flashlight, and Lou's lighter. If we don't get out of here soon, we're here for the night, like it or not."

Barry tried to nod, which with a dislocated shoulder, was a dumb choice. "So, we split into groups. Walt can keep working on his equipment to get a signal out. Janna can stay with him. Lou, Betty, and Lisa can search this floor. Amanda, Brittney, and I will check the cellar. Then we'll all go upstairs together."

Barry still thought he was in charge. He wouldn't be for much longer. The three went into the kitchen. I gave a silent prayer that the stoners had the munchies and would check the cabinets for snacks. Barry bravely went down the cellar stairs first, followed by the twins, who did not look happy to be part of a group participation project. I decided to wait and wait for the inevitable. Right on schedule, I heard the snap as the jock stepped on the trap hidden on the cellar stairs. There was a blood-curdling scream followed by a thud and more screaming, this time in close harmony. Two hysterical cheerleaders came running upstairs. The kitchen exploration team came rushing back. Poor Pete was still undiscovered in the cabinet.

One of the cheerleaders was crying hysterically. The other one seemed in slightly better shape. "B-Barry stepped on some sort of a trap and then fell down the stairs and landed on his bad shoulder.

 Help me get him back upstairs. He's bleeding." They all headed downstairs.

I strolled out of the wall and took the electronics. Just for fun, I took the food and the flashlight too. I left the bottled water and beer. The house predated indoor plumbing, which meant people would have to wander off to secluded corners of empty rooms to commune with their bladders. I like people with nervous bladders. Wandering off alone made my life easier and their lives shorter.

I could hear them arguing about whether to move him or take the trap off first. In a flash of genius, I took the black candle and stuck it on the Ouija board, then lit it. Then I went back behind the wall. I hadn't had junk food in over a year, so the cookies were a nice change from rabbit stew. Unfortunately, there was no ice cream. Someone would pay for that oversight.

Brainy and Stoner Guy were helping Barry into the room. Dye Job saw the candle was lit and screamed. Brainy and Stoner Guy were startled and let go of Barry, who went down face first. The cheerleaders saw Barry take a face plant and screamed too. The little blonde just leaned on the door jamb looking amused. Stoner Girl was not there. She must have stayed in the cellar to explore. I decided to see what she was up to. Between Brainy's hysterics over the missing equipment, cheerleaders shrieking about the candle, and Barry's groans about a broken nose, things were a little too noisy up here.

The basement was only lit by some small windows and the window wells were pretty much filled with weeds and debris, so visibility ranged from "mostly dark" to "pitch black." But popping out of the wall was still a little risky. If she saw me first, she could warn the others. I cracked open the hidden door. She was sitting in a corner surrounded by musky smoke. Thanks to my friends up in Rhode Island, I knew she was smoking what those formerly cool kids called weed. I stepped out into the shadows.

She looked up. "Lou, is that you? I got one rolled with your name on it, Baby."

I walked up to her.

"You're not Lou."

I just smiled and brought my hatchet up.

"Shit. This house isn't haunted. We're in a slasher flick."

That seemed like a good place to end the conversation by burying the hatchet into her skull. After years of practice, I knew how much force is required to penetrate a skull. I did a nice job if I say so myself, but I was going to feel it in the morning. The old shoulder just doesn't handle swinging a hatch like it used to. I decided to leave her sitting on the floor where she ended up. I also decided to leave the hatchet in place for aesthetic reasons. Barry would be the only one not squeamish enough to consider taking it as a weapon, and he wasn't exactly much of a threat anymore.

Now that I was in an artistic mood, I decided to recruit Pete, or at least his head, for a performance art piece. I'd grab him out of the cabinet and bring him upstairs. When the survivors decided to explore the second floor, I'd roll him down the stairs from the third floor. That should be a most interesting audience reaction. I loved performance art with body parts. If I got the chance, I might even reconnect a trap on the stairs.

I slipped upstairs to grab Pete out of the kitchen and take the hidden stairs up to the third floor. I rounded the corner and stopped. One of the cheerleaders lay sprawled on the floor of the kitchen, very dead. I may be crazy, but I never forget a kill, and this wasn't mine. It was nice work, speaking as a professional. It was a single clean slice across the throat that provided a quick and silent death. This was not somebody's first rodeo. However, that somebody was rudely poaching my victims from inside my personal charnel house. I could hide the body and throw the competition off his game, but all that blood was a problem. I dragged Amanda into the hidden library (I couldn't tell them apart, but she was wearing an A monogram necklace). I looked at the puddle and one of the voices had a marvelous idea. They thought they were in a haunted house, so I dipped my finger in the congealing pool and then scrawled GET OUT on the wall.

I heard footprints and ducked into the passage. The hysterical shriek told me it was the surviving cheerleader—no one shrieks like a hysterical cheerleader. I looked out the other peephole in time to see Brainy, Blondie, and Stoner head into the kitchen, leaving Dye Job with Barry. Frankly, Barry looked terrible. His arm was limp in his sling, a tee-shirt was wrapped around his ankle, which based on the blood soaking through, was not helping. His nose was stuffed with fabric, probably from stoner boy's flannel. The plaid was a nice touch against the blood smears. It was delightful.

The three half-carried, half-dragged the cheerleader into the room. She was almost catatonic with fear. And Brainy didn't look too steady either. They sat her against the wall and gave her some water. I noticed a number of cans of beer were missing. Someone's bladder was going to be the death of them.

Brainy was close to a breaking point. He was muttering under his breath as he paced the room. Finally, he stopped and looked at Blondie.

"You! You're the key to getting out of here alive." Brainy's voice was getting a little shrill. "You're the good girl. The good girl always survives the slaughter. If we eliminate the good girl, we shift the paradigm and someone else survives."

He suddenly charged at the blonde. She grabbed him and spun around, flipping him over her shoulder. Someone knew some martial arts. Good to know ahead of time. Unfortunately for Brainy, his momentum carried him toward Barry. The two guys slammed together with a sickening thud. The only thing that kept me from laughing out loud was that I wasn't sure which walls were soundproof.

Brainy was out cold but Barry was writhing in agony, clutching his groin with his good arm. He turned and threw up, which was a bad choice with a dislocated shoulder. He jerked back in pain. The new trajectory of the vomit was impressive as it landed on the cheerleader.

The cheerleader stood up and screamed again. Stoner was tending to Brainy. Dye Job was trying to comfort Barry. Blondie relaxed from a defensive posture. Cheerleader went running down into the cellar. A few seconds later, she screamed again. I assume she found Stoner Girl. She came running up out of the cellar and ran upstairs. If she wasn't careful, she was going to hurt her throat with all the screaming. I slipped upstairs to see where she ended up. She kept climbing to the third floor.

It occurred to me that I didn't recall if I finished disabling all the traps up on the third floor. If I did disable them, she might make it to the attic and the tower access. The tower was technically a way out, assuming you didn't mind a 50-foot drop straight down.

She kept screaming and kept running up the stairs to the third floor. At least until she hit the tripwire guillotine on the top stair. The bad news is that is still didn't cut the victim completely in half, but I was getting closer. The good news was she finally stopped screaming.

I headed back to the rapidly diminishing gang in the parlor. Bad Hair Job was able to get Barry into a sitting position. Stoner and Blondie were standing near Brainy, who was still sprawled on the floor.

Blondie glanced toward the stairs. "Brittney stopped screaming. She must have found a place to hide."

Stoner glanced that way. "Pete, Amanda, and Betty are missing, Brittney is hiding, and Walt is a head-case. Barry can barely move. Now what?" Barry didn't look up. Apparently, he no longer believed he was in charge.

Blondie looked around. "Well, we need to find them. Maybe we start with Brittney since we know where she went."

Stoner tapped Brainy with his toe. "We can't leave Walt alone. If he goes nuts again, Barry is no shape to protect Lisa."

Dye Job stood up. "I can take care of myself."

Blondie looked at her. "I believe you can. But can you hold off Walt if he goes after you and Barry?"

Stoner walked over and looked up the stairs. "What about we take him with us?"

Both girls looked at him. He shrugged. "I see doors up there. What's he weigh? I doubt he's 120 pounds. I carry him upstairs, lock him in a room, and we leave him there until he calms down. It gives us time to look for everyone and maybe find a way out."

Dye Job looked at Barry. He raised his head and nodded. He looked like he was breathing funny. I wonder if his collision with Brainy had also broken a rib or two.

Blondie didn't look happy. "Okay. Lisa, you stay with Barry. I'll go with Lou. No one goes anywhere alone until we figure this out."

Stoner picked up Brainy and tossed him over his shoulder like a sack of wet laundry. He and Blondie went slowly up the stairs. Dye Job sat down next to Barry. "Well, you finally got your wish. We're all alone."

Barry raised his good arm toward her. She stood up and moved away. "Yeah, in your dreams. That was sarcasm, you moron. I doubt you have enough working parts left to even consider it."

She picked up the Ouija board and went and sat on the pile of logs. According to Brainy, Dye Job was the easy one. To get turned down by her must have stung more than the fox trap. Of course, she was right. Old Barry was barely in good enough shape to sit upright, never mind anything strenuous. She silently played with the planchette. Considering I'm the only one haunting this place, she wasn't going to get results.

About ten minutes passed. Blondie came down the stairs. "Did Lou come back down here? After we locked Walt in a room, he decided he had to take a leak and ducked into one of the rooms. I haven't seen him since."

That gave me a moment of panic. If he had found a passageway, he could be in one of my rooms, and I had weapons stashed everywhere. Dye Job shook her head.

"Lou hasn't had a toke since we got here. He's probably ducked into a closet to light up without sharing."

I decided to make sure and headed upstairs. If he pissed in the old library, he was already a dead man—that was my main entry, and urine stinks in the summer. The room was empty of stoners and puddles.

46

He was still a dead man, but it would be quicker. I went into my library. Then I caught a whiff of his smoke drifting in. He was in one of the rooms in the far end of the corridor. I slid open the secret panel. He was right in front of me, facing the door. I slipped to his left and tapped his right shoulder. He went to turn to the right. I grabbed his head and twisted left. The crack when his neck broke was most satisfying. Nothing is more rewarding than working with your hands. But now my shoulder was really aching. It was time to up the game and maybe grab a machete. I do like the classics.

I locked the door from the inside and went back downstairs. Blondie was sitting on the stairs. Dye Job apparently didn't know she was on the blonde's spot.

Dye Job kept looking at Barry and then looking at the stairs. Blondie saw her looking. Finally, Dye Job couldn't stand it anymore. "Janna, we need to get out of here. Barry needs a hospital."

"Lisa, I agree, but every time we separate, someone disappears. Everyone is missing. Based on that blood in the kitchen, something bad has happened to one of us. If we go looking for a way out, Barry is alone. We may need to stick together and hope someone comes looking for us."

Dye Job looked upstairs again. "What about Walt?"

Blondie looked at here. "Walt? As in 'Let's kill Janna' Walt? No thanks."

Dye Job looked at Barry. "How about I go upstairs and see if he's cooled down? You can stand on the stairs and keep an eye on both of us."

Blondie thought about it, then nodded. Dye Job went up and unlocked the door. She stepped in and screamed. Blondie went running upstairs, Barry forgotten. I went scampering up the hidden stairs as well. Brainy was lying on the floor. His face had a very unhealthy blue tinge, probably due to someone wrapping his belt around his neck—quite tightly from the look of it. I was outraged—this was not my work. I was also amused. Brainy had definitely cooled down.

Blondie knelt and picked up a reefer by the body. Dye Job looked at it. "Lou is a killer? Where's Betty?"

Blondie put her arm around Dye Job's shoulder. "I don't know. The last time I saw her was in the basement."

They walked down the stairs and went over to Barry. Dye Job dropped to her knees. "Barry, Lou is the killer. What do we do?"

Barry didn't look particularly chatty. My amateur diagnosis was he was in shock. "Where is he?"

Blondie stood and looked down. "We don't know."

Dye Job stood up. "We need to forget escaping and worry about surviving. Can we find any weapons?"

Blondie gestured toward at the woodpile. "Maybe we can throw kindling at him?"

Dye Job looked at the wood and then the cellar door. "What about the trap that Barry stepped on in the cellar?"

Blondie nodded. "Lou must be upstairs looking for Brittney. So, we put the trap on the stairs leading down here. Seems like fair play turnabout to me."

As soon as they said cellar, I was halfway there. I had a real Rube Goldberg type trap on the cellar stairs I had been dying to test (not that any of these kids would know who Rube Goldberg was). I found the Barry trap and placed it in plain view on the bottom of the stairs as bait. Then I attached the tripwire and waited. Dye Job opened the door and looked down the stairs. "I see the trap. I'll grab it. You just keep an eye on those stairs to make sure Lou stays on the second floor."

I stayed behind the fake wall. If this worked, it would be gloriously messy. If it didn't work, I didn't want to be anywhere near the stairs. She cautiously crept down the stairs and picked up the trap, then turned to head back up. That was enough for the tripwire, which then released six arrows from behind the stairs. Dye Job caught four of them. I don't know which arrow was the fatal blow. My money was the one through the throat, but the one in her eye would have done it too. She went down fast and silently.

I detoured through the kitchen to grab poor Pete, who was still sitting patiently in the cabinet. By now Blondie should have been calling down the stairs to Dye Job to see what was taking so long. Something was amiss. I unsheathed my machete, and Pete and I walked into the living room.

Blondie stood there next to what was left of Barry. His intestines were spread out on the floor, arranged to spell out "Kilroy was here." I glanced at her and the dripping knife, then the Barry graffiti.

I looked at her. "I love what you've done with the place."

She smiled without mirth but didn't lower the knife. "Thanks. I was worried it was a little over the top."

I smiled, and I think I faked sincerity better. "Art is the work of a finite being seeking to make an infinite statement." I glanced as the cooling entrails. "Literally and figuratively in this case."

A brief smile crossed her face. She knew a kindred spirit. "Now what? We drop our weapons and hug? We battle for supremacy? You unlock the door and we go our separate ways?"

I glanced at Pete's head and tossed it in the corner. "I'm not a hugger. And if you somehow killed me first, you'd never get out of here."

She nodded. "So, we head off in different directions. It was nice working with a master artist."

Neither of us had lowered our weapon. I looked at her and pretended to appear empathic. "You're Janna." She nodded. "Well Janna, you're an artist as well, at least at the killing people part. That one in the kitchen was a textbook kill. And framing Lou as the killer was brilliant. It even fooled me. But your staging is weak. You're not instilling terror first, and that's half the fun. Also, as a pointer, that knife is too big for your hand. If your hand gets slippery with blood, you're going to lose it in someone's ribcage before you finish them off."

She looked thoughtfully at the knife. "You're absolutely right. Would you consider a new trainee?"

I looked at her. She had deep blue eyes—a pretty color, but soulless like a shark. And she certainly wasn't squeamish. Definitely a full-blown psychopath. I liked her already. I decided retirement was overrated.

I made a decision. "All right, let's give it a try. We can talk on the walk to Ferrisport."

She looked at me. "Ferrisport? What's in Ferrisport?"

I smiled. "Ice cream. I'd kill for some ice cream."

She smirked. "I have killed for ice cream. Three times, as I recall."

Yes, I do believe this is going to work out quite nicely.

David Bernard is a native New Englander who hightailed it to South Florida as soon as he was informed that grown-ups can live anywhere they want, and that in spite of opinions to the contrary, he was considered to be an adult. He does still keep an ice scraper by the door, because you never know. His previous works include short stories in anthologies such as *Alternative Apocalypses* (B Cubed Press), *Snowbound* *with Zombies* (Post Mortem Press), *Legacy of the Reanimator* (Chaosium), and *The Shadow over Deathlehem* (Grinning Skull Press).

Monster Teach Back
by Rosalind Barden

"I see you didn't attend the Pep Spirit Committee's 'Decorate Your Lockers Uplift' event that I asked you to," the school's Vice Principal intoned, head looking into Jordon's file. "I'd hoped it would help uplift your spirit too, Jordon." The Vice Principal pursed his lips and looked up at the 16-year-old boy in question.

"Um." Jordon slouched as low as he could in the chair across from the Vice Principal's desk. The chair had black padding, and hopefully, maybe, with Jordon dressed head to toe in black, he would somehow blend in.

"Well?"

"Um."

"Is 'um' a leader's response?"

Not that again. Jordon sunk lower into the chair.

Back to the file. "I see you've been nodding off in class. Fourth time in a week." Eyes up and staring at Jordon again. "It's not the monster under your bed keeping you up at night again?" A wry smiled added to the stare.

"No, absolutely not!"

But it was true. Every night since he was ten, since his new stepdad moved Jordon and his mom into the rundown apartment. Every night, the thing that somehow had known his name right away slid out from under his bed, a smudge like a cat-sized dust ball that was darker than his dark room, opened its two red blobs that stood for eyes, opened the gap that stood for its mouth that was darker than even its dark self, and said, "Oh, hi there, Jordon!"

Even after the stepdad ran off with another mom and another kid, leaving Jordon and his mom the ratty apartment and a pile of debt, the thing still slid nightly from under his bed, "Hey, Jordon! Miss me?"

But he'd given up telling anyone. No one believed him. His stepdad laughed at him: "You're a nasty little boy. You deserve a monster under your bed." His mom tried to be sympathetic. Nowadays, she was so exhausted from working two jobs, it was pointless trying to bother her about the thing.

Jordon called it Percy, after the stepdad.

"Here's what we're going to do." The Vice Principal smiled in a way that Jordon knew he wouldn't like whatever was coming next. "You will attend our next weekly "Reinforce Your Motivation Seminar," which is today, after lunch, in the lunchroom. Convenient, huh? Eat your lunch, then kick back and relax and let yourself become motivated. Before long, you'll be asking yourself, 'Who's the leader now?' Then you can do Teach Backs to other struggling kids, just like yourself." The Vice Principal spread his hands at the apparent wonder of it all.

Jordon stared at the man.

The Vice Principal cleared his throat. "And that's mandatory for you. No show, and we will have to send your parent a letter. Understood?"

That meant intercepting another stern school letter at the apartment mailbox and forging his mom's signature again. That meant he'd risk getting caught, another stress Jordon couldn't deal with right now. "Yeah, fine, whatever."

In the lunchroom, Jordon endured the usual, "Doom. It's Dr. Dooom," from the bullies. Plenty of non-bullies tittered too. They were all in on it. Jordon was the weird kid in all black with hanging head, dark circles under the eyes. Not long after Percy began popping out from under his bed, the school inhabitants assigned his new name: Dr. Doom.

"Hey, Doom, are they making you go to the dumb leadership thing too? I'm skipping!" Lots of wiggling into the lunchroom chair across from Jordon accompanied these words, along with an annoying giggle. It was his lunch companion, his only friend, such as he was. Doom Jr.—assigned that name by school inhabitants because he too wore all black and hung out with the original Dr. Doom. Only, he had no Percy. So he had no bags under his eyes, no hanging head.

Doom Jr. was the only person who ever believed in Percy. Was jealous, even, which made no sense to Jordon. Why would anyone want to be tormented on purpose?

"You skipping? Come skip with me!" Junior said excitedly. "There's this house a couple of blocks from here that's for sale and it's vacant and the internet says it's haunted, maybe. Let's go! I'm thinking of posting adventures online, like going to haunted places and skipping school. That'll be our first post. We'll call ourselves Doom Bros! Get it? Get it?"

Doom Jr. talked in this rapid-fire way all the time. It made Jordon's head swim. But if he didn't tolerate Doom Jr., whose real name he vaguely recalled might be Robert, then who would talk to him? No one. Except Percy.

"Nah. I'll just get into deeper trouble."

Doom Jr. was disappointed, but only for a moment. "Oh, well, I'll go adventuring on my own then. I guess you have so much paranormal fun already with Percy, huh?"

Off he went, leaving Jordon alone as the lunchroom emptied of all but the eager-eyed motivation groupies who attended every one of these weekly seminars without fail. The seminars used to be required for all students, but after an unfortunate incident involving a trust exercise, where a student fell backwards into the supposedly waiting arms of her fellow students, the seminars became optional only. Except for cases like Jordon. Then, in his opinion, they were meted out as punishment.

As the motivation groupies pushed aside a table and rearranged chairs into a circle, Jordon felt himself nodding off. He estimated he only got at most three hours of sleep a night. No one can function long with such sleep deprivation. He made it up by dozing in class, dozing during lunch if Junior's chatter didn't jar him awake, and sleeping on the couch as soon as he got home. He tried sleeping all night on the couch, but Percy figured it out and moved under the couch. "Peek-a-boo, Jordon! You can't hide from me!" He tried everything: ignoring Percy, ear plugs, pulling the covers over his head, but he could no more ignore Percy's chatter than he could Junior's.

Last summer he found respite in a job working for an all-night dry cleaner. His mom was against the night job, but finally came around because a cousin's wife owned the cleaners. Jordon slept during the day, like a rock, then worked all night. He felt reborn. It was fantastic. But after a couple of months, just in time for school to start, Percy overcame his fear of daytime and popped out from under Jordon's bed at high noon, "Guess who, Jordy-boy?"

"Who's the leader now?"

Jordon was startled awake. He looked toward the sound coming from the circle of chairs. All hands were up. The voice spoke again, "Wonderful!" It was the Guidance Counselor who periodically forced him to come into her office where she asked how he felt, pointedly.

"Who wants to recite the 'Leadership Qualities?'" she asked, cheerfully. All hands shot up again, except Jordon's. "Wonderful! Let's recite together then."

All eager-eyed groupies and the Counselor pulled something up on their respective phones and read:

Leaders Take Chances
Leaders Share
Leaders Take Care of Business
Leaders Reach Out to Those in Need
Leaders Don't Look Back
Leaders are Huge Helpers

It was like a cult. Spooky. But he was used to spooky. He felt himself drifting again.

"We have a guest!" The Counselor's perky voice shocked him awake. "Say 'Hi!' to our guest."

"Hi, Jordon!"

That was interesting. The only people who called him by his real name were teachers, the Counselor, the Vice Principal, and the like. Never students.

"Tiesha, why don't you give Jordon the 'Uplift?'"

A girl left the circle to trot over to where Jordon slumped at the lunch table by his half-eaten peanut butter and jelly sandwich. "Welcome aboard, Jordon." She shoved several stapled-together papers into his hands. "You can be a leader too." She was a sincere freckled girl he'd seen in the halls and previously ignored.

He noted the groupies didn't ask him to pull anything up on his phone. Everybody in school knew he didn't have a phone. Couldn't afford one. Besides, the last time he had one, Percy kept popping up on it and cackling, "Who's my Boo?" This groupie knew to give Jordon stapled paper.

The freckled groupie girl was still standing next to him. "Come join our circle."

"Uh."

"Come on!" from the circle, all smiling.

"I think you're ready to be a leader," from the Counselor.

The freckled girl actually tugged his black sleeve.

Since he wasn't, clearly, going to get sleep, he scooped up his half-eaten sandwich, the printed manifesto, or whatever it was, and shuffled to the circle. A couple of kids pulled a chair into the circle for him. That was thoughtful, he supposed.

"We'll do the tree today," the Counselor smiled. Ohhs and ahhs from the circle.

"Close your eyes."

Oh, good. He could get some sleep now.

"Imagine you are a leaf," she said in a dreamy voice barely above a whisper, "in a vast tree filled with thousands, millions, billions of other leaves. All the leaves are different, yet the same. They are all connected to branches that join to the same vast tree. See the tree, its trunk, the branches, and all the leaves. You are one of the leaves, and are connected to every single one of the others. Feel the connection, reach out to the other leaves. Do you feel it?"

Weirdly, he did. Maybe because he was so sleep deprived, in a hazy state between sleep and waking, he felt a strange electricity between him and the Counselor, the freckled girl, all the kids in the circle, Doom Jr., wherever he was frolicking in the haunted house, the Vice Principal, all the teachers, all the students in his school, all students in every school, even bullies, on to his mom, his cousin and his wife who owned the dry cleaners, all customers who came to the cleaners at 2 a.m. (not many), all the bosses at his other after-school jobs who fired him for falling asleep, even his step dad Percy, and even that other Percy, the thing that tormented him under his bed.

"Breathe deep. Let it go. And open your eyes. How do you feel?"

Jordon opened his eyes and noticed all the other eyes staring at him, the guest, apparently expecting something.

"Weird?" he ventured.

Smiles. They liked that answer. "It is a weird feeling at first, isn't it?" the Counselor smiled. "You are on your first step to becoming a leader."

Jordon shrugged and tried to be indifferent, though it was a change being paid attention to, and in a nice way, not a shoving, "Dr. Doom, I vomit on you!" kind of way.

"Everybody, take time today to reach out and communicate with someone—one of our fellow leaves—and ask, 'How are you feeling?'

55

Do a Teach Back about what we learned today, about the leaves. Feel your mission. That's what a leader does." And the seminar was over.

Jordon was in deep thought the rest of the school day. During class, he had trouble doing his usual napping and instead snuck peeks at the printout. It listed the leader qualities the motivation groupies recited, plus lots about communication, and the "How are you feeling?" thing. Hmm.

He read the printout as he walked home from school. He ignored the usual neighborhood dogs wildly barking and growling at him because they smelled Percy clinging to him. Animals hated him since Percy came into his life. But now he wasn't glumly dwelling on it like he usually did.

At home, stretched out on the sofa, sleep eluded him as his mind raced over the day's revelations. A leader. Was he one? An idea formulated in his mind. He wasn't sure where it'd go, but he'd been out of any other ideas for a long time.

Leaders Take Chances

That night, lights out, he sat up waiting for Percy. Before long, its face, or what stood for its face, slid out from under his bed. "What's up, pussycat?" came the sniggering voice from its mouth, or what stood for its mouth. Then it stopped, stared. Jordon was usually cowering under his sheets. Now he was sitting up, exposed in the darkness.

Much as he hated to, Jordon took a deep breath, tried to feel as a leaf in the tree, looked at the dark blob with its shimmering malevolent eyes, and asked, "How are you?"

The red eyes popped wider than their usual wide stare and it twitched. Was it stunned? Certainly seemed to be.

"What can I do to communicate our connectedness on the tree of life?" Jordon added.

Percy was silent, then a soft, "Wha ...?" slipped from the dark spot that stood for its mouth.

This had never happened. Jordon had never gotten the upper hand, silenced the thing. It felt good. He plowed on, talking about the tree, connection, leaders, sharing Teach Backs. And feelings.

"I've always wanted you to just go away, leave me alone so I never saw you again. That's how I feel."

The thing's silence broke with a more adamant and louder, "Wha ...?" and, "But why?"

"Why? You've tormented me since my ex-stepdad brought us here to this dump. I can't sleep, can barely eat. I'm falling apart. Can't you see that?"

Its red blob eyes drooped in a way Jordon had never seen before. Could it be sad?

"But, but, you're the only boy I torment. No other! I'm here for you every night. Only you. You're all I think about. When you're gone, I'm, well, I turn into a dust ball and I'm nothing. You're everything to me."

What the Guidance Counselor would think of this communication, Jordon could only guess. But he hoped she'd be impressed.

"Really?" Jordon asked.

"Oh, yes!"

"But I still don't sleep. You've scared the wits out of me every night since I was ten."

Shyly, Percy purred, "Thanks. I do try."

Before Jordon could think what to say next, Percy grabbed hold of Jordon with its ice-cold dust-ball body. Jordon cringed and pulled away, hating when Percy touched him.

"We're going to share, Jordon, share and communicate, and we're going to do a Teach Back at the Monster Convention!"

It was Jordon's turn to say, "Wha ...?"

In an instant, he and Percy were inside a large shadowy space. Jordon made out shapes milling and jumping around, grotesque, tiny, huge, horrifying. All monsters. It took a few moments for Jordon to realize they were inside the school's old auditorium annex building. But that was impossible. It burned down years ago.

"It did burn down," Percy said cheerfully, reading Jordon's mind, as it did with startling frequency. "But you can't come here on your own, only with me. This here is the frozen moment right before your friend Doom Jr. torched it."

Jordon always suspected it was Junior, but, "How do you know I know Junior?"

"You think about how he annoys you often enough. All the time, in fact."

Percy grabbed Jordon's arm in an icy grip, then floated forcefully forward, tugging him up to the stage. "Make way! Make way! Me and my human are going to do a Teach Back! A good one that'll have you asking, 'Who's the leader now?' You!" Percy shouted toward a huge green monster that scraped the ceiling and was staring with its massive purple eyes at its purple toenails on the ends of its long orange feet perched across several auditorium seat backs. "Pay attention!"

It looked up, squinting its glowing purple eyes sleepily.

After more shouting until enough monsters were more or less paying attention, and a spotted monster the size of a rabbit, who seemed to be in charge, made an explosion go off and screamed, "Shut up!" it was time for Percy's and Jordon's Teach Back.

Percy shoved Jordon forward with its icy body. "You're the expert. Do the talking. I'll nod and things like that."

Jordon stumbled with another shove from Percy. When he straightened up, he saw all the glowing eyes on him. Oh, how he wished he had the leadership manifesto as a cheat sheet. But he didn't. So he did the next best thing: "You are leaves."

The Teach Back was a resounding success. The monsters got into the leaf bit, and Jordon sprinkled in enough of the communication and "How are you feeling?" to actually bring tears to some of their glowing eyes. The massive green monster declared with passion, "I'm bringing my human here right now and we're gonna communicate!" Lots of "hear-hear" and shrieks of delight and a wave of monsters vanished then reappeared a moment later with an assortment of ashen, shaking, sobbing humans. "Do the leaf thing again!" the green monster demanded.

So Jordon did.

There was lots of hugging by the monsters of their humans. Unfortunately, that didn't go over too well with the humans, and Jordon was a bit reassured that he wasn't the only one who hated being touched by an ice-cold monster. Some humans broke loose and ran about, arms flailing, tripping over auditorium chairs. But that did not dampen the monsters' enthusiasm. The auditorium trembled with their excited roars. The green monster became so excited, declaring, "I am one with you!" to its human, that it swallowed the poor woman in one gulp.

A few other monsters caught the fever and swallowed their humans too. The screams increased to an alarming level, both of the delighted monster variety, and the terrified human variety.

"You know what they say," Percy said, grabbing Jordon in an ice-cold hug, "leave 'em wanting more." With that, they were back in Jordon's room. Dawn was barely making an appearance outside the window.

"Time for shut-eye for me," Percy said. "That was a great Teach Back. We make a dream team, don't we?" Then Percy disappeared under Jordon's bed.

It was time for Jordon to go to school again, with no sleep whatsoever. He felt nearly delirious, but he had another idea.

Leaders Share

"Hey, Junior, can I talk with you for a sec?"

Junior was trying to shove a wad of gum through the vents of someone's locker, but he was easily distracted. "Oh, sure." He popped the wad of gum back into his mouth.

Jordon led Junior to a secluded hallway near a back-exit door. "You know that thing under my bed?"

"Percy?" Junior was instantly excited.

"Want to meet it?"

Jjunior started hyperventilating. "Can I? Can I really? Can we skip out? Now?"

"Can't see why not."

All afternoon in Jordon's room, Junior hyperventilated and chattered and nearly fainted with anticipation. When night finally arrived and Percy popped out from under Jordon's bed, its "Surprise!" faded into a "Sur ... prise?" when it noticed Doom Jr. was also sitting on the bed.

"Oh, My, God! Are you serious?" Doom Jr. became so excited, he grabbed Percy in a hug. Jordon noted Junior didn't cringe when he touched Percy's icy-dust-ball-ness. It was Percy who cringed.

"What is this other boy doing here?" Percy demanded.

Doom Jr. giggled. "Love how you talk, Percy." Doom Jr. still held Percy tight in a hug and showed no sign of releasing the monster.

"Percy," Jordon explained, "we're sharing. You already know about Junior, so that makes you connected. Remember the leaf and the communication and all that?"

Percy's dark spot that stood for a mouth made what Jordon thought was a frown. "I'm a one-boy monster. I think I told you that."

"Is that how a leader talks?"

The frown continued, but Jordon thought he detected signs of melting as Doom Jr. cooed, "Oh, Percy, you're the greatest, the coolest ever, ever, ever."

"I was thinking," Jordon continued with what he felt was his new leader's voice, "we can go to the Monster Convention and do another Teach Back. Remember how empowering that was, Percy?"

"Fine," Percy grumbled, though its red spots that stood for eyes glanced in a less hostile way at Doom Jr.: "Oh, Percy, you're the most monster, monster, ever."

In a flash, the three of them were in the shadowy auditorium.

"Hey, I thought I burned this down," Doom Jr. said, but then in the next second, his attention was consumed by the monstrous goings on. "Oh, Dr. Doom, way, way cool!"

Monsters of various sizes, shapes, and material manifestations swung from the ceilings, vomited multicolored pixies across the auditorium, and tore up seats to toss for their unhappy humans in a hideous game of fetch. It was a party. The only sad one, besides the fetching humans, was the huge green monster who'd eaten its human last time. Curled up in a ball in the far corner, obscuring the blinking Exit sign, it sobbed heavily, purple tears cascading from its glowing purple eyes.

The spotted monster in charge was busy hissing at a similar rabbit-sized monster, but with stripes. Jordon took advantage of their power play drama, and ran up the steps to the stage, leaving Percy and Junior behind. "Have a seat!" he called back to them. "I want the two of you to participate in the audience to get the full motivation impact." Clutching Percy tight, Junior happily sat in a front row seat. Percy's red blob eyes stared at Junior, softening, softening.

"Hey everybody! Ready for another Teach Back?" Jordon called to the crowd. The monsters came instantly to attention this time and roared with approval. Jordon felt his leader confidence rise. "You are leaves."

It rankled him.

Doom, Jr.—yes, the kids still called him that, but in a fun, chummy way, not the cruel tones of times past—had a following now, both at school and online. "Doom, Jr., your puppet is so cool. You're so cool!" Always walking around school now with his phone, recording himself and the "puppet," a.k.a. Percy, chatting with new friends, a.k.a. the bullies who used to torment him, but now popping into Jr.'s shots to smile and wave and laugh amusing things for the wide world to see and appreciate with comments like, "Doom, Jr., how can I get a puppet like yours?"

It rankled.

And what about him? There were positives, of course. Jordon felt truly awake for the first time since he and his mom moved into the stepdad's apartment. The world seemed lighter; colors came out. Jordon actually felt the breeze outside, and he wanted to be in the sun, the air, instead of hiding inside, dreading the night. If he could afford to buy all new, non-black clothes, he would.

The bullies, the other kids? They still called him Dr. Doom, but with less venom than before. Mostly, they ignored the new him. The other Doom and his puppet had caught their fancy.

Rankled.

Leaders Take Care of Business

Jordon approached Doom Jr. during a pause in his phone filming, when his new bully fans were briefly not there. "Hey, Junior!"

Junior's face was guarded. "Hey," he quietly responded while his attention went back to his phone. Percy's red blob eyes didn't even look up at his ex-human.

"I'd love to go to the next Monster Convention with you and Percy. I kind of miss hanging out there. It'd be cool to say 'Hi' to some of the crew and all, you know? How about it?"

"Ahhhh ..." Junior looked at Percy, who looked up at Junior from his snug perch in Junior's backpack. "Welllll ... we're kinda involved in a new committee there, and, Jeez, I'm not sure about our time ..." They both made eye-avoiding half-shrugs.

Jordon had a feeling neither of them would want him lurking around, but still. Being blown off by these two he'd brought together, it rankled. A lot. On the positive, it reinforced his motivation. Jordon couldn't go to the Monster Convention on his own. Only Percy had the ability to pull a human into that realm.

"I hear you. No problem. I'm not meaning I'd be glued to you guys every minute. I was thinking we could do a Teach Back to everyone about how well things have worked out with you two. What do you think?"

Jordon knew this Teach Back would be way beyond what the Junior-Percy team would tolerate from Jordon the uncool. In comparison, Jordon hitching a ride with them was less toxically annoying. Plus, cleverly reminding them that it was he who'd hooked them up was meant to play to whatever bit of guilt might be rattling around inside either of them.

61

Big sighs from both. "Oh, I guess we could pencil in time for that. We leave promptly at 20:00 hours from my room. Be late, and you'll miss the train," Junior said with a bored rise of an eyebrow. Percy huffed and turned about in the backpack, leaving what stood for his backside to face Jordon.

"Oh, absolutely."

At the appointed hour, in the appointed place, Jordon grabbed Doom Jr. and Percy, the two of them cringing at his touch. In an instant, they were in the old school auditorium.

Junior and Percy quickly left Jordon to join the spotted and striped rabbit monsters, who appeared to have formed a truce, along with a huddle of excited creatures and their humans planning a Teach Back on "Breakthroughs in Motivated Monster-Human Communication!"

More monsters were coming into the shadowy auditorium, the buzz was rising. Here and there Jordon spotted more humans, not all of whom were feeling the breakthrough motivations, and were sobbing to prove the point.

The one who sobbed most of all was not a human, but the large green creature who'd eaten its human in the initial burst of enthusiasm when the leadership concepts first hit the monster world with a little too much force. It was still in the back by the Exit sign, alone with its huffing tears.

Leaders Reach Out to Those in Need
Jordon sat next to it. "How are you feeling?"

In the next few weeks, life lightened up even more for Jordon. The Dr. Doom moniker was forgotten. He had a new after school job—no, business—as a dog walker/cat feeder/plant waterer for the traveling and chronically busy people in the neighborhood. Pets no longer growled or fled in terror from him because Percy's scent no longer clung to him. With funds from his enterprise, Jordon bought brighter clothes, tropical even. It was Jordon's mood nowadays. The black clothes? Donated to charity. He bought a phone too and posted photos of his new shirts online. His only follower was the shirt manufacturer, but he had to start somewhere.

Jordon was still mostly ignored at school, but hoped his Teach Back at the next "Reinforce Your Motivation Seminar" called "Total Breakthrough: Change Your Life," might help in that area, at least among the motivation groupies. Jordon would welcome any friends at this point. Later, he could afford to be more choosy.

Doom Jr.? Nowadays, Jordon felt sorry for him. Hard not to.

Drooping face, feet dragging, dark circles under the eyes. Percy was nowhere to be seen, always hiding in the backpack. Gone was Jr.'s phone filming of clever bits with his puppet for posting.

The bullies weren't amused. "Hey, Doom Jr., why aren't you posting? Where's your puppet? What's your problem?"

Leaders Don't Look Back

Setting aside how much of a jerk Doom Jr. had been post-Percy, Jordon sat next to him as Junior sat clutching Percy in the backpack, head hanging, on a bench in the far corner of the school grounds next to the scorched foundation, all that remained of the burned auditorium.

"Hey, Junior, how are you feeling?"

A long sigh, and another long sigh echoing from somewhere inside the backpack. Not the annoyed sigh when Jordon asked to go to the Monster Convention. But a sigh of hopelessness.

Jordon put his arm around his once friend, who didn't cringe this time. "Junior, I want you to know I'm here for you. Come to my motivation Teach Back today about breakthroughs."

Doom Jr. flinched and cringed. A groan from the backpack. "That's a bunch of crap. You're not seriously believing that anymore?"

"Hey, look at what leadership did to me. Do you know a shirt manufacturer is following me on social media?" Jordon raised his eyebrows and tugged his orange shirt dotted with palm trees. "My life is becoming amazing."

Another simultaneous sigh choked with a sob: "A big green monster moved under our bed."

Jordon stifled a grin. "That's rough. But think about coming to my Teach Back. Maybe it'll help."

Doom Jr. gave him a dark look. Percy peeked its red blob eyes out of the backpack to glower.

No matter. Jordon walked away and did not look back. That's what leaders do.

Leaders are Huge Helpers

That night, Jordon drifted to sleep pondering a move to Florida post-high school. It would fit his new, tropical palm tree lifestyle.

Suddenly, his bed heaved up to the ceiling, jolting Jordon awake. An ice-cold grip encircled him. He screamed.

By the glow of the thing's massive purple eyes, Jordon saw it was the huge green monster from the auditorium. Gone were its tears, replaced by an orange tusk-filled smile. It icily hugged Jordon close.

"Junior said you were lonely too, and he said we can help each other from now to forever. Percy said that's what leaders do."

"Monster Teach Back" is **Rosalind Barden's** sixth story in the *Strangely Funny* series. Mystery and Horror, LLC has also included her stories in their anthologies *History And Mystery, Oh My!* (FAPA President's Book Award Silver Medalist), and *Mardi Gras Murder*. Her humorous Young Adult mystery novel set in Depression-era Los Angeles, *Sparky Of Bunker Hill and the Cold Kid Case*, is an Author Academy Award Top Ten Mystery Finalist and a Critters Annual Readers Poll Top Finisher in both Best Mystery and Best Young Adult categories. Dozens more of her stories have appeared in print anthologies and webzines, including the U.K.'s acclaimed *Whispers Of Wickedness*. Ellen Datlow selected her short story "Lion Friend" as a Best Horror of the Year Honorable Mention after appearing in *Cern Zoo*, a British Fantasy Society nominee for Best Anthology, part of DF Lewis' award winning *Nemonymous* anthology series. *TV Monster* is her print children's book she wrote and illustrated. Her satirical novel *American Witch* is available as an e-book. In addition, her scripts, novel manuscripts and short fiction have placed in numerous competitions, including the *Writers' Digest* Screenplay Competition and the Shriekfast Film Festival. She lives in Los Angeles, California. Discover more at www.RosalindBarden.com

A Nice Place to Visit
by A.L. King

The little tourist trap drew a great deal of attention.

EXPERIENCE HELL—JUST 5 MILES! a sign by the highway read, a painted-on arrow pointing toward the desert.

Wayward travelers at first considered it a joke, yet still they drove down the makeshift path until they reached a rickety shed. Another sign had been erected outside the hastily built shanty. This one read, HELL: A NICE PLACE TO VISIT.

When asked, "How much?", the man inside always answered with a grin, "The first trip is free!"

There were only four walls and a flat ceiling. The floor was the same desert dust it had always been, but for a deep six-foot wide by six-foot long hole at center. The proprietor pointed each guest toward the pit, even if it wasn't their first trip.

Weeks after this strange new roadside attraction sprang up, it was common for lines of cars to stretch for miles. Months into the existence of the business, traffic began backing up on the highway.

There were many skeptics initially. Memes about the shed were shared online, mocking the strange new business while serving as a free source of advertisement.

Journalists reported that one clever Nevadan was profiting from a blatant satire of the Las Vegas Strip. Evangelical pundits suggested the man behind it was, in reality, Satan himself. The proprietor, however, rejected both notions. Any time the cameras were on him, he simply smiled and said with a wink, "I'm not the Devil, but I am a capitalist. It's the real deal. Come see for yourself. The first visit is free."

Visitors who were interviewed gladly confirmed the legitimacy of the business. Among them was a former congressman recently released from prison. He explained how humbled he was following his trip to Hell.

"I served my time for sexting that teenage girl, but there is a far worse sentence in store for me if I don't sincerely turn myself around. I used to believe there was no such thing as Hell. Now I do believe, and I think everyone should visit."

"Even the Pope?" asked one snarky reporter.

"Especially the Pope," the disgraced politician replied. He then appeared to consider that belittling the Holy Father may well be a sin, and he quickly backpedaled. "Because, you know, he needs to see firsthand what happens to people who are not saved."

Paparazzi and spectators took video of the supposedly saved ex-statesman as he entered the shed at least once a week. When questioned about why he felt the need to return, he responded with another question.

"Why do Catholics return to confession?"

Soon the road was paved. Painted boards were plucked from the ground, and posts holding large neon signs were cemented in their place. The shanty fell so a building strongly resembling Fort Knox could go up around the portal to Hell.

The gift shop sold souvenirs. People walked out wearing t-shirts that stated, HELL IS A NICE PLACE TO VISIT! Keychains shaped like cute little devils danced as happy customers turned keys in ignitions. Horned hats—the equivalents of caps with Mickey Mouse ears—could be seen through rear glass, bobbing on the heads of kids as their families drove away from their new favorite vacation destination.

A rest stop, a few gas stations, three hotels, and a Denny's sprang up around the literal Hellhole, but it was with the arrival of casinos, strip clubs, and licensed brothels that a critical eye turned on the economic progress.

"If this place is supposed to scare people toward salvation, isn't it contradicting to tempt them once again only a few doors down?" asked detractors. Those in opposition never failed to point out how a former representative was building a condo on the outskirts.

The proprietor offered a somewhat philosophical response.

"Do not drug rehabilitation facilities exist across the street from liquor stores and pharmacies? We should be sympathetic of relapse as a society. After all, such setbacks are a huge part of the recovery process. Besides ... those naughty places aren't necessarily meant for those who have already gone to my business in order to be humbled. They are for those yet to enter the hole. Many people want to come here and experience one last hurrah before going through Hell and seeing the light upon their return."

One appeal for visiting was how the experience seemed to differ for every person, the landscape of Hell also changing with each trip. Some theorized that the amount of goodness versus sin determined just how harrowing the experience. The better you behaved prior to entering the hole, the less painful the experience. The worse you were ... well, you get the point.

One brave documentarian vowed to explore the depths of Hell by committing one atrocious act after another. For thirty days straight, his crimes escalated. At the end of each day, following his latest and greatest sin, he walked into that infernal pit. He shared dramatic tears with the cameras upon each resurface.

"It was so much worse that time! I swear to God ... at the end of this month-long stint, I'm going to turn things around. I'm going to ask the Lord for forgiveness and avoid going there for eternity. It's true what they say ... Hell is a nice place to visit, but I wouldn't want to stay."

Satanize Me was a massive hit. The sequel, De-Satanize Me, in which the producer/documentarian/subject attempted to counter his dark deeds with Christian-like behavior, was less financially successful. It did, however, make a lasting cultural impact.

Although camcorders would not work in Hell, and although the filmmaker reported that Hell softened with each good deed, he came to a startling conclusion after his thirty days of virtue had lapsed.

The film ended with an emotional profession.

"I'm still going to Hell," the star of the documentary said. "I could dedicate the rest of my life to doing only good, and it wouldn't put a dent in that uppermost level. It may be different with each visit, but I still end up there." He pointed at the pit. The camera followed his finger. "If someone walks into that hole in the ground and doesn't experience anything but that hole in the ground, I'd like to see if that person can also walk on water."

Of all the film's clips to surface on YouTube, that excerpt was the third most-viewed. Two behind his near-breakdown after going three weeks without masturbating, and just barely behind the scene where he buys and donates a Girl Scout troop's entire stock of cookies to the homeless.

The belief that you could not escape your destination no matter how hard you tried had a profound effect on society. First, there was a remarkable shift toward decadence. Second came the inevitable leveling out as the new status quo settled like cement.

"According to most experts, the fate of your eternal soul can always get worse," said one interviewer to a kindergarten dropout who released mustard gas on her babysitter. "So, I have to know ... aren't you afraid of Hell?"

The gifted little chemist, speaking like the leader of a terrorist cell, gave a confident response.

"There's no need to be afraid. After I do something a lot worse than I've ever done before, I just visit Hell. It gives me the chance to get used to my fate. I'll cut as many throats as I have to in order to be rich. Then I can visit Hell whenever I want to! I'll be immune to its punishments by the time I die!"

She then offered a devilish smile. Watch the clip closely enough, and you'll see the interviewer shudder.

As it turned out, the founder of the business only discovered the portal as the result of digging a hole to dump a prostitute he'd slain. But once he realized the potential of the otherworldly gateway, he buried her two-hundred yards away. Ironically, it was the success of his entrepreneurial efforts that resulted in outing his crime. They'd been expanding the Denny's parking lot when they dug up the corpse.

The murder would have been a major scandal before the Hellhole opened, but times had changed. Not as much as a warrant was issued for the arrest of the wealthy entrepreneur, who practically shrugged off what little outcry reached him.

"I do apologize, but I can only apologize so much for my actions," he said, as assertive as ever. "I say that, but a part of me finds it difficult to really be too, too sorry. After all, my sin led to the salvation of millions, soon to be billions. I include myself in those numbers. Praise Jesus!"

He died of dehydration about a week later, face down in vomit on the bathroom floor of the penthouse overlooking his empire. He had accidentally stepped on a bark scorpion and mistakenly thought he would be fine when the sickness caused by the venom cleared up in a day or two.

The debate about the fate of his soul persisted for some time.

Until the discovery of the second Hellhole, the largest investments in property were primarily for mineral rights. That all changed when investors knew they had a chance at striking something much deeper and darker than oil.

One was found in Japan, at the base of Mount Fuji. Another was found in Quebec, Canada. North Korea claimed it had a Hellhole, but nothing was ever substantiated. A few celebrities discovered or purchased their own, private slices of Hell.

The mass media fueled debates about the affordability of visiting Hell. Long gone were the days when peoples' first trips were free.

Politicians were quick to pander.

"Going to Hell is a basic human right!" one presidential frontrunner started out each campaign rally. "Just like healthcare and housing and food and a vehicle and access to the Internet."

The infamous ex-congressman who served time in prison for sexting a teenager got in on the debate.

"I was on the Hellhole bandwagon to begin with, so while I respect the senator's position and wish everyone could experience it for free, he's not saying how we'll accomplish that. Our party needs to be practical in the primary if we expect to win the general. We need to be specific."

A member of the opposite party unsurprisingly opposed the proposal of free Hellhole visits, speaking instead in support of free-market Hellholes.

"I don't see Senator Socialist using his vast wealth to purchase and hand out millions of tickets to Hell. I say he puts his money where his mouth is if that's what he really believes. Besides, it would bankrupt our country if we tried to pay for everything that's not a basic need."

One commentator gave pause, then asked a follow-up question. "So, you're saying that people don't have the right to know the fates of their eternal souls?"

"I ... uh ... um ... I guess that's for the voters to decide. I for one ... um ... just think we need to be careful with how we redistribute wealth in this country."

A law was passed to place a minimum age on visiting Hell.

"Used to be I could go down to the corner store and buy my mom a pack of cigarettes," said the bill's sponsor. "But times change for a reason. The vast majority of children can't handle the effects of visiting Hell. Many of them don't even know what Hell is yet!"

On the opposite end, the speaker of the house said the passing of that particular legislation was not only ageist, but it also dealt a devastating blow to parents' rights. "It's a sad day when a parent can't put their kid through Hell!" she said.

The same girl who once caused permanent damage to her babysitter's health by exposing her to mustard gas vowed to murder the families of every politician who voted in favor of the bill.

"I'll do it, too!" she promised. "I'm not afraid of going to Hell! If they don't call a special session and do the right thing by overturning that silly law, they can kiss their husbands and wives and kids goodbye!"

She made partial payment on her promise ... until a sniper took her out, thus freeing the surviving hostages.

The public obsession lasted for some time. However, as Mom and Pop shops went out of business due to shopping malls and those malls closed doors due to the prevalence of online shopping, Hellholes eventually became things of the past, nostalgic nuggets occasionally referenced in television shows.

Several years after the first Hellhole in Nevada was boarded up, the hole resembling the remains of a shutdown mine, a group of youths broke into the building.

On their way out, one of them remarked, "I don't get what my parents are always going on about! It's just a friggin' hole in the ground! Wait ... did the rest of you experience anything?"

Alexander Lloyd King (publishing as **A.L. King**) is an author of horror, fantasy, science fiction, and poetry. As a fan of dark subjects from an early age, his first influences included R.L. Stine, Edgar Allan Poe, and Stephen King. Later stylistic inspirations came from foreign horror films and media, particularly Japanese.

He is a graduate of West Liberty University in West Virginia, has dabbled in journalism, and is actively involved in his community. Although his creativity leans toward darker genres, he has written a children's book titled Leif's First Fall.

He was raised in the town of Sistersville, West Virginia, which he still proudly calls home.

Platinum VIP
Kelly Gould

It was a brisk autumn morning as Rachel Post left her house for her morning jog. The sun was out, but she could see her breath in the air. A quick stretch, a heavy sigh, and she was off.

Rachel hated running. Even though she had friends who swore they loved it, she never understood how someone could enjoy the sensations that came with pounding the pavement. The burning legs, the difficulty breathing, and the pain in most every joint convinced her that her friends must be dirty liars. She was only a couple of years removed from gaining her college Freshman Fifteen, and she wanted to make sure those pounds never returned. Running on the sidewalk was cheaper than a gym membership and certainly fit her meager budget.

She was already gritting her teeth at the half-mile mark, trying to put the discomfort out of her mind and lose herself in her music. Wireless earbuds and her smart phone, gifts from her parents, streamed Motivating Jamz from the radio app she had downloaded just for running.

Downtown Irvington went by her, but Rachel hardly noticed. She kept her eyes on the ground in front of her feet. Traffic, both pedestrian and vehicle, was light so early on a Saturday.

This time she made it a little more than a mile before she slowed to a walk. The song on the radio was going much faster than she was.

Static from her earbuds interrupted Rachel's fledgling body aches. At first, she assumed it was due to the tall buildings around her, but it only got worse as she went on.

A voice, faint at first but quickly becoming clearer, came through the static.

"...atinum VIP experience starts on 34th street in Irvington, Oregon. Longtime fans will recognize the address, but not the building's current configuration. In 2021, the now famous Butkus Club on 34th and Schmidt was a combination tattoo parlor and marijuana dispensary."

What the hell was this? The voice took Rachel's attention away from her exercise ordeal. She stopped and found herself looking across the street at Big Tim's Tattoo and Cannabis Supply. The two street signs she stood under told her she was on the corner of 34th and Schmidt.

"The Butkus Club," the voice continued, "was the site of Abigail LaFleur's big break. She was first discovered there, performing with her band Spoiler Alert. The band's bass player, Stephen Mackey, would later join her on Voyager 6."

Rachel crossed Schmidt Street to examine Big Tim's more closely. She must have passed by dozens of times but never really noticed it. Nobody was in there now and she tried to picture how the building could be remodeled into a concert venue.

"Our next stop on your BTWF Platinum VIP Tour is Campbell Square, just three blocks south of the Butkus Club."

Hesitating only a moment before breaking back into a jog, Rachel made her way towards Campbell Square. She actually didn't know her south from north, but she knew where the square was. Her pace, now that she had a destination in mind, was quicker than before.

Campbell Square was almost empty when she got there. A few transients milled around the cobblestone courtyard in the middle of downtown. There was a small group of people gathered around the statue of a well-dressed man in the center of the square. They seemed out of place, taking pictures of themselves like tourists but dressed business casual, like they were going to the office.

Rachel, still breathing heavy, walked over to them. "Hi, folks. Good morning." She smiled big and tried to not look as awkward as she felt. "Taking pictures, huh? You from around here?"

The group, there were six of them, regarded her with worried looks. "No, we're just here visiting family," said one of the two men. Rachel couldn't see a family resemblance in any of their faces. She gave an unintentional skeptical frown.

"We ... were just leaving. Don't want to get a parking allegation on our automobile." The man seemed to struggle to find the right words, like someone speaking a second language not quite as well as their first.

Parking allegation on their automobile? What strange phrasing, she thought, but kept to herself.

Her earbuds came back to life as she watched the visitors leave. "Campbell Square was prominently featured in the movie 'From Nowhere to Here'. LaFleur's performance in this film earned her a second Oscar to go with her four Grammys. The iconic scene of LaFleur's character, Patrice, and her rousing speech to an audience of zombie apocalypse survivors was filmed in Campbell Square and has become a classic piece of Americana. The statue of former Irvington Mayor Charlie Campbell is now on display in the Smithsonian."

The plaque on the statue in front of her read:
CHARLIE F. CAMPBELL
IRVINGTON MAYOR
1985-1994

"What hell is going on?" she thought out loud. None of this made any sense. Was this some sort of new podcast or a really elaborate prank? Before Rachel could even begin to wrap her mind around the situation, the now familiar voice filled her ears again.

"Thank you for choosing Before They Were Famous Tours for your unique, exclusive meet and greet opportunities. Only with BTWF Tours can you have the ultimate in fan experiences. Meet your idols with no crowds and no pressure. We only ask that you remain within the guidelines set forth in your orientation."

Rachel pulled her phone from its carrier on her arm. On the screen, in the place of the usual radio app logo, was a digital hourglass. The sand in the hourglass was slowly falling to the bottom one grain at a time. The bottom of the screen read: "Abigail LaFleur Tour, 5 Star, 2021." She was too afraid to touch the screen; she didn't know what might happen if she did.

She carefully put her phone back as static replaced the voice of the tour guide. The strange tourists were gone but Rachel headed in the direction she had seen them last. The city was waking up. The day was beginning to get warmer. Shops were opening for the day's business.

The people of Irvington were generally a friendly lot, and this morning was no different. Rachel received several warm smiles and greetings as she made her way through downtown. Her responses were perfunctory. The surreality of this particular morning jog made her too preoccupied for regular social interaction.

With all thoughts of a morning workout now gone, Rachel wandered. She quickly realized that she was searching. Searching for the tour guide's voice or another glimpse of the strangers from the statue. Up and down the streets, she was slowly but surely losing hope. She strained to hear beyond the white noise in her earbuds. There was nothing.

Rachel shook her head and muttered to herself. Then she turned around and went back the way she had come, taking the quickest route that would lead her back home.

She didn't make it far before the static started to change. At first, she thought it was just her imagination. Her desire to hear something through the nothingness tricked her mind into thinking something was there. Then she managed to make out a garbled word. Then another. The voice came through the static once again.

"We have now reached the final portion of your VIP tour." Like before, the tour guide became clearer as she walked. She must be going the right direction. "In the fall of 2021, 19-year-old Abigail LaFleur worked as a barista at a locally owned coffee shop called The Coffee Hut."

The Coffee Hut? Rachel knew right where that was. She had never stopped there but several of her friends swore that it had the best coffee in town.

"On this day in 2021, the day of your Platinum VIP Experience, Ms. LaFleur is working the ten to two shift at the Coffee Hut. Her specialty drink is the Cinnamon Roll Double Shot. Today it is six American dollars including gratuity. As some of you may remember from the fourth volume of her autobiography, this is the drink she claims she still made for herself even while in the Oval Office. Ms. Lafleur said that nobody else could quite get it right."

Rachel covered the distance to the coffee shop faster than she would have previously thought possible. She was breathing heavy, but paused for only a moment before she went in.

There were plenty of empty tables at the Coffee Hut. The early morning rush for caffeine had given way to a late morning lull. Rachel looked around the room, barely noticing the half dozen or so patrons. Behind the counter, she found what she was looking for. The blonde girl stood near the cash register, smiling and chatting casually with a co-worker. She wore a name badge that read ABBY in big, bold letters.

The girl looked even younger than the 19 years Rachel knew her to be. Despite that youthful appearance, the girl behind the counter radiated a confidence and self-assurance that drew people to her while making them comfortable at the same time. She was instantly likable. This was Abigail LaFleur.

An older couple sat at a corner table whispering conspiratorially to each other. Their matching grey hair and the way they held each other's hands suggested they had been together for a very long time.

The woman stood up suddenly, gently twisting out of her husband's grasp. "Donna, don't," he said, shaking his head at her. Donna stood up straight and nervously adjusted her long-sleeved red sweater. Taking a deep breath, she walked purposefully across the room to Abigail.

The older woman reached across the counter, taking the younger woman's hand in hers. From her spot across the room, Rachel couldn't hear what was said. Abigail looked confused but not frightened. There were tears in Donna's eyes as she spoke. Whatever she said only took her a few seconds but seemed much longer.

A man emerged from the opposite side of the coffee shop. He must have been at one of those back tables this whole time, Rachel thought. He wore a generic baseball cap to go with his nondescript windbreaker and jeans.

"We have to go," was all he said. He took Donna, sternly but not harshly, by her arms and ushered her towards the front door. Rachel had to practically jump out of their way as they hustled out of the building. Donna's husband kept his head down and followed a short distance behind.

"This timeline has been compromised." A new voice immediately came to life in Rachel's ear. This one lacked the melodic tone of the tour guide. It was rougher and all business. "Initiate emergency protocols."

Rachel tensed at that. She didn't know what to expect but the new voice's tone and choice of words made her anxious. Those remaining in the coffee shop were just going about their everyday business. Generally, people don't notice what is going on around them. The Coffee Hut was no exception. If they even noticed anything was amiss in the first place, they just shrugged their shoulders and moved on.

Gradually, Rachel let herself relax. Nothing happened. She felt a little embarrassed even though she wasn't sure why.

"I can help the next person." It was Abigail. She was looking right at Rachel as she spoke. Nobody else was in line. Rachel could feel her face turning red.

Rachel approached the counter and cleared her throat. "Yeah, hi. Um, I'll have a large Cinnamon Roll Double Shot."

"One Cinnamon Roll Double Shot coming right up. Will that be all?"

"Actually, yeah," Rachel said as she removed her phone from its case. "This is going to sound really weird, but would you mind taking a selfie with me?"

Kelly Gould lives and writes in Oregon with his wife and children. He is an avid fan of the Chicago Bears and Van Halen (w/ Sammy Hagar). When he isn't writing he is usually enjoying good whiskey and bad horror movies.

His work has been included in anthologies from Lycan Valley Press, A Murder of Storytellers, Deadman's Tome, Lycopolis Press, Aphotic Realm, and Weirdbook. His story, "Hopelessly Devoted," was a part of the anthology *Stories of the Dead: A Tribute to George Romero*.

Road of Bones
by C.D. Gallant-King

"Don't go that way."

The old man's face contorted and twisted like a cow as he chewed a wad of ... something. Maybe it was tobacco, maybe it was tough meat, maybe it was strips of flesh from the inside of his own mouth, sloughing off from the rot. Honestly, Antonio didn't want to know either way.

"Excuse me?" Antonio asked. He was sitting at a table with his groomsmen, drinking far too much wine at a filthy tavern in a village he had never even heard of. Saint's Cave? Salty Cove? He had no idea and was too drunk to care. The five of them were celebrating Antonio's upcoming nuptials. It was a newfangled sort of gathering the folks up in Dyskovenia called a "bachelor party."

It was Antonio's best friend Thorvald's idea, this bachelor party business. All Antonio knew was that he'd been loaded for a week, and if his fiancée found out they'd spent enough coin on booze and whores to buy a summer cottage, she would be pissed.

"Don't take the Almoner's Road." The old man was grey and bent, with a wild look in his eyes. He was seated alone at a table a dozen paces away from Antonio's party. When he spoke, the whole tavern grew quiet.

Thorvald, a scrawny rake with the arrogance and loudness of a man three times his size, sneered at the old-timer. "We're trying to get back to Whyte-upon-Rice. They say the Almoner's Road is the fastest way."

"We got a wedding to get to tomorrow!" added one of the other revelers. He was a young fellow named Drebin, called "Titmouse" by his friends on account of both his terrible haircut and because of the night he got drunk and tried to nurse from the teat of a vole. Titmouse was barely old enough to shave, and unfortunately thought himself a bit of a wit. "Though why anyone would want to stop this party to have a chain clamped around their balls is beyond me."

The men at Antonio's table laughed and clanged their flagons, but the old man didn't so much as crack a smile.

"Aye, it's faster." The old man nodded, then spat something horrific onto the sawdust of the tavern floor. Antonio tried not to look directly at it. He was pretty sure it was moving. "But you'll regret it. No one who goes up that way at night ever comes back the same."

"Are there highwaymen?" Antonio asked, quite earnestly. Antonio was a plain, simple man, a little older than Titmouse and not as brash as Thorvald. He had always held a fear of being robbed on the road, ever since a gang of bandits had ambushed his father and uncle when he was but a boy. His uncle said the bandits had stripped his father bare, buggered him with a mace handle, then chopped him into little pieces and fed him to the gang's pet boar. Antonio hadn't seen any of this of course, but his uncle had painted quite a picture. Literally. Uncle Auk was an accomplished artist, and had painted a triptych of the event which still hung over the fire in the family's ancestral manor. The scene had haunted Antonio since he was three years old.

"Nothing so banal." The old man continued to chew. "You go up there and you'll wish you were only buggered by a mace, chopped up and fed to a boar."

Antonio shuddered. Either the old man was a seer, or that must be the preferred, and very specific, method of banditry in these parts.

"Have you heard about the Nunnery of the Damned?"

"Sounds like a minstrel's troupe." Thorvald guffawed at his own joke.

"Laugh all you want, but what happened to those poor women is no joking matter." The old man leaned back in his seat, and everyone in the tavern unconsciously leaned closer. There was a feeling in the air, the unmistakable, universal understanding that some crazy old coot was about to tell a ghost story. It was a primal instinct, like blood turning cold at the sound of a wolf's howl or running from the room covering your ass when your father reached for his belt. The tavern grew deathly quiet.

"I don't know how long ago it happened, but this was an old story when my grandpappy told it to me as a lad knee high to a pubic louse. There's an old nunnery up on the hill along the Almoner's Road,

80

about a league and a half from here. They say it used to be called the Convent of Sacred Salvation, or some bullshit like that. Maybe it was Holy Heart Nunhouse, I don't remember, the mind isn't what it used to be."

"What did it used to be?" asked Titmouse. "A potato?"

"Shut up, Drebin." Antonio was on the edge of his seat. He hadn't taken his eyes off the old-timer, who continued his tale.

"The important thing is that now it is only known as the Nunnery of the Damned, and this is why: Many years ago, on a full moon just like this, a gang of bandits rode up to the nunnery, looking for something to ease the boredom of the backwoods roads. Now, even the most vile and bloodthirsty robbers will usually steer clear of a nunhouse, for to harm the anointed sisters will surely bring the wrath of the gods. But these men were not just vile and bloodthirsty, they were drunk, and desperate, and had not seen a coin or a whore's embrace for many days. They were not thinking clearly when they kicked down the nunnery door and the bandit leader demanded the mother superior suck his cock."

The tavern was silent but for the sound of the fire crackling and the old man chewing. No one laughed. They all knew this story was about to get as dark as a witch's asshole.

"The sisters pleaded, and begged for mercy, but their cries fell on deaf ears. The bandits raped and murdered every one of them, some of them many times over. The mother superior was the last, who had watched all of the others butchered and defiled, and with her dying breath cursed the bandits. She swore that from that night forward any man who stepped within sight of the convent would be struck with all the fury and vengeance of the gods, and that any who felt their wrath would beg for the solace of death, which would be a mercy compared to what horrors they would wreak upon their souls."

Antonio contemplated the story. He did have a question about how someone could be murdered many times over, but he let that one slide and asked another instead. "What happened to the mother superior?"

"The bandit leader cut off her head and fucked the stump of her neck."

Now there were uncomfortable coughs and mutterings throughout the room. The bartender put a tankard down hard on the bar and half the room nearly leapt out of their seats. Antonio squeezed his fists together so tightly in his lap he nearly broke his own fingers. This was getting far too close to his nightmares of his father's death.

81

The old man spat on the floor and continued. Several people pushed their chairs a little farther away from the growing black stain. "The bandits piled the corpses of their victims in the chapel and collapsed at dawn, exhausted from their slaughter orgy. They slept through most of the day, for when they woke the sun was once again low in the sky. If they had left right away, perhaps they would have survived, but instead they went about cleaning out the rest of the nunnery's stores, taking whatever food and wine and brass candlesticks they could carry. When the sun set, the ghosts came."

Thorvald rolled his eyes. The thin man with an even thinner mustache and eyes that looked like two piss holes in the snow did not believe in ghosts, Antonio knew. Never mind that Thorvald's own mother had been a fortune teller and soothsayer; Thorvald always called her a filthy thief and liar. "So, I suppose the ghosts killed them, then? Magic invisible ladies stabbed them with glowing daggers?"

Still the storyteller would not rise to the rattish man's bait. He remained level-headed and calm, laying down his wisdom as but a courtesy, leaving those in attendance to decide whether they would heed his warning. "No. They lived. But the men who walked out of the nunnery the next morning were not the same. They were broken, their lives and souls crushed. They say that within a week, one by one, each of them perished by his own hand, begging for forgiveness and peace in the next world."

"And how do 'they' know this story, old man?" Thorvald's question dripped with disdain, like the oil that dripped from his slick-back hair. "Sounds like a made-up story to scare babies."

Antonio had never heard a children's story about fucking a dead nun's neck stump, but he held his tongue.

"I know it because they say the bandit leader himself climbed to the roof of our temple, just across the town square from this very inn, and he confessed his sins at the top of his drunken lungs before throwing himself down to smash his head like a rotted gourd on the cobbles below."

They had seen the temple outside before they stumbled into the tavern. It was plain and perfunctory as far as places of worship went, but the spire was pretty tall. A good twenty, thirty feet at least. Antonio's stomach lurched at the thought of it. He hated heights, on account of his Uncle Auk making him re-shingle the roof when he was a child.

The old man continued. "But I don't need to know the story, because we've all heard the ghostly voices from up the Almoner's Road.

We've all known the foolish men who dared to go up that way at night, and seen them come back broken the next day. Folk don't go up there much at all anymore, most use the new road down by the river, but every few years some dipshit—usually from out of town—gets too drunk or too careless and takes the Almoner's Road. If they live to regret it, they don't regret it very long."

"Because they get over it?" asked Titmouse, thoughtfully.

"Because they don't live," said Antonio.

"Your groom is a wise man," said the old man, beginning to rise. "You all best listen to his counsel. Or not, bugger if I care. I've got to take a shit."

The storyteller shuffled out of his chair and around from behind his table. The groomsmen all watched him for a moment, then realized he was an old man who moved with the velocity of a crippled sloth, so they turned their attention back to their own table when he was about a quarter of the way across the tavern.

"What a sodding load of shit." Thorvald chuckled and downed half a mug of ale.

"I don't know, Thorvald, I'm not particularly fond of ghosts." Titmouse looked more skittish and pale than usual. "Perhaps we should listen to the crazy old coot."

Thorvald slammed his tankard down on the table. "There's no such thing as ghosts!"

"No, but there is a such thing as bandits," said Antonio, diplomatically. "Perhaps taking an old, overgrown road at night is not the best plan anyway."

"It's the only way to reach Whyte-upon-Rice by morning." Thorvald shrugged. "If you want to be a coward and listen to a dysenteric codger ..."

"He shit himself on the way to the door." Titmouse's face twisted horribly.

"Fuck you," called the old man, still only two-thirds of the way across the room, but the smell wafting from him was unmistakable. "We'll see how well your bowels work when you reach three score and ten!"

While Titmouse did some arithmetic on his fingers, Thorvald continued. "I'm sure Melissa would be very understanding if you miss your wedding."

Antonio sighed. "It's not Melissa I'm worried about. It's her very wealthy father who is just looking for any excuse to call off his only daughter's wedding."

"Seventy." Titmouse nodded, satisfied. "He doesn't think much of you, does he?"

No, he did not. The family had taken a river boat journey to celebrate the engagement, and when Antonio fell overboard, Melissa's father had only tossed him a rope after someone assured him the other end wasn't tied to anything. Never mind the fact that Antonio was pretty sure his future father-in-law was the one who had pushed him over in the first place. Melissa's father would be more than happy to call off the wedding if they arrived late tomorrow, and Antonio would be out all the lands and gold the union would have brought him.

And Melissa's love, of course. He would also lose that, probably.

But the gold and lands ... with that kind of wealth he could lock himself in his manor and never have to leave and worry about bandits again.

"We take the Almoner's Road," Antonio announced to the table. "How soon can we leave?"

Thorvald smiled. "Right away. Just let me go vomit first; the smell of that old man is turning my stomach."

Shortly, after Thorvald and one of the other groomsmen had emptied their dinners and a gallon of wine and ale in the latrine behind the tavern, the party was on the road again. Antonio rather wished he had emptied his own guts. He was feeling queasy himself, but whether from the drink, the threat of ghostly murder, or just nerves over tomorrow's wedding, he could not say. He felt as he did that time as a boy when Thorvald dared him to eat a live sparrow, and Antonio swore he could feel it fluttering and clawing around in his stomach for hours afterward.

The Almoner's Road was dark, and narrow, overgrown with years of alder bushes. It had taken them over an hour just to find it, even with the directions from the obnoxious farmer who had laughed at them the whole time.

"Follow Hackett's farm up to Frisky Hare Rock," the farmer had explained after asking them several times if they were sure they wanted to go that way. "You can't miss it, it's a big rock shaped like two rabbits rutting. Then take the East road toward the forest, that'll take you straight to Almoner's Road.

"Then, bend over, put your head between your legs, and kiss your ass goodbye. 'Cause you won't be coming out of there alive."

"Actually, the old man in town assured us we would live, but be forever changed." Titmouse smiled, but he didn't have the usual jovial tone to his voice.

After finding the road (Frisky Hare Rock actually looked more like two badgers wrestling, at least according to Titmouse), their travel went swift enough through the woods. It was ominous, and the sky was so dark from overcast clouds they had to rely fully on their lanterns to lead them through. The swinging lamps cast dancing, constantly shifting shadows that made the trees around them appear to be alive with movement. The only sound was their labored breathing and the crunch of their boots on dry leaves and dead branches.

Though it was a warm late summer night, Antonio felt cold. Icy sweat ran down his back and his hands were trembling. This was not right. This was not natural. At Uncle Auk's wake, young Antonio had been so terrified of the corpse that he hid in a cupboard. He fell asleep there, so when the family left for the night they accidentally locked him in the old funeral parlor with Uncle Auk. Terrified and beside himself with horror, Antonio pounded on the door until the townspeople, certain that Auk had risen as a bloodthirsty ghoul and was trying to escape, set fire to the house to destroy him. Antonio survived the ordeal, but the combination of being trapped in a funeral parlor with a corpse and nearly dying by arson had without a doubt been the worse, most nightmarish night of the bridegroom's life.

Until now.

There was something in these woods. Something besides the five drunken, scared men who kept looking over their shoulders and jumping at shadows.

The trees thinned and parted, and the forest gave way to a sloping rise on their left. Atop the grassy, overgrown hill sat the ruins of a monolithic old structure, as big as a small castle. The Nunnery of the Damned.

"We should go back." Antonio's words felt sharp and scratching in his throat, like he was choking on gravel.

Thorvald guffawed. "You're afraid of an old nunhouse? We're halfway home, my friend; no sense turning back now."

"Help me."

The voice came from the trees behind them. Or Antonio thought it came from behind them. Titmouse pointed at the nunnery. "There!" he said. "There's someone in trouble up in the ruins."

"No, that way!" said someone else, pointing at the opposite side of the road.

"Let's go!" Thorvald called, waving them to continue on the road. Only once before in their long lives together had Antonio heard that kind of fear in Thorvald's voice. It had been the night Thorvald crept into his room and told Antonio that his father found out he'd gotten his cousin pregnant. Antonio didn't see Thorvald for two years after that, until his cousin had moved away with her ugly, rattish baby, and Thorvald Senior had died in a freak millinery accident.

They turned back toward the road to Whyte-upon-Rice and found a woman blocking their way. A young woman, dressed in nun's whites and blacks. Her dress and face were soaked in blood, her eyes glistened with tears. "Help me," the voice came again, but it didn't come from the woman. It came from all around them.

"Begone spirit!" Antonio howled. "We mean you no harm!"

"Help me," said the voice again. "Help me pave the road."

The men saw that she had a knife in her hand, and they ran. They scattered in every direction, some into the forest, some back the way they came. Titmouse even ran blindly toward the nunnery.

The ghosts caught every one of them.

Antonio staggered through underbrush, alder branches scratching at his face and hands. Something tore at his eye and drew blood, but he just kept plowing ahead, cursing under his breath.

When he tripped and fell, he rolled down a small hill into a ditch, landing face down in foul, knee-deep water. He suddenly had a vision of childhood, when his father tossed him off a bridge into the Rice River to teach him to swim. He could not remember how long he sat on the bottom of the stream, but he vividly remembered a trout swimming up to his face and poking its nose against his as if to say, "My, you're an ugly friggin' fish, get out of my river." Eventually his father pulled him out, gasping for breath, three-quarters drowned. He had been about two years old.

Antonio came up sputtering out of the ditch, and immediately rather wished he'd drowned. The woman was standing over him, her ethereal, misty form staring down at him with a wicked smile on her face, the kind Uncle Auk had when he'd drunk too much and came to visit Antonio's sister, Bernice.

Antonio tried to run, but he felt the ghost nun's fingers in his hair and his head snapped back as if a troll had grabbed him by the scalp. Her fingers felt like cold, hard marble. He came off his feet and landed back in the filthy water, then scrambled backward as she yanked him out of the ditch with impossible strength. Antonio wasn't sure what was going to tear off first—his hair or his head. He didn't particularly want to find out.

The ghost nun held him down with one hand on his chest. It felt like a blacksmith's anvil, threatening to crush his ribcage, just like the anvil Bernice had pushed off the stable onto Uncle Auk. It held up a long, slender knife in front of Antonio's eyes. He noted that it glinted like polished silver, which struck him as odd since it was ethereal and semi-transparent, not to mention there was no light for it to reflect.

"Please!" Antonio begged. "Spare my life!"

"It's not your life that I want."

The knife moved down past Antonio's throat, across his chest, until it hovered above his crotch.

The ghost went to work, and Antonio began to scream.

Just before dawn, five ghostly nuns left five small new mounds alongside the Almoner's Road, just outside the Nunnery of the Damned. The mounds joined dozens, possibly hundreds, of other tiny piles of dirt and rocks that lead halfway back to the village. The five new victims stumbled out of the forest at Whyte-upon-Rice later that day, pale, shaken, and forever changed by their short journey.

As the old man had foretold, none of the five survived the week, and all of them died by their own hand. Titmouse drowned himself in the Rice River, coincidentally the very same spot that Antonio's father had tried to drown his toddler in twenty years prior. Thorvald threw himself under a carriage racing down a main thoroughfare. The first pass only broke an arm and a leg, so he had to drag himself up and throw himself in front of another one to finish the job.

Antonio went through with his wedding to Melissa, though he looked sick and half-dead through the whole ceremony. The next morning Melissa went back to the town priest and demanded an annulment on the grounds that Antonio could not consummate their marriage, nor sire any heirs. When they went looking for Antonio, they found him dead in his ancestral home, hung by his neck in front of the triptych depicting his father's dismemberment.

On maps the old road between Salty Cove and Whyte-upon-Rice is named the Almoner's Road, as it was once where nuns and monks would beg for alms from passing travelers. But the locals of Salty Cove have a different name for it, a secret name that they don't share with travelers.

They call it the Road of Bones.

C.D. Gallant-King wrote his first story when he was five years old, and he made his baby-sitter look up how to spell "extra-terrestrial" in the dictionary. He now writes stories about un-heroic people doing generally hilarious things in horrifying worlds. A loving husband and proud father of two wonderful little kids, C.D. was born and raised in Newfoundland and currently resides in Ottawa, Ontario. There was also a ten-year period in between where he tried to make a go of a career in Theatre in Toronto, but we don't talk about that.

C.D. has self-published two novels, including *Hell Comes To Hogtown*, which was a semi-finalist in Mark Lawrence's 2018 Self-Published Fantasy Blog-Off. This is the fourth time his work will appear in the *Strangely Funny* series.

Lake Flaccid
by B. David Spicer

The sun fell behind the hills just as the four teens galloped out of the woods and yanked off their clothes. The boys laughed and the girls squealed when they dove into the chilly water. The lake looked black in the weakening light; they might as well have been swimming in a pool of ink.

Tommy, a muscular towhead, captain of the wrestling team, hoisted Jan, his tiny brunette girlfriend, into the air and tossed her further into the lake. "Did you see her fly? Come here, Jan. Let me see if I can throw you all the way to the other side!"

She aimed a splash in his direction. "Ha-ha muscles. How about I drown your ass?"

"You wanna try?" He aimed his naked backside at her. "Do your worst!"

Kevin, the other guy in their group, pointed at Tommy and brayed like a donkey. "How cold is this water? Or is that bait for the bluegill?" He dodged a splash from Tommy, then looked at his girlfriend, Sabine. She stood waist-deep in the lake with her arms crossed over her modest bosom. "What's wrong, babe? Did Tommy's little worm scare you?" He dodged Tommy's next splash by diving underwater.

Sabine glanced around her, aiming a squint at the darkened woods. "I just don't think we should be doing this."

"Stop being such a stick in the dirt." Jan shook her head sadly.

Sabine's eyes rolled. "Stick in the mud."

"What?"

"It's 'stick in the mud' not stick in the dirt."

Jan and Tommy frowned at each other for a second, then shrugged and started chasing each other through the black lake water.

Kevin stared at his girlfriend as he floated on his back, looking for all the world like he was being eaten by an eel. "Everything's fine, babe. Try to have some fun!" He held out his hand, beckoning her to come deeper into the lake. "Come on, we'll swim out to the island."

Sabine's eyes widened. "We're naked! We can't swim all the way to the island!"

"Swim to the island! That's a great idea!" Tommy turned toward the dark mass of the little island that sat in the middle of Rose Lake. It wasn't much of an island, just a couple of acres of dry land with a few trees and picnic tables. Tommy paddled hard, barely keeping ahead of Jan, who, despite her petite frame, swam like a fish. "Last one there is a rotten fish!"

Sabine's eyes rolled. "It's egg, you mor ..." She lost interest halfway through the sentence. She aimed her disapproval in Kevin's direction. "This is a seriously bad idea."

He shrugged. "Yeah, but it'll be fun! That makes it okay!" He turned and started across the lake.

"Why do I stay with you?" As she watched the eel following her boyfriend, she remembered. "Hey, wait for me!" She waded deeper into the lake, then dove underwater and swam for all she was worth. She made it to the island after everybody else was already there. The other three were standing on the edge of the lake, looking at their feet. Sabine had just enough time to wonder what they were looking at when she heard a stranger's voice.

"Aha! Here's another delinquent! Get over here!" A bright white light blinded her for a second, then somebody roughly grabbed her arm and dragged her over to the others. "Just what the Pete Hill did you four think you were doing?"

Sabine's eyes rolled. "Sam."

The light blinded her again. "What did you say?"

"It's 'Sam Hill', not 'Pete Hill'."

"No, it isn't!" The light moved away and illuminated her friends. "You four are in a ton of trouble! A ton of trouble. I'm Ranger Gribble, and you have been caught performing a lewd act on land owned by the great state of Maine." He strutted in front of them like a drill sergeant. "Yep, you are in a ton of trouble!"

Kevin frowned. "What lewd act are you talking about?"

Ranger Gribble aimed the beam of his flashlight over the group to indicate their general state of undress. "You four degenerates are all ..." He halted as he slashed his flashlight over Kevin's naked body.

90

"Wow. Good for you, son." He paused to clear his throat before continuing his tirade. "Naked! You are all naked!"

Tommy chuckled. "It's hard to go skinny dipping with your clothes on!"

Ranger Gribble blinded Tommy with the flashlight. "Oh, you think this is funny? This is a joke to you? Well, we'll see how much you four like spending the night in jail." He shook his head to knock the disgust out of it. "A ton of trouble, that's what you're in!"

The sound of a splash carried across the water. Sabine peered into the darkness that covered the lake, but couldn't see anything. "Did you guys hear that?"

The blinding light hit her in the eyes again. "You'd better keep quiet missy, you're in a ton of trouble."

Her brows creased as she tried to squint the light out of her eyes. "So you keep saying. There it is again!"

This time, they all heard it. Ranger Gribble turned to face the water, aiming his flashlight over the lapping waves of the inky lake. "What the Pete Hill was that?"

Two things happened simultaneously: Sabine's eyes rolled, and something enormous leapt out of the lake and snatched up Ranger Gribble. The water was churned to froth, and the high-pitched screaming of four teenagers could be heard from the far side of Rose Lake.

Sheriff Gallagher steered the motorboat toward Rose Lake Island. He'd been across the county dealing with a car that had hit a deer and was late to the party at the lake. He tied up at the dock just as the sun rose, and found the wrinkled mug of his deputy. "How bad is it, Carl?"

"Bad. Three dead, with one more trying hard to join them."

"Any witnesses?"

"One, girl named Sabrina."

"It's Sabine, not Sabrina!" Sabine strode up to the sheriff wearing a white sheet that somebody had given her. "I'm Sabine!"

Sheriff Gallagher looked her up and down before he spoke. "Why are you wearing a sheet? You out here for choir practice?"

Deputy Carl grinned through his wrinkles. "They were all naked, boss."

"Naked!" The sheriff shook his head in disbelief. "You have any idea how much trouble you're in, young lady?"

"A ton. Ranger Gribble made a point of telling us that." She sighed in exasperation. "Can we please get to the part where the monster popped up out of the lake?"

"Monster!" The sheriff shook his head in disbelief. "You're not gonna get out of trouble by making up stories about sea monsters."

Sabine'e eyes rolled. "Lake monster."

"What?"

"It was a lake monster! I saw it kill my friends and Ranger Gribble. It almost killed my boyfriend."

"Boyfriend!" The sheriff shook his head in disbelief. "You got a boyfriend?"

"Uh, yeah." Sabine tilted her head and looked at the sheriff. "He's over there."

Sheriff Gallagher and Deputy Carl walked over to where the medics were loading Kevin onto a gurney. They hadn't given him a sheet, so he was still wearing only his skinny-dipping outfit. The sheriff stopped in his tracks when he saw Kevin. "Wow, good for you, son." Then he turned to Sabine. "Is that your boyfriend?"

She just nodded.

"Oh, you poor girl. How do you two even ..."

"Sheriff!" Dr. Stevens, the county medical examiner, waved his hands in the air. His assistants had just zipped up the mortal remains of Tommy, Jan, and Ranger Gribble into plastic body bags. He limped over to where Sheriff Gallagher stood. "Sheriff!"

"What do we got, doc?"

Dr. Stevens struggled to catch his breath. "Three dead, one injured. There are some strange tracks in the mud, though."

"Tracks!" The sheriff shook his head in disbelief.

Sabine turned to the doctor and aimed a thumb at Gallagher. "Is he always in a permanent state of surprise?"

Dr. Stevens ignored her. "Sheriff, you've got to see these tracks for yourself!" He led Sheriff Gallagher and Sabine down the embankment to the water's edge. Large round shapes contoured the mud. "See what I mean?"

Sheriff Gallagher took off his glasses and knelt to peer at the mud. "Just looks like mud to me."

Dr. Stevens shook his head vehemently. "No, no, no! Something made these tracks! Something big!"

"Something!" The sheriff shook his head in disbelief. "What made them? A crocodile?"

Sabine's eyes rolled. "A crocodile in Maine? That's so stupid that I can't even believe you said it."

"Stupid!" The sheriff shook his head in disbelief. "What are you saying doctor?"

Dr. Stevens rubbed the stubble on his jaw. "Something is in this lake, an animal that shouldn't be here. Those tracks are like nothing that I've ever seen, and I've lived here my whole life."

"What do you propose we do?"

"Well, sheriff, I think we should call in an expert."

"Expert!" The sheriff shook his head in disbelief.

"Yeah, and I think I know just the guy we need to call."

Dr. Stevens put his cell phone into his pocket and grinned. "He's on his way."

Sabine frowned at him. "Who is this guy anyway?"

"He is the world's leading marine biologist. Or, at least, he was."

"Was!" The sheriff shook his head in disbelief.

Sabine adjusted her sheet. "He's no longer the world's leading marine biologist? What happened to him?"

Dr. Stevens scratched his chin thoughtfully. "As I recall, there was a disagreement at a marine biology conference. His theories on the mating habits of krill were, ah, unorthodox, to say the least. He was drummed out of the marine biology field by his colleagues. He crawled into a bottle and he's been living in a third-world shithole ever since."

"You mean Detroit?"

"Cleveland."

"Cleveland!" The sheriff shook his head in disbelief. "What that poor man has had to endure!"

Dr. Stevens nodded sagely. "I still think he's the best shot we have of identifying the beast that killed those people."

Sheriff Gallagher was counting on his fingers. "How long is a flight from Cleveland?"

"He's here!" Dr. Stevens trotted over to the dock. "Welcome, Dr. Dammett!"

Dr. Jack Dammett stepped out of the dinghy and onto the dock. He dropped a heavy duffle bag onto the ground beside him and slowly took off his sunglasses. Sweat glistened on his tanned skin, and the breeze ruffled the sun-drenched curls of his hair. He looked like Charlton Heston and Ursula Andress' love child, with maybe a dollop of

Matthew McConaughey thrown in just for seasoning. His Burt Reynolds tattoo seemed to wave at them as the muscles moved beneath his skin.

"Which one of you is Sabine?"

Sabine raised her hand, almost dropping her sheet.

He nodded in her direction. "I saw them loading your boyfriend into the ambulance. You poor girl, how are you even standing ..."

Dr Stevens rushed up and shook Jack's hand. "Dr. Dammett, thank you for coming, especially on such short notice."

"You must be Dr. Stevens. I saw the victims on the mainland. Crushed to death by something large and heavy, right?"

Dr. Stevens nodded. "That's our initial assessment, yes."

Sheriff Gallagher stepped forward. "I'm the sheriff. What do we have in my lake? Some kind of hog gone monster?"

Sabine's eyes rolled. "Dog. Dog gone."

"That's what I'm here to find out." He hoisted his duffle bag onto his shoulder again. "Show me the tracks."

They led him to the lakeshore, and he spent several minutes examining the marks in the mud. After a few minutes, he stood up straight and nodded slowly. "I know what we're dealing with. I recognize these marks."

"Marks!" The sheriff shook his head in disbelief. "It's a crocodile, isn't it?"

Jack raised an eyebrow. "It's a Trichechus manatus."

The sheriff, the doctor, and Sabine stared at Jack blankly for a moment. Finally, the sheriff spoke. "Is that a crocodile?"

"No, it's a manatee. A big sucker too!"

"Manatee!" The sheriff shook his head in disbelief. "What is that?"

Jack took a deep breath. "A manatee is an aquatic mammal that feeds mostly on plants. This particular species is native to the Caribbean. Quite a few live in Florida."

Dr. Stevens looked impressed. "You can tell all that just by looking at some muddy tracks?"

"Of course. Once you've seen a manatee belly print in some mud, you can always recognize them."

Sabine looked less impressed. "If this thing is an herbivore, why did it attack my friends? It couldn't have been trying to eat them. Could it?"

Jack stroked his chiseled jaw. "No, your friends were crushed, not eaten. I'd say they were snuggled to death."

"Snuggled!" The sheriff shook his head in disbelief. "Huh?"

"Manatees in captivity are notoriously affectionate. This one probably saw a group of people standing at the water's edge and just wanted some attention."

"This one isn't in captivity." Sabine straightened her sheet.

"Not anymore. How do you think it got into the lake?"

Dr. Stevens nodded. "Somebody put it there!"

"Exactly." Jack unzipped his duffle bag and pulled out a sleek, deadly looking, rifle. "This is a tranquilizer gun. We'll lure the beast to us, trank it, and put it on a flatbed truck headed for home."

"Flatbed!" The sheriff shook his head in disbelief. "Why not a plane?"

Jack's eyebrows rose. "That's a stupid question."

"What do you need from us?" Sabine stroked the rifle with her fingertips.

Jack grinned. "You get to be the bait."

Sabine sat amongst several dozen heads of cabbage right at the edge of the lake. "Tell me again why I couldn't put my clothes back on?"

Sheriff Gallagher shrugged. "Dammett said that we had to recreate the scene as much as possible. You were naked last night, so you have to be naked now."

"Can I at least have the sheet back?"

"No. It'd maybe get wet."

She rolled her eyes. "We can't have that now, can we? I'm never going skinny dipping again."

Jack Dammett strode over to her, the tranquilizer rifle on his shoulder. "Ready?"

Sabine frowned. "No. What's with the cabbage?"

"Manatees love cabbage. This particular cabbage is special. A plant biologist I know produced this hybrid, optimized it for its delicious taste. She used to grow the heads in the campus greenhouse. She gave me a little head there once. It was mind-blowing."

Sabine blinked. "I don't doubt it."

"Now, are you ready?"

"As ready as I'm ever going to be." She spat out a huge sigh and waited for the lake monster to find her.

Jack had made a barricade of picnic tables and hid behind it with the tranquilizer gun. Sheriff Gallagher sat beside him with a shotgun, just in case things went south. Dr. Stevens sat behind them with his black medical bag on his lap.

They sat, waiting. After Sheriff Gallagher sighed for the sixth time, Dr. Stevens waggled a finger at him. "A botched pot never boils."

Sabine's eyes rolled. "Watched. A watched pot ..."

At that moment a huge wave crashed against the shore, soaking Sabine's unclothed skin. The manatee lurched ashore, snapping up cabbages in its maw as it shambled toward Sabine, who scuttled away from the lurching blob that threatened to crush her. The manatee was enormous, a monstrous specimen by any metric. Jack aimed carefully and fired two darts into the bulbous neck of the manatee. It chuffed out a squeaking chirp, advanced another two feet, then stopped. Its eyes rolled back into its head, and it didn't move again.

Sheriff Gallagher stepped closer to the beast, his shotgun at the ready in case it moved. He nudged a fin with his foot, but it didn't respond. "I think we got it."

A dripping Sabine stood beside the sheriff. "Can I please put some clothes on now?"

Jack Dammett peered at the mud on the shore intently. He squinted as he rubbed his fingers over depressions in the earth, shaking his head slowly. "Is it possible?"

Just then, with another titanic explosion of lake water, a second manatee, much larger than the first one, shambled ashore. It snapped its head around, which caught Jack in the torso, and threw him to the ground. The tranquilizer gun soared out of his hands and into the lake. The enormous beast squawked and began to nuzzle his prone form, threatening to snuggle him to death. "Dammit, Dammett! Of course there were two of them!" Jack brought his hands together in a loud clap, which startled the beast enough that for a second it shied away from him.

Jack twisted his body out of the bulbous beast's embrace, and used its head as a springboard to leap over its bloated body, and end up in the lake behind it. The manatee swung its head toward Sabine, and made a happy chirp as it wallowed in her direction.

The naked girl ran far enough inland to avoid the brute's deceptively soft and inviting flesh. Sheriff Gallagher aimed the shotgun at the beast, but nothing happened when he pulled the trigger. His mouth hung open and he shook his head in disbelief. The manatee bowled him over with a swipe of its massive flipper, and nuzzled his body with the side of its face. Soon, the sheriff would be crushed beneath the bulk of the behemoth.

Sabine hunkered down beside Dr. Stevens in the barricade. "What do we do, doc?"

"We need to draw it away from Sheriff Gallagher before he gets pulverized!"

"Great! How do we do that?"

"You'll have to run out there and distract it!"

"What?" Sabine scowled at the doctor. "Are you nuts?"

"Just give it a wide earth."

Sabine's eyes rolled. "Berth. A wide berth." She heaved a gigantic sigh and ran toward the manatee. "Hey, over here, blubber-for-brains!" The manatee saw her and heaved itself away from the sheriff. It squealed savagely as it ambled toward her. From a lack of other options, Sabine led it back toward the water.

As the ponderous bulk of the thing approached the lake edge, the water almost seemed to part and Jack Dammett rose from beneath the waves, the tranquilizer gun in his hands. "Smile, you son of a bitch!" He fired three darts into the demonic creature, and finally, it stopped moving. With one final groan, it closed its eyes and took a long nap.

Sheriff Gallagher sat down next to Jack and Sabine at a picnic table. "The state wildlife officers are loading both of those things onto a flatbed truck as we speak. I also just had a very interesting phone call with Mrs. Gribble. She tells me that her husband is responsible for the wallabies being in the lake."

Sabine's eyes rolled. "Manatees."

He waved that away. "That's what I said. Anyway, he stole them from some sort of zoo down south a few months ago. Been feeding them nothing but that super-cabbage ever since."

Jack slipped on his sunglasses and stood up. "That explains their enormous size."

Sabine frowned. "It does?"

"It does indeed. Each head is packed with nutrients. Getting a never-ending supply of head like that is bound to make anyone impressively large." He zipped up his duffle bag and slung it over his shoulder. "You know, you could probably put some clothes on now, Sabine."

She smiled. "I know, but I think I'm gonna go for a swim first."

B. David Spicer graduated from Ohio University, earning a BA in English. His first name is Brian, but he thinks B. David sounds more artsy and pretentious. He's had short stories in more than a dozen anthologies, including *Cosy Crime* from Flame Tree Press, *Out of Phase* and *Wicked Deeds: Witches, Warlocks, Demons & Other Evil Doers* from Sirens Call Publications, *Strangely Funny II* and *III* and *VI* from Mystery and Horror, LLC, and *Pernicious Invaders and From the Corner of Your Eye* from Great Old Ones Publishing. *Big Shots and Bullet Holes*, his first novel, was recently published by Mystery and Horror, LLC. He lives in Ohio and owns more books than ought to be legal.

StarbucksFishboy
by R.C. Mulhare

"So, Bob, what do you do at the end of the day? Jump into Arkham Harbor?" Quinn asked me.

I should expect questions like these, especially since my eyelids atrophied and gill slits started folding in the sides of my neck, making unfashionable turtlenecks necessary. That or wear a scarf around my neck, which gets in the way. The wrong shift leader will get on my (metaphoric) tail about the ends, no matter how short, dipping into someone's coffee. If anyone but Quinn had asked, I'd say I crash with a bag of chips and Netflix. But Quinn's going through their own change, so I felt more at ease. "Usually, I soak in the tub after I mix salt into the water."

"Sounds like a good evening; like taking a bubble bath?"

Mavis, today's shift leader, called out, "Folks, we've got a rush coming. Bob, come up front." I drew in a breath—through my nostrils—and came up. Given my looks and some people's attitudes, I usually stay back making the drinks.

A guy in a blue suit at the head of the line looked me up and down, barking out his order too fast for me to jot it onto his cup.

"Could you please repeat that, sir?"

He reached out and thumped the side of my head, hard enough to rattle me. "You lost your hearing along with your eyelids, fishboy?"

"It's a little noisy in here, sir, and I want to get your order right."

He repeated the order, then added, with what he probably thought sounded like a teasing voice, "Now don't get any salt or scales in it."

I tried hard not to stare at him as I jotted his order on his cup and passed it down to Quinn. "That'll be $6.25, sir," I said calmly.

A welcome sight for my sore eyes walked in next: Jim Maitland, one of our local weird fiction writers (as in the fiction is weird, not the writer; Jim is the definition of a kind soul), approached the counter, a manila folder of what looked like posters under his arm. I reached for a cup, writing it up for him.

"Venti, black, three Splenda for ... Dagon?" he asked, announcing his usual order. Mavis, working alongside Quinn, gave us an odd look, which Jim met with a smirk. "Long day, Bob?"

"No longer than usual," I said, passing the cup down the line and ringing up his order. "WeirdCon posters already?" You'd think a convention for all things weird would be right up my alley, but I have my reasons for staying on the fringe, and it doesn't always hinge on the Old Gent's outdated philosophies.

"Yeah, think you can get August 20th off?"

I darted a look to Mavis out of the corner of my eye. "Wish I could, but the boss lady always wants all hands on deck when there's a weekend event. Try coming here the last weekend of Haunted Holiday."

"Like the time the customers asked about your make-up job?" he asked, solemnly.

"It'll be worse when the Cthulhu fanboys mob the streets of witch-haunted Arkham. What happened to Providence hosting it?"

Jim took his coffee from Quinn. "The hotels down there are ... less than thrilled after the last time, between the Deep One body makeup that clogged some shower drains and gummed up a pool, and the riot that broke out when the Stormfront idiots showed up. The mayor of Providence pulled the plug. But if any town can handle big crowds and crazy stuff, it's Arkham."

"Could I have a small soy latte, ten Splenda?" said a soccer mom with a baby on her hip.

"Won't keep you from your customers," Jim said, beckoning Mavis aside to speak with her.

"You looking forward to WeirdCon?" Quinn asked, as we restocked the pastry display later.

"Hardly," I said. Coming up from the depths two years ago, in my opinion, is one of the worst things that (some of) my mother's side of the family could have done in this crazy world. But it's a channel marker bell that can't be unrung. "The extra hours would be great, but the extra work will be hell."

"Maybe I can convince the warden to let you work the back," Quinn offered.

"You succeed in convincing her, and I'll owe you one."

"Nah, don't worry about that. This is what friends do," Quinn said. I took a cinnamon scone left over from the morning, wrapping it in a paper napkin. "You gonna have that at your break?"

"Yeah?" I said, puzzled as to why they'd ask, since Mavis lets us nosh on the leftovers.

"Shouldn't you be on a fish-based diet now?" Quinn asked.

"I've barely got my gill slits, and I'm not in a hurry to transform," I said, going to the back room.

"You ever wish Mom's people never made it clear what they are?" I asked my dad that evening, as we loaded the dishwasher at home.

He looked at me, his gray eyes in his weather-beaten face concerned. "Anyone giving you more trouble on account of yah looks?" His Coast Guard training had kicked in, the way he set his jaw and his shoulders in a "Who do I have to school now?" way.

"No one but the usual cranks, but ..." I told him about the convention next month.

He clunked a skillet into the rack and slid it in harder than usual before he stood to his full height and kneed the door shut. "I worry aboutcha, boy, and what people could do to you. I'll ask Mack and Fenton to keep a close eye on the shop while this shindig is on."

I wasn't sure I wanted his cop buddies hanging around my workplace, but I couldn't help appreciating the concern. "Thanks, Dad."

"Anything to take care of yah, Bobby." Only he can call me that these days. "You still hanging out on those forums?" he asked, as I turned to head up to my room.

"For the artwork and the fiction, yeah."

"Just be careful." Dad wasn't thrilled over the number of people squealing in delight over the Fish Guy in *The Shape of Water*, after his own odd experience with a Deep One during a Coast Guard mission. That had resulted, nine months later, in my turning up wrapped in a bundle of seaweed on his then main, now sole, lady friend's beachside back porch. Mom's kind coming up from the depths brought up a lot of things. "Can't help feeling it's like picking at a scab, but yer grown and I can't tell you what to look at and what not to. Want me to draw up yah bath tonight?"

"Sure, thanks, Dad."

He stepped around me, heading upstairs and I heard him go into the bathroom next to my bedroom. I went to lay out my clothes for next day's shift, then went to soak for a while.

Dad must have emptied a half a carton of Market Basket iodized salt into the water: I had to stir the water more than usual, to dissolve it faster. I hopped in to soak for an hour, my tablet in its waterproof case in hand, trawling the website and forum of Suzanne Morrey, one Lovecraft-inspired writer I gladly read. Besides studying marine biology, she'd spent time with a colony of Deep Ones, learning their ways and their culture. She even acted as an ambassador after a fashion between the locals and the Deep Ones who introduced themselves to the North Shore towns a year or two ago, after a particularly bad summer nor'easter sent some Deep One youngsters packing onto dry land. Sounds corny, but her books helped me feel closer to my mother's side of the family, even more than meeting the colony just off Rowley when Dad brought me down to the shore to meet my kin (I got the feeling they wanted me to grow more scales before they'd take me in).

In a new blog post, she announced that WeirdCon had invited her as a last-minute addition to the guests of honor, when another author had flounced out in a huff after behaving rudely to the organizers. Among other events, she would read from a new novel to be released there, *The Tides Shape the Land*. I don't put a lot of stock in Lovecraft, since the guy had so much backward thinking for someone so clearly intelligent, but I love what she did with the back story on the people of Innsmouth. I'd planned to avoid the con, but I went to their site and bought a one-day ticket for Friday, the first full day, when she'd give her reading.

The morning of August 20th, I found an unmarked police car parked near my Starbucks, two of Dad's buddies on the force sitting inside. One of them, Jim "Mack" MacElroy looked up from his newspaper to wave at me, while his partner, Trina Fenton, gave me a double take before relaxing.

"Having a good day so far, Bob?" Mack asked.

"So far, so good, though I bumped into several weirdos in Cthulhu shirts as I walked here."

"Want us to drive you to and from work?" Fenton asked.

"Thanks, but, nah, my boss might get weird about it. Hope it doesn't come to that."

I went in, stowed my bag in the office, then pulled on my apron, adjusting the scarf around my neck before I punched in.

The counter already buzzed with customers by the time I got up front. Mavis stepped back from the drink station as I approached. "Bob, you're in luck; you're on drink prep."

"Thank heavens," I said, going back to scrub up and pull on a pair of food prep gloves.

"Thank God, Jesus, and the deep, Fishboy is here," Manny, the new guy on the register, said. Mavis and Quinn, stocking the front display case, shot Manny a look.

I stayed off the register that entire shift, but among the people collecting their drinks, I spotted plenty of folks of all kinds sporting Cthulhu shirts and hats, and for some reason, a lot of fezzes, some with the Yellow Sign. A guy whom I took for a Robert E. Howard cosplayer chatted with a dark haired, bespectacled woman wearing a black tee-shirt reading "STRAIGHT OUT OF DUNWICH" like that Straight Out of Compton logo.

"Wow! Great Deep One makeup!" a guy with an "Innsmouth Swim Team" shirt said. "You do that yourself?"

I handed him his latte. "Kind of." Not a lie, but not letting on that my looks hadn't come out of a plaster mold, either.

The next customer, dressed like a Gibson Girl with seashells surrounding the crown of her cartwheel hat, straight up asked: "Oh, are you part Deep One?"

What I usually say to questions like this: "Eh, I look like this because of a glandular condition. It ain't catching."

What came out of my mouth: "Uh, yeah, I am."

Beachside Gibson Girl's eyes lit up. "Oh, wow! Do you feel a spiritual connection with the sea or just water in general?"

Dunwich Shirt Woman collected her matcha smoothie. "Well, I always liked Our Lady, Star of the Sea."

"Oh," Beachside Gibson Girl said, getting a weird look from that Dunwich girl, and asked no further questions.

Next came a guy wearing a ball cap with a plush Cthulhu head on the front. "So, you swim anywhere near Devil's Reef?"

"Well, no, I don't swim well, but I take a bath in salt water, to help my skin."

"Do you use any special salt?" asked a woman in a Wonder Woman tee shirt over an ankle-length hemp skirt behind him. "I know a place that sells Dead Sea salt. I can get you a jar, if you like."

103

"Well, um, you can tell me where you get it," I said. She jotted something on a napkin and stuck it into my tip jar.

The rush barely let up that day. But not all the questions from the fanfolk weirded me out.

"Can you talk to fish?" asked a little girl in a "C is for Cthulhu" shirt, as I handed a black coffee and a tiny chocolate milk to her dad.

"Gee, I wish I could," I said.

"Aww, that's sad."

"She wanted to ask if you know Ariel. My sister showed her *The Little Mermaid*," her dad said.

"Aw, cute! I've loved that movie since I was a kid."

I crashed when I got home, flopping onto the couch. Dad, watching the six o'clock news, looked over at me. "Coffee beat you up?"

"Yuh."

He let me stay put, bringing supper to me. When I'd managed to choke some of it down, he helped me upstairs and into a bath. I don't remember falling asleep in the tub, but I dimly remembered waking up as Dad pulled me out, toweling me off. He helped me into my room and then to my bed, tucking me in like I was six years old. I fell right back to sleep.

Somehow, I woke up earlier than expected. Just as well, as I needed time to dig in my closet for a costume: gray pants with suspenders, a lighter gray shirt, newsboy cap, and the sandal soles I'd worn for a dance recital (I know, why not water ballet??), then pulled my sneakers over them.

Dad, cooking eggs in the kitchen, threw a double take at me. "Going somewhere?"

"Going to the con: Suzanne Morrey's giving a reading."

"Thought you were dreading it?"

"Suzanne's the exception to the rule."

"And you're going dressed like something out of *Shadows Over Innsmouth*?"

"Good way to blend into the crowd."

I expected a line to the check in desk at Arkham's Hawthorne Hotel, and after my customers' reactions the day before, I anticipated a lot of attention and comments from the con-goers in line: "Great Deep One costume!" One guy called out "Iä, Dagon! Iä, Mother Hydra!" One girl called out, "Eeee! A fish!" I playfully croaked at some of them.

At length, I got to the desk, handing over my ID and showing the confirmation email on my phone. The registration lady looked from my ID to my face and back, raising one eyebrow, then handed me the welcome packet: con badge on a lanyard, a pin with the Sign of Dagon, programming booklet, then a complimentary book of art, essays, and some fiction commissioned for the con, including a new Innsmouth story by Suzanne Morrey. I slipped the lanyard over my head and tucked the goodies into my messenger bag before taking off my shoes and shambling into the con hall.

The dealer room hummed with people browsing the booths, chatting with friends and the hucksters behind the tables. I passed booths of resin-cast figurines of weird fiction characters, then a table of antique books from a local bookstore. The girl with the Dunwich shirt, now dressed like the movie version of Herbert West in a lab coat over a blood splattered shirt, stood with a stocky, chin-bearded man in a black Court of Thorns tee shirt behind a table loaded with books.

At the next table, Suzanne, sporting blue-green and blue streaks in her black hair, sat with two other people, behind stacked copies of several anthologies, along with her new book.

"Wow, with that cosplay, I think I know what book you're looking for," Suzanne said. I've seen author photos that looked better than the author themselves in real life, but I could honestly say the reverse of her, and that's not me fanboying, either.

I croaked something meant to be, "You got that right", which I only half intended to do. Pulling my jaw off the floor, I repeated myself, saying actual words this time. "I came to the con just for this, and, well, you. I mean your reading. I'm Bob Harnden, StarbucksFishboy on the Forum."

Her green eyes brightened. "Ahh, you're the guy who's impressed with my research. I hope it makes the fiction stronger, and it pleases you."

"If anything, it makes me feel closer to my mother's people."

She gaped. "Whoa. Here I thought you had a really good makeup job. I hope I didn't offend you."

"Naw, beats people at work accusing me of dropping scales or fish slime into their coffee."

She took a book from the stack before her and wrote in it before handing it to me. I took my wallet from the inside pocket of the messenger bag. She waved it away. "An offering to a son of Mother

Hydra and Father Dagon," she said in a mock spooky voice. I took it from her. "I have to ask, have you ever LARPed before?"

"Not really, not officially, anyway."

"Ahh, I was going to offer you a spot in my group tonight. We got permission to end the campaign by Arkham Light, about 7.30."

"I'd like that, actually. Better than just watching a show."

"Good! We'd love to have you in our mob of Deep Ones. See you then?"

"And at the reading." I tucked the book into my bag and shambled on.

I was one of the first into the room set aside for the readings. Someone, probably her, had decorated the space with large bits of driftwood surrounding the storyteller's chair and the rostrum next to it. More people trickled in behind my spot in the front row, talking among themselves, some pointing and staring at me, only to have more conscientious people whap their hands.

Suzanne had the third slot on the roster of readers, all with Innsmouth stories. One guy from Florida set his tale in the Keys rather than New England, while another writer set their story in the Great Lakes.

Then Suzanne had her story. Like the fanboy that I am, I hung on her every word, mesmerized by her tale of a clan of Deep Ones on the West Coast, helping Chinese immigrants escape from a detention center on an island in San Francisco Bay.

I applauded a bit later than the rest of the crowd, I got so wrapped in her reading. She glanced my way. For a moment, I worried she might call attention to me. Thankfully, she didn't, aside from reaching out to take my hand in hers as she passed me when she opened the chair to the next author.

I chilled the rest of the day, taking in the weird art gallery in the Museum Place arcade, across from the Essex Museum, then grabbed a tuna melt (it's no different from people eating pork or steak) at the family pizzeria also in the arcade.

At around seven that evening, I wended my way to the maritime site, past the *Companionship*, the replica of a schooner that had belonged to some merchant back in Arkham's heyday as a shipping city, docked in the harbor. I must have started out earlier than I thought, as the crowd hadn't gathered at the small lighthouse, pretty much a light on top of a tower about the height of a typical house, at the far end of the pier. I sat on the stoop to watch the sky and the footpath leading to the light.

I must have dozed off. Something, probably a large fish, splashed loudly in the harbor, startling me awake. Ahead of me, a stream of black figures wended their way toward me. If I still had hair on the back of my neck, it would have stood right up. I rose, tempted to bug out of there, till they got closer and I could see they were regular folks, dressed in black robes and wearing odd headdresses and collars cobbled from dollar store tiaras and other golden plastic gewgaws

The tallest and biggest guy, a stacked tiara on his head, looked me up and down. "Suzanne wasn't kidding when she told us to look for a guy who looked like an extra from *Shadow over Innsmouth*. Hey there, fishboy. You here for the LARP?"

"Fishboy?" I said, still on the verge of getting out, for a different reason. I couldn't take one more would-be joke, even from kindly folks.

"Whoa, hey, we cool," the big cultist said, holding up his hands disarmingly.

I breathed easier. "Hey, sorry, I knew to expect company. But I usually hear 'fishboy' from not exactly well-intentioned people."

"Gee, sorry about that. From us, it'd be a friendly nickname."

"It's like N-word privileges," said a Black girl wearing a mermaid-like fish tail dress under her robes.

A skinny, dark-haired cultist with thick glasses peered over the big cultist's shoulder. "Hey, are you StarbucksFishboy on Suzanne's forum?"

"Matter of fact I am."

"Cool! I love your posts."

"Nice seeing someone with Deep One heritage commenting on her fiction?" I asked, dryly.

"I wanted to say that, but I wondered if I should."

"Hey, here she comes!" a cultist keeping watch called out.

Suzanne approached, a black cloak covering her from neck to ankles, but not quite covering a blue-green hemline below.

"Hail, Mother Hydra!" The big guy kowtowed toward her, the other cultists joining in.

"Rise, my minions," she replied in a comically deep, imposing voice.

They briefed me on the plot and coached me on my part. I'd be at the back of the pack of cultists as they surrounded the base of the lighthouse, where Suzanne's Mother Hydra would sit enthroned. When the investigator players arrived, we would surge forward, trying to block them.

The twilight closed in, the light fading behind the rooftops of Arkham. A radiant train of lanterns bobbed toward the lighthouse, the glow cast up at a group of players dressed like *Boardwalk Empire* background actors. The sight set the back of my head prickling.

Our group advanced, calling to the interlopers: "Iä, Dagon! Iä, Mother Hydra!" One girl burbled something I wouldn't want to spell out. I croaked as convincingly as I could.

The big guy roared, "You shall not approach the sanctuary!" I glanced back to the doorstep.

Suzanne-Hydra sat poised on the doorstep, the last light gleaming on her. She'd cast aside the cloak, revealing her gown, blue sheer material draping a skirt covered in black and green spangles like scales covering her skin.

On cue, we surged forward. Then, one investigator who looked like Central Casting would hire him to play a Mob heavy shoulder-checked me. My feet, despite their size, lost traction on the grass. I skidded backward toward the edge of the land. *I'm not falling into the harbor*, I thought, as the surface rushed up to meet me. I hit the water with a deafening splash.

The surface broke under me, I felt the deep pull me in. You'd think with all the time I spent floating in a tub of salt water, I'd relax the minute I sank like the proverbial rock. The adrenaline from our acting kicked in. My mind ordered my limbs to relax so I'd float. Up turned to down, and down turned into up. Instead, I flailed, fighting for the surface, and failing. The dark line of the shore against the lighter darkness of the twilit sky receded, as the undercurrent pulled me away.

Something tugged my ankle. I told myself I'd snagged junk on the sea floor. My panic turned it into a nameless, eldritch entity rising from the deep to devour a tasty Deep One juvenile. I kicked, but whatever attacked me grabbed my other foot.

I did the stupidest thing you could do underwater. I screamed. Water filled my lungs. Something tore in my throat.

Something else caught my waist and I sank even deeper, the last air escaping my lips. I've heard when you drown, a sense of peace fills you. That sense engulfed me as I went limp in my predator's grip. Like your typical Lovecraft protagonist, I blacked out.

For a long, dark time, I thought I'd died, and nothing awaited a hybrid like me. I'd thought wrong. Warmth and wetness awakened me.

My eyes burned despite soft light reflecting off water up to my waist as I lay in a shallow but wide tub.

"What ... where?" I asked, eloquently.

Susanne, clad in a terry cloth bathrobe, leaned over me. "You came back."

"How did I ...?"

She took my hands in hers. "I dove in to save you when you fell in. I shouldn't have asked you to tag along with that bunch."

I looked at my hands. The webbing between my fingers looked wider, more obvious. "What happened to me?"

She flexed my hand. "I was afraid of this. The trauma sped up your transformation. I've seen it happen in juvenile Deep Folk, after shark attacks or run ins with boat propellers or some other threat."

"The seas warming?" I asked dryly.

"That's contributed to it. A colleague of mine suggested that Deep Folk might be a key to humanity's survival, if more Deep Folk intermingled with humans, allowing their offspring to live on land and off."

I pulled away from her. She smiled at me reassuringly. "Don't look worried. I'm not one of those weirdos who'd beg you for a water baby."

"Good. I mean, I'm not anywhere near ready to become a father, not till I'm sure I'm cut out for it."

She reached to the tub-side table and offered a clear plastic cup of iced tea to me. I took it carefully, negotiating the webbing on my hand, and drank. She took the cup back. "You better rest. You had a long night and tomorrow will be a long day."

"I should." I settled in the tub, my head heavy. I figured the near drowning had worn me out, and so I leaned against the side of the tub.

I woke, my head still heavy, when something tugged my foot. I came fully to—can't say I opened my eyes—and looked down.

For one thing, I lay in different tub: a deeper, tiled affair, the size of a small swimming pool, the bottom sloping down into the shadows concealing the far end. A breeze on my face hinted at an exit.

A Deep One, or a Deep Folk or whatever they were, and I mean a big, bony-finned, scaly-skinned fish dude, a good hundred pounds heavier than me, twiddled my webbed toes. I recoiled. The fishman took this as joke and grabbed my other foot, tickling the sole.

"Stop that!" I yelled.

He croaked. Short, quick noises, as if he laughed at me, the scaly pest, and kept tickling me. I tried yanking my feet away, but he pulled me back.

"Suzanne! Help! There's a Deep One!"

A voice spoke, subsonic, vibrating through my chest. *She isn't here, but we are.*

"I really should leave," I said, a nervous squeak cracking my voice.

A second Deep One rose from the water, the facial features differently, even delicately carved. They—or maybe she—laid her hand on my chest. *This is your home now. You will dwell with us.*

I pulled away. "I'd rather dwell with my father Bill Harnden for a little while longer."

Suzanne emerged from the shadows beyond the pool, padding close to the edge. "Oh, you woke up to meet your kin."

"Suzanne, call my Dad. His number's in my phone—"

"Which fell from your pocket when you fell into the harbor," she said. "You're better off with them, especially since you've transformed so much in the last 24 hours. Going back to your old life is near impossible. No one would recognize you."

"He'll look for me. He's a cop. It's what he does."

"He thinks the Coast Guard and the State Police never found your body. You know you're going down to the sea to stay. It just happened sooner." She said this with something like regret, but I saw a cool curiosity in the set of her eyes and mouth, like I'd expect from a scientist examining a particularly interesting specimen.

"I wish it had happened later." I couldn't deny the pull of my own curiosity drawing me toward the pair of Deep Ones. At the same time, I wanted to hate her for this situation, but she couldn't have foreseen it happening like this, could she? Then again, she knew more about my mother's people than I did. I needed her knowledge, and she needed another juvenile Deep One to study for her research.

And, like any good Lovecraft story, it got weirder. The water rippled from the far end to the near end, from the shadows to the lit end. The air hummed with a subsonic tone. My cousins looked toward the darkness, flexing their lips.

A wave rose, rolled across the surface, breaking over me. A large, dark shape surged from the gloom toward me. I scrabbled for the edge of the pool, but my cousins pulled me under and toward the shape.

A large Deep One with especially wide fins on his back and on the sides of his head where his ears had been, rose toward me. I wriggled free of my kin and tried to backpaddle, but he had a lot more years of swimming on his flippers. He grabbed me around the waist, dragging me into the darkness, into the deeper end of the pool. The water grew cooler and the darkness deepened. We rose to the surface, a wave breaking over my head. I gasped, drawing a lungful of fresh air, letting it out in a scream at the night sky above. "Haaalp!"

Hush, little fingerling, no one will hear you out here, Grandpa Deep One communicated to me. I tried to yell again, but he dunked me. I gagged on the water, the gills on the sides of my neck flaring. Talk about getting tossed in at the deep end and being over my head. I'd take a line out the door or a dozen weird fans asking me questions about my (non-existent) love life over this one-way ticket to Yah-hanith'leh. I guess I'm going to need to learn how to spell that, now that I'll soon call it my mailing address.

R.C. Mulhare was born in Lowell, Massachusetts and grew up in one of the surrounding towns, in a hundred-year-old house up the street from an old cemetery. Her interest in the dark and mysterious started when she was quite young, when her mother read the faery tales of the Brothers Grimm and quoted the poetry of Edgar Allan Poe to her, while her Irish storyteller father infused her with a fondness for strange characters and quirky situations. When she isn't writing, she moonlights in grocery retail, and enjoys hiking in the woods of New Hampshire's White Mountains and browsing the antiques shops one finds all over New England. A two-time Amazon best-selling author, contributor to the Hugo nominated *Archive of Our Own*, and member of the New England Horror Writers, her work previously appeared with Atlantean Publishing, Off the Beaten Path Press, Macabre Maine, FunDead Publications, *Deadman's Tome*, and *Weirdbook Magazine*.

She's happy to have visitors online at:
https://www.facebook.com/rcmulhare,
on Instagram at https://www.instagram.com/r.c.mulhare/,
on GoodReads at https://www.goodreads.com/matrixrefugee
and on Tumblr at https://www.tumblr.com/blog/rcmulhare .

Eddie's Apocalypse
by Zach Friday

Dear Traveler,
Please read this.
    - Carrie
P.S. YOU WON'T BELIEVE THIS ONE TRICK!! SLUGS HATE
THIS MAN!!
    - Eddie

5 HOURS BEFORE THE END

My date, Carrie, sat across from me staring at the TV in the corner of the little Italian restaurant's bar. Her blonde hair spilled down her shoulders across a pretty green sweater, which highlighted the fact that only one of us had spent time on our appearance. Everyone in the restaurant was locked into the shocking news on the TV. Except me. I just couldn't take my eyes off the last breadstick sitting in the middle of the table. It was technically hers; there had only been four and I'd already had two, but they were so good, and the salty, buttery sheen called to me. I wondered if she would notice if I snuck it away. Would that make me a bad person in her eyes? Did it matter if the news broadcast was true? Would that last breadstick be my biggest regret if we all died in an hour? The reporter's voice echoed loud through the restaurant. "I repeat, we are receiving confirmation that the pit is growing. It has now consumed all of Chicago. Chicago is no more." The reporter took a moment of silence while my eyes lingered on that beautiful breadstick.

"New information coming in now; I have confirmation that another hole is currently opening under Los Angeles. I repeat, A second pit has opened beneath downtown Los Angeles. If you are in the area, it's recommended to leave immediately."

"Oh my God," Carrie said. She looked back at me only to follow my gaze toward the last breadstick as my greedy fingers closed around it and slowly lifted my ill-gotten gains to my plate. "Are you fucking kidding me right now, Eddie?"

"I know, I know. I've already had my two, but you seemed so distracted and I didn't want it to go to waste, ya know?"

"What? I don't care about the breadstick. I can't believe they're saying the world is ending and you're worried about a damn breadstick."

I shrugged. "Chicago and L.A. are hardly the world."

She tossed her napkin onto the table and folded her arms. "What if one of those pits open up here?"

"Here? I don't think whatever cosmic event is unfolding cares about our little town. I'd put money on New York next. Want to bet on it?"

Her face told me that no bets would be placed.

Gasps came from the crowded restaurant as we turned our attention back to the TV where the reporter was franticly trying to describe the scene on the screen. The footage came from a helicopter hovering over a hole stretching for miles where downtown Chicago used to exist. Fires burned out of control in dark neighborhoods surrounding the pit. Far off from the helicopter, Lake Michigan had turned into a new Niagara Falls spilling into the freshly opened earth.

"I— I don't know how to adequately explain what we're seeing here." The reporter said over the harrowing images. I took a bite of my breadstick, catching a disapproving look from Carrie in my peripheral vision. "We are now viewing live footage of the pit in Illinois. We're receiving reports of mass looting, shootings, and a mass exodus as people try to leave the area. Wait a minute, what in the holy hell is that?" The spotlight on the helicopter illuminated what looked to be shadowy wisps of smoke pouring out of the pit. One of the shadows stopped in the beam of light and flew towards the helicopter as we watched. As it got closer, it looked like two yellow embers for eyes were set deep in the shadow heading towards us before the wisp of smoke transformed into a solid, dark beast. The camera was engulfed with a crash, there was a brief sound of struggle, and then the camera went dark.

Screams filled the restaurant. People pushed and pulled as they sprinted for the door, where a pileup happened immediately. People climbed over the poor souls on the bottom of the pile, some restaurant staff trying to pull people off while other staff contributed to the mass of humanity occupying the doorway. Carrie stared at me, her jaw hanging down in disbelief.

I stood up and grabbed her hand. "Let's get out of here."

She nodded, and we made our way towards the kitchen. Pushing thorough the double doors, I spotted a few cooks running through an exit in the back. I grabbed a basket of breadsticks waiting on the expo line and took a bite as we left the restaurant.

We exited into a city full of pandemonium. Cars sped past, sounding horns and flying through red lights. Across the street someone was flinging everything they had into the back of a minivan until someone else jumped in the driver's seat and sped away, leaving the man at the back yelling and cursing as he chased his car.

"Holy shit," I said. "That didn't take long." We made our way to my car down the block. It was old, beat up, and literally held together by duct tape. I felt safe that no one would be looking to steal it as things went haywire around us. Sirens blared as a cop car rushed one way and an ambulance the other. Ten steps from my car, an SUV slammed into my little hunk of junk. The driver wasted no time throwing the SUV into reverse, taking my bumper with it and leaving the front wheel at an odd angle as they sped away into the night.

"Well, that's a bummer," I said as I took another bite of my breadsticks-to-go. "At least they didn't get out, though. I don't have insurance." I could tell I was not impressing Carrie.

"Come on, my apartment is only a half mile away. Let's just go there."

"Hold on." I reached into the backseat of my car and pulled out an overnight bag. I tossed the remaining breadsticks into the top of it. Carrie threw an accusatory glance towards me and the bag. "What? I uh, I always keep one of these with me. I just like to be prepared," I said, hoping I had saved a little face.

"Uh huh. Just follow me."

4 HOURS AND 30 MINUTES BEFORE THE END

The jog to her apartment felt longer than a half mile to me. I wished I had run more than the occasional once a month when I inevitably had the 'Get Your Life Together' pep talk with myself before promptly abandoning all hope. I was breathing hard by the time Carrie slowed up in front of her apartment building. She pushed the door open into a nice little foyer that ended with a staircase. I couldn't help but notice the lack of elevators. Carrie bounded toward the staircase and I thought about sitting down for a minute, but eh, who knew? Maybe she was only on the second floor.

She was not on the second floor. As we finally reached the landing on the top floor, I thought my heart might explode. Carrie pushed open her door and invited me in. The apartment was put together well, clean, and smelled good. I was happy this was where we ended up instead of my place. If the world did end, it wouldn't have been fair for this poor girl to die in my nasty apartment. It also seemed like a good place to have a heart attack, which I was fairly certain I might have soon.

Carrie immediately sat down on the couch and opened her laptop. I sat down next to her, pulled my breadsticks from the bag, and bit into one as Carrie gasped next to me.

"Sorry, did you want one?" I asked as I reached for another breadstick.

"Look at this, Eddie," she said as she passed the laptop to me, which was playing a video titled, "THE RAPTURE IS HERE!!!!" A shaky camera filming a dark street in Chicago full of gunshots and screams greeted me. Without going into too much detail, the video chronicled a poor man's attempt to run away from one of the shadow beasts after watching it rip his friend in half. The video ended with the sound of the man's sobs as the shadowy beast loomed over him.

I slid the laptop back to Carrie, not knowing what to make of that. I stared at the breadstick in my hand, its jagged edge where I had torn into it reminding me of the image of that man being torn in two. We sat there quiet for a few moments before she started to cry. I looked at her, unsure of what to do. I had no experience in consoling people about imminent doom. I pushed the breadstick towards her, and to my amazement she smiled, laughing a little.

"You're an idiot, you know that, Eddie?" She wiped away a tear.

"Oh, I know that," I said as I put an arm around her. "I'm sorry you're stuck with me for this. Do you have anyone you need to call?"

"No. I don't have much family left anymore. What about you?"

"Nope. I mean, I wonder where my roommate, Jessie, is in all of this. But, if he wants to say any last words to me, he'll just show up, trust me. He'd probably only say 'fuck you' anyway, so I'm not that disappointed." We sat in silence for another little while. The sound of the town going crazy crept into the apartment from the street below.

4 HOURS BEFORE THE END

Carrie looked up from my shoulder and kissed my cheek. "Listen, I'm not usually like this, but I don't know. I don't know how to say this." I felt my heart start racing just a little. "Don't read into this or anything, but if we're going to die from all this, do you want to have a little fun first? I just haven't been with anybody since I moved here, and I don't know, it sounds better than sitting here waiting to die."

She waited for my answer, and I'm sure saw the stupidest-looking man ever staring back at her with complete disbelief on his face. "I uh, I eh, what I meant is—" Carrie stood up from the couch, took my hand, and led the way to her bedroom while I stuffed the last bit of breadstick in my mouth.

3 HOURS AND 57 MINUTES BEFORE THE END

"Oh! Oh, God. I'm sorry."

3 HOURS AND 30 MINUTES BEFORE THE END

Carrie nestled in the crook of my arm as we laid in her bed. I felt bad about my two-and-a-half minutes of glory, but she didn't mention it again after the embarrassing moment. I'm not sure if that was better or worse. She was on her phone looking through post after post about the apocalypse.

"Oh my God, Eddie, look," Carrie said as she sat bolt upright in the bed. The sheet sliding off her chest sent blood rushing through my body, making me think I might get a redemption round. Instead, she shoved her phone in my face, a headline stating that a new pit had opened only an hour north of us.

"See? I told you it wouldn't open under this shitty town," I said.

I could tell she wanted to hit me. "If it opened that close to us, that means those shadow things will be here in no time."

"And? What do you suppose we do about it?" I asked, honestly hoping she had an answer since she was clearly more intelligent than me. I had no hope of making it through the night. She looked like she was about to answer when a heavy knock came from the door. Carrie jumped up and grabbed her pants, threw on a tee shirt, and picked up a baseball bat from behind her nightstand all before I had even thrown my legs over the side of the bed. The knocking on the door came again louder this time. Carrie looked ready for war.

"It's okay," I said. "I don't think those things from the pit would knock."

117

"No shit, Sherlock. But in case you hadn't noticed, the world has gone to shit out that window and it's not like it's a big secret that I live here alone."

"Oh," I said. "That makes way more sense. I thought you were going to try smacking a shadow with a bat."

"Later, I might try that too."

The knocks on the door came louder and longer this time. I pulled on my jeans and walked to the front door to look through the peephole. What I saw surprised me and didn't surprise me all at once. I threw open the door to see Jessie standing there with a grocery bag full of what seemed to be Morton table salt. At least ten of the big containers of it.

"Finally, man. Jesus, you take forever to walk anywhere now. Also, fuck you," Jessie said as he stepped into Carrie's apartment, looking from me to the scared woman in the bedroom doorway, holding her bat at the ready.

I looked to Carrie, sighed, and accepted that Jessie had indeed found me to say, "Fuck you."

"See? I told you. Jessie, this is Carrie. This is her apartment we're standing in, by the way. Carrie, this is Jessie, my roommate." Jessie is actually my brother—well, stepbrother, but we call each other roommates because neither of us like to discuss how and why we've been living together for fifteen years. He is everything I'm not: fit, tanned, tall, fair-haired, well put together, doing stuff with his life. It's often a contentious point between the two of us, leading to many screaming matches later between me and my mirror where I usually lose. "And by the way, Jessie, it's the end of the world. You have to tell me, seriously; how the hell do you always find me?"

"Oh, I put a pet tracker in your shoe a couple years ago. I have a couple of extras since I thought I'd have to replace it when you changed shoes, but you know, you haven't. Really, buy new shoes, man."

"Are you shitting me? Like a tracker for a dog?"

"Yeah. They sell those collars with them. I just took the tracker part out and slipped it into the tongue of your sneakers one day. I use the app to find you."

"Okay. But why?"

"You're kind of like a puppy, man. Sometimes you just disappear, so I did the tracker thing. Besides, if you drive off and kill yourself, I didn't want to lose the car."

"Well it was nice of you to bring some groceries," I said, looking at the bag full of salt and vowing to myself that if I ever did kill myself, I was going to push the car into a river first.

"I think I hate both of you, but yeah, I definitely needed ten pounds of salt, so thanks for that," Carrie said.

"Oh, I like her, man," Jessie said. "I was watching videos from Chicago when I saw a guy throw some old road salt at one of those things, and it seemed to hurt it. I figured this was better than nothing."

"Great. We'll just sit around and wait to throw salt at monsters," I said.

Carrie finally set the bat down in the corner of the room, looked the two of us over and said, "Eddie, this has without a doubt been the worst date of my life."

I shrugged. "This is definitely top five for me."

2 HOURS BEFORE THE END

Carrie and Jessie sat on the couch watching videos of the outbreak on their phones while I sat at the window on lookout. More pits had opened across the country and we were watching the apocalypse happen through our tiny pocket computers. Their screens lit their faces, showing me two very different reactions to the whole scenario. Carrie looked worried and scared for the fate of humanity, while Jessie looked excited, grinning just a bit like a kid watching a horror movie. He is a sick, sick, man.

I still felt indifferent to the whole ordeal. It just felt like another day at this point. Sure, demons might swarm my town at any moment to ravage our little group, but eh, I didn't have anything going on tomorrow anyway. I watched the scene below, where wrecked cars lined the street. There were at least two bodies I had been watching to see if they would get up again. So far, they hadn't. Gunshots rang out in the distance every few minutes, while a man marched down the street playing a trumpet, shouting about the End of Days.

We had watched the video Jessie had mentioned, and sure enough, the man threw road salt at the shadow thing in his garage, causing it to scream when the salt passed through it, leaving little streaks of red as the salt fell through the shadowy mass. Carrie, being smarter than either me or Jessie, had pondered that maybe these things were some form of demon, her reasoning being that salt apparently had deep religious ties to cleansing damned souls. Jessie agreed of course, shaming me for being so thick as to not make the apparent connection. Whatever the reason, it seemed to work, so we each had a can of the table salt next to us.

"Well, there go the phones," Carrie said.

"Yeah, my connection just went out too," Jessie said. He saw the breadsticks in my bag next to him on the couch, pulled one out and started to munch on it.

"Hey, toss me the last one," I said to him, knowing he would eat them both if I didn't act quickly. He grabbed the last one and threw it overhanded at my face where it landed with a thud. "Thanks," I said wiping the salty butter from my cheek.

"I can't believe I'm going to die with you morons," Carrie said.

"Hey, we might not die. The salt thing could work," Jessie managed through a mouthful of breadstick.

"Sure. But what then?" Carrie asked. "Say we throw salt at these things and they leave us alone. For how long, though? Until we're out of salt? Where do we go? What happens when we're out of food? We can't live in my apartment for more than a couple of days."

"That is a very good question," I said as I watched the street. A woman was walking down the sidewalk, quickly pulling a suitcase behind her. A wispy shadow lingered above her about fifteen feet in the air, floating beside the building across the street. I picked up my can of table salt, opening the little spout. "I think we're about to find out if the salt thing even works though, then we can worry about the rest." The shadowy thing descended on the woman. It rapidly turned into a solid monster and picked the woman up by the ankle. She screamed and tried hitting the beast holding her. Her punch seemed to depress its dark skin before drifting into the blackness underneath. She screamed, pulling out a bloody stump where her hand used to be while blood sprayed the sidewalk beneath her. I felt my stomach churn and fear rise in my throat. I watched the beast expand its dark mouth and swallow the woman whole. No more screams came from below.

I felt Jessie and Carrie standing behind me, looking down on the horrific scene just in time to see the woman disappear into the gaping maw of the beast. Jessie squeaked briefly before Carrie grabbed him from behind and covered his mouth with her hand.

"Shut. Up," she hissed in his ear, but it was too late. The shadow monster turned its head towards us. I locked eyes with those beady yellow embers somewhere deep in the darkness as it floated towards Carrie's apartment building.

1 HOUR BEFORE THE END

"Shit, shit, shit! What do we do?" I paced back and forth in front of the window. "It saw me! I'm sure it did. It's coming up here for sure. That lady punched it, and her hand was dissolved or something, I don't even know!"

"Just chill, man, we have the salt. We'll find out if it works." Jessie said, entirely too calm.

"Chill? This is your fault. What the hell was that squeak?"

"I don't know, sometimes I squeak. I didn't know they had super hearing."

"Just shut up! Both of you just shut up," Carrie said. "Let me think."

"I would suggest thinking quickly," Jessie said pointing to a thin film of black smoke sliding through the cracks around Carrie's front door.

"Shit!" Carrie exclaimed as she grabbed her salt and moved to the side of the front door. "Distract it!" she whispered to me and Jessie.

I ran to the other side of the door, where my back was to a small kitchen area. "Yeah! You distract it, Jessie. Just remember we can't touch it!"

Jessie flipped me off, picked up his can of salt, and got into what looked like a Kung Fu stance someone would take if they had never seen a Kung Fu stance before. We watched as the shadow poured under the door and began to rise in front of us. It filled the entryway; two yellow embers peered out toward us. Jessie made a sound that, to this day, is an intense argument between us. To me and Carrie it sounded like he squeaked again, a sound I can only describe as a chipmunk being strangled, but if you ask him, he will assure you he yelled the best one liner ever yelled. But this is my account of events, and in this one, it goes like this: Jessie squeaked at the monster in front of him and threw his entire can of salt, unopened, at the beast. The can of salt passed through the shadow without it so much as noticing. Then came an ear shattering scream from the beast as red lines appeared all along its side. Not from the can that Jessie threw, that was pretty much useless, but from Carrie's can of salt as she shook it back and forth over her head, hurling lines of salt at the thing.

The monster began to turn from shadow to solid in front of us. It lurched toward Carrie, as another scream that I thought might burst my eardrums filled the apartment. I shook my can of salt at the beast's back. In its more solid state, the salt didn't just fall through it, but ate

121

into its dark skin, leaving little craters glowing red. The monster picked up a table next to the door and flung it at me. The table seemed to fly at me in slow motion, which helped very little as it smacked me square in the chest and sent me sprawling backwards into the kitchen.

I scrambled upright, looking for my salt, only to see it roll to Jessie's feet. The monster was bearing down on me as I stood and looked for anything I could use as a weapon. I threw a pot that had been soaking in the sink at the beast. The pot bounced off and clanged to the floor, but where the water from the pot touched areas where the salt had already wounded the monster, its skin bubbled, popped, and glowed a dark red color. The monster slapped at its new injuries, the dishwater and salt acting like acid to it, eating away at its flesh. It all clicked for me at that moment.

"Throw more salt!" I yelled. Way ahead of me, they were already pelting its back with more of the loose salt. I turned the sink on full, grabbed the spray nozzle and blasted the monster. The thing screamed and slapped at the water as it began to burn and melt. It backed away from me and stumbled over the couch, crashing through the coffee table. Jessie and Carrie dumped the last of their salt cans onto its gooey mess of a body. The screeching grew louder and louder, while its yellow eyes grew brighter. I walked up behind them with a cup of water from the sink and dumped it over the beast. The yellow embers extinguished as the monster continued to melt in front of us, leaving a dark puddle stinking of sulfur in the middle of Carrie's apartment.

"Well, damn," Jessie said. "That worked better than I expected. Who knew we could melt it Wicked Witch style? I guess they really don't like water."

"I don't think it was the water," I said. "The water only hurt it where the salt was already eating into it."

"So, that makes sense. The water just made it easier for the salt to get deeper into that thing," Carrie said.

"Right. Yeah, this all makes complete sense," I said.

The smell of rotten eggs was filling my nose as they both turned to me. I could feel that this was my chance; I could solidify myself as a leader, step up and take charge, change the downward spiral of my life. Instead, I threw up into the black goo at our feet. My dinner of breadsticks now swimming and mingling with the remains of whatever the hell we had killed.

"Nice," Jessie said. "Insult to injury. I like it, bro."

"I think I have an idea," I said. "It might be the dumbest idea I've ever had, but Jessie, is that shit from your birthday still in the back of the car?"

His eyes lit up.

15 MINUTES BEFORE THE END

We ran back to my car, taking a backpack full of water bottles and the remaining salt with us. The journey back was uneventful for the most part, until we watched one of the shadows go into someone instead of killing them, which was unnerving. The young man that was invaded by the shadow grabbed his own head, twisted it around so that it faced backwards, then crab walked down a dark alley screeching. Jessie, of course, was sure we had just watched someone get possessed. He deemed any future people doing anything similar or that we saw get invaded by a shadow as a PP. PP standing for possessed person, of course, because he's a moron. He also took it upon himself to name the shadow demons flying around 'Slugs' due to their reaction to salt. Carrie and I didn't have the energy to argue with him, so now we're stuck with those names. Avoiding Slugs and PPs, we eventually made it to my car and opened the trunk to our salvation. Jessie and I pulled out a mess of water guns and super soakers. We loaded our colorful plastic weapons full of saltwater and walked deeper into the apocalypse.

THE END

There it is. That's how the apocalypse went down for me. I hope you had a better time than we did. If you're reading this, then I assume you've survived through some miracle. It was smart of you to come to the hospital, look at the big brain on you. We also came here first hoping for any sort of disaster relief or information, but, like you, we also found it empty of life and full of death. If you're still looking to go a little further, come join us. Carrie, Jessie, me, and a small ragtag group we picked up along the way have all decided to head south to a salt mine in East Texas where Carrie grew up because it seems safer than anywhere else, right? Follow the road south and I'm sure you'll find more of my notes, or not ... we might all be dead. But who knows? Gotta take a leap of faith every now and then now that the world has ended, right? What, do you have something better going on?

If you don't want to join us, I completely understand; I wouldn't either. Take any useful information you can from my tale, I only ask that you leave it up for the next traveler to read. By the way, the super soaker thing works great. I highly recommend it. Beware Slugs and PPs on your journey. Too-da-loo fuckers.

-        Love Always, Eddie

Zach Friday is a fiction writer whose work focuses on horror and comedy, sometimes merging the two. His short stories have appeared in publications around the world. He lives in North Texas where he works as an editor for DBND Publishing, spending most of his time reading and writing horror stories or watching hockey with his dog, Bosco. To follow his work, visit @ZachAFriday on Twitter.

Caterwaul
Larry Hinkle

Marlin Hambrick opened the front door to find a dead cat on his porch.

This was troubling for two reasons: one, it was Wednesday, which Marlin considered the least likely day on which to find a dead cat on one's porch. Two, the cat in question wasn't just dead; it was also missing its head.

This was not good. Not good at all.

He was already late for work. And to make matters worse, Marlin had recently had a bit of a tiff with his neighbors over the very feline that now rested—sans noggin—at his feet.

When Marlin first moved in, they'd fought over the cat's habit of leaving dead animals on his porch. As disgusting as he found the habit to be, he now accepted them as gestures of the cat's goodwill; the feline equivalent of saying, "Look, I know my owners are horrible people, so here, have a dead bird. I pulled its eyes out for you."

The most recent fight concerned the cat's propensity for half-burying its shit in his wife's garden.

This morning, though, it appeared someone had taken it upon themselves to plant the pooper in question upon his front porch.

Marlin considered his options. Obviously, he couldn't just leave it there. His wife might step in it. Marlin Jr. might want to play with it. And what would happen if the neighbors walked over and saw what was left of their precious fur baby splayed across Marlin's welcome mat? Certainly they wouldn't think *he* did it, would they? Even people as awful as they were would recognize it made no sense for him to leave their dead cat on his own porch. If he'd planned on making such a blatantly bold and bloody declaration of war, wouldn't he leave it on their porch?

Marlin hadn't read *The Art of War*, but he imagined there had to be an entry on the stupidity of attacking yourself with the dead cat of your enemy.

Marlin grabbed a rag, picked up the cat, and tossed it into the dumpster in the alley. On his way back, he stopped and snatched the dead cat's collar from around his garden gnome's neck.

"I'll deal with you later," he said to the gnome. He took the collar into the garage, and threw it in a shoebox full of bloodstained collars.

Later that evening, Marlin went out to the garage and opened the box. The number of collars had grown considerably over the past six months. Mostly cats, but also a few he thought might come from those little yippy dogs so many young women seemed to carry around as fashion accessories.

"What's the matter, Marlin? Cat got your tongue?" his garden gnome asked, leaning against the doorway to the backyard.

"Shut up, Gnick," Marlin said, making a point to pronounce the gnome's name "Guh-Nick."

"No, you shut up, Marlin," Gnick hopped on a footstool, then climbed up onto a cooler. "If you're going to talk to me, at least have the decency to say my name correctly. It's pronounced Nick. The 'G' is silent."

"Whatever. Why'd you do it?"

"Do what?"

"You know."

"I know lots of things, Marlin." Gnick tamped tobacco into his pipe. "Except whatever it is you're talking about right now."

"Fine. That's how you want to play?" Marlin put the lid back on the box of collars and sat down across from Gnick. "Why'd you kill my neighbor's cat?"

"I think the question should be: why do you care so much about this particular cat, Marlin?"

"Because you left this one on my porch," Marlin said. "I don't know what you did with the other ones. And I don't care. But you left this one on my porch."

"Look, Marlin, this is a quiet street."

"And ...?"

"And I'm just doing my part to make sure it stays that way. When those cats start fighting or fucking or whatever else they do when the sun goes down, it makes me crazy! I can't take the constant caterwauling!

I hate it!" Gnick stood up on the cooler. "This is my neighborhood, Marlin. My house, my yard, my garden ... It was mine long before you got here, and it'll be mine long after you're gone."

"But I own the house. My name is on the mortgage. So technically, I own you, too."

"That sounds good on paper, Marlin, but we both know I really own this place. And anyone who lives in it." Gnick wiggled his fingers at Marlin. "When you moved in, you moved under my spell."

"That doesn't even make sense."

"The point is, when something—or someone—makes too much noise around my house, I'll put a stop to it."

Gnick took a deep breath and closed his eyes for a moment. "That aside, do you know what I hate even more than caterwauling, Marlin?"

"Doggerwauling?"

Gnick's eyes popped open. "What?"

"Doggerwauling. It's like caterwauling, except with dogs—"

"You think it's funny, Marlin?" Gnick jumped onto Marlin's lap and poked him in the chest. "You think it's funny that my ears are seventy-five times more sensitive than yours? Does it amuse you that I hear things you can't, like whose name your wife whispered when you used to have relations? Never mind," he said, before Marlin had a chance to answer. "That was a low blow. She only whispers your name, stud." He climbed back down onto the cooler.

"I thought you said fifty."

"What?"

"The last time you complained about your ears, you said they were fifty times more sensitive than mine. This time you said seventy-five."

"Fifty, seventy-five, whatever Marlin. I'm a gnome, not a mathematician."

"Sorry. So, what is it?"

"What's what?"

"What is it that you hate more than caterwauling?"

"Besides stupid questions?"

"Yes."

"Getting shit on, Marlin. Call me crazy, but I hate getting shit on. And that cat tried to take a dump on my foot last night."

"He's been doing that in the wife's petunias a lot lately, too."

"I know. But just like every other time something needs done around here, I'm the only one with balls enough to fix it."

"That's great, Gnick," Marlin said. "But what if the neighbors saw it? I'd be in a complete world of shit, instead of just a flower garden full of it."

Gnick shrugged.

Marlin sighed. He knew arguing with Gnick was as pointless as trying to get rid of him, but sometimes he couldn't help it. Despite being cursed with a killer garden gnome, Marlin loved his house. He had since the day they first saw it. And there was no way he was going to move out, no matter how hard Gnick made it to stay.

He got up to leave. "I have to go in now, Gnick. Marlin Junior has a cold." At the door, he turned back toward the gnome. "Please don't leave any more cats on my porch."

The sound of Marlin Junior's coughing echoed over the backyard. "That sounds like a real bad cough there, Marlin," said Gnick. "I sure hope your boy feels better soon."

Marlin turned off the light and went inside.

Marlin Junior did not feel better that night. Nor did he feel better the next several nights, despite visits to two different doctors and an urgent care facility. The nurse at the urgent care told them the flu was going around town, and cough syrup, ibuprofen, and rest was the only thing they could recommend.

The flu was going around Marlin's plant, too. They were so short-staffed, Marlin's boss told him he'd have to pull a double shift.

Marlin protested. He told his boss about how sick Marlin Junior was. But his boss didn't care. "Those widgets ain't gonna widget themselves," he said over his shoulder as he walked away. Marlin called his wife, let her yell at him a bit, and went back to work.

The next week was a blur. Marlin pulled a double shift every other day. Marlin Junior coughed and cried every day and night. And Gnick sported a new collar nearly every morning. Marlin had no idea there were so many cats in the neighborhood. He hadn't heard a single one the past few nights. Of course, thanks to the double shifts and some sleeping pills, he hadn't heard much of anything. Even Marlin Junior's coughing fits seemed like a distant memory.

Until this morning. This warm, windy Wednesday morning.

"What do you mean, he's gone?" Marlin asked his wife, rubbing sleep from his eyes.

"I mean he's gone! He's not in the house! He's not in the yard! He's not anywhere!"

She meant Marlin Junior. He'd been coughing when Marlin had got home the night before, as usual. And Marlin had taken a sleeping pill and gone to bed, as usual. What wasn't usual, however, was his wife waking him up, hysterical, screaming that Marlin Junior was gone.

Marlin got out of bed, threw on some pants, and together they searched the house, the yard, and the garage. Then they called 911.

Marlin had never been inside an interrogation room before, but he'd seen enough of them on TV over the years to knew someone was watching from the other side of the mirror. What he didn't know was why the police seemed more interested in his box of collars than his missing son.

"Let me get this straight," Marlin said to the two detectives sitting across from him. "My son's missing and you want to talk about a box of cat collars? Why aren't you out looking for him, instead of wasting time with this?"

"Patrols are looking for him," said the first detective, a tall, skinny blond man Marlin decided was the Starsky of the two. "And the sooner we get this out of the way, the sooner we can all get back out there and help."

Marlin leaned back in his chair and sighed. "Fine. What would you like to know?"

The second officer, who by default became Hutch, despite being chubby and bald, asked Marlin about the bloody fingerprints they found on the collars and the box.

"They're mine," Marlin said. "It's not my blood, though. It's not even human. It's cat. Maybe a little dog. Just check the DNA like they do on TV. You'll see."

Starsky looked up from his yellow legal notepad. "Cat blood? You get off on killing cats, Marlin? Got some unresolved pussy issues?" His partner stifled a laugh.

"What about dogs? Unconditional love not enough for someone like you?" asked Hutch.

"No! I mean, yes, unconditional love is more than enough for someone like me."

129

"Then why kill them?" Starsky set down his pen. "You have to get something out of it."

"This is ridiculous! I didn't kill them." Marlin couldn't believe the questions they were asking. He'd been "Employee of the Month" three times in the past year alone. And while three-time "Employees of the Month" were a lot of things (loyal, hardworking, and dependable sprang to mind), they were definitely not psycho cat killers.

Unfortunately for Gnick, three-time "Employees of the Month" were also honest.

Marlin took a deep breath. "It was Gnick," he said in a low voice. "Gnick killed the cats."

"Guh-nick? How do you spell that?"

"G-N-I-C-K. It's actually pronounced Nick," said Marlin. "The G is supposed to be silent. I call him Guh-nick because—never mind, it's not important right now. The important thing is finding Marlin Junior, which is why I don't understand your fascination with Gnick's box of dead cat collars."

"Did he just say the cat collars were dead?" Starsky asked Hutch.

"No, I think he meant the collars belonged to dead cats," Hutch said.

"Cats that a Mister ..." Starsky checked his notes. "...G-N-I-C-K, pronounced Nick with a silent "G," killed. That sound about right, Marlin?"

"Yes."

"And who is this Gnick?" Hutch asked.

"Our garden gnome."

Starsky set his pen down. "Your garden gnome killed the cats?"

"No."

"But you just said he did."

"I mean yes, he killed them, but no, he's not my garden gnome. He just came with the house. I tried throwing him away at first, but he was always right back in the garden the next morning. I used to think the neighbors were playing a trick on me."

"Used to?"

"Yeah, until I found out Gnick was just walking back on his own every night."

"Your garden gnome can walk?" asked Hutch.

"That's not all he can do. He can walk, talk—"

Starsky snickered. "Can he chew bubble gum at the same time?"

Marlin cocked his head. "At the same time he's talking? How would I know?"

"Not when he's talking, Marlin. That would be rude. Can he walk and chew bubble gum at the same time?" Starsky asked.

"Why does that matter?"

"Because that would make him a pretty special gnome, Marlin."

"That's not the type of gnome you'd want to just throw away," said Hutch.

"He's not special! He's an albatross!"

"An albatross?" Starsky picked up his pen. "I thought he was a gnome?"

The speaker above the mirror clicked on. *"It's a figure of speech, guys. I think Marlin means Gnick is the albatross that hangs around his neck."*

"Exactly!" Marlin pointed his finger at the speaker. "She gets it. I can't get rid of him, no matter how hard I try. That stupid gnome is a curse. A mean, nasty, cat-killing curse."

Hutch reached into an evidence box sitting on the floor and pulled out a large plastic bag. Gnick was inside the bag. "You mean this garden gnome? He doesn't look that cursed to me." Inside the bag, Gnick put his forefinger over his lips and winked at Marlin.

Marlin blanched, then nodded at the officers.

"You wanna explain all the red around his mouth?" Starsky asked. "Did you put lipstick on your gnome?" He turned to Hutch and pursed his lips. "I think maybe Marlin here has a thing for Gnick."

Hutch laughed. "You may be on to something. Sure doesn't look like a g-normal g-nome to me."

"That's cat blood, too," Marlin said.

"Of course it is. Say Marlin, do you happen to know why Gnick killed all these cats?"

"He said he couldn't stand their caterwauling." Marlin rubbed his temples. "According to Gnick, a gnome's ears are fifty to seventy-five times more sensitive than ours."

"Fifty to seventy-five?" Hutch whistled. "That's a pretty wide range, Marlin."

"He's a garden gnome, not a mathematician."

"Duly noted."

"So, if I heard cats making a ruckus at night, I knew I'd find a collar around Gnick's neck the next day, like a little trophy. I don't know why I kept them. I just did."

"What can you tell us about this?" Hutch pulled another bag out of the box, then slid it across the table to Marlin. In it was a binky, splattered with red. "Is that cat's blood, too?"

Marlin's blood froze. "That's Marlin Junior's binky. Where did you find it?"

"It was in the box of collars. Another of Gnick's trophies?"

Marlin lunged across the table and grabbed at the bag. "What did you do to Marlin Junior? Answer me!"

Starsky snatched Gnick back out of Marlin's reach, while Hutch ran around the table, grabbed Marlin by the shoulders, and pushed him back down into his seat.

Inside the plastic bag, Gnick flipped Marlin the bird.

"Did you see that?" Marlin shouted. "He stuck his middle finger up at me!"

"I didn't see anything," Starsky said, "except a grown man trying to attack a garden gnome in a police evidence bag."

Hutch slapped Marlin on the back of the head. "You can't touch the evidence, Marlin! Don't you watch TV?"

"I'm sorry," Marlin said. "But Gnick did something to Marlin Junior. I know he did."

"How do you know that?" Hutch asked as he returned to his seat.

"Because Marlin Junior's had a cold the past couple weeks. He's been up coughing every night, and I'm sure the noise was bothering Gnick. I just didn't think he'd do anything to my little boy."

"Why would you think that?"

"Because Gnick's a dick, but he's not a murderer. At least I didn't think he was."

Hutch looked at Gnick, then at Marlin. "You know what I think, Marlin?"

"No."

"I think *you* think we're a couple of yahoos you can fool with some story about being cursed with a killer garden gnome."

Starsky snorted. "I'm insulted, Marlin. A killer gnome? That's the best you got?"

"It's not a story!"

"You're right, it's not." Hutch slammed the table with both hands. "It's a friggin' cliché!"

Marlin slunk back into his seat. "W-w-what?"

Starsky sighed. "A killer garden gnome is one of the oldest tropes around, Marlin. You're certainly not the first person to use it."

"Yeah, why not try something a bit more original?" Hutch asked.

"Well, the cursed part at least showed a little imagination," said Starsky.

"Seriously?" Hutch waved his hands in the air and imitated Marlin's voice. "Ooh, a killer gnome haunts my garden. I tried throwing him away, but he just keeps coming back. Ooh, he must be cursed!"

"Well, when you put it that way, it does seem pretty lame," Starsky said.

Marlin frowned. The detectives' new tack confused him. "What are you talking about?"

"I'm talking about of all the ideas you could've tried, you picked one of the lamest ones out there," said Hutch. "Why not tell us Black *Annis* broke into your house and ate Marlin Junior?"

Marlin made a face. "Black anus?"

"*Annis*, Marlin. Black *Annis*. She was a bogeyman-type creature in English folklore with iron claws and a taste for the succulent flesh of young children."

"Mind you, we wouldn't have believed that either," said Starsky, "but at least it would have showed some more imagination on your part."

"But it's the truth! Gnick took Marlin Junior!"

"It's not the truth, Marlin. It's lazy." Hutch pointed his finger at Marlin to punctuate his point. "If I came across your story in a book, I'd hunt the author down and kick him in the nuts for being such a lazy hack. But since he's not here, I guess yours will have to do." He walked around the table and gestured for Marlin to rise. "Come on, stand up."

"I will not!"

Starsky grabbed Marlin under the armpits and lifted him out of his seat.

"You can't do this!" Marlin turned his head toward the mirror. "Tell them they can't do this!"

The speaker on the wall above the mirror crackled to life.

"*Nah, it's okay guys. Go ahead and kick him in the nuts.*"

The speaker switched back off.

Hutch swung his leg back, while Marlin tried to cross his to soften the blow.

"Stop!"

Hutch's foot stopped mid-kick. He looked up at the speaker. "Was that you, chief?"

133

"*No.*"

"Then who was it?" Starsky looked around.

A ripping sound filled the room as Gnick tore his way out of the evidence bag. "It was me, you stupid fucknuts! Haven't you been listening?" He jumped across the table and snatched out both of Hutch's eyes. "So, I'm a cliché, am I?" He lowered his head and rammed Starsky in the stomach. "I'm lazy, huh? Could a lazy cliché do this?" He punched his clay fist through Starsky's abdomen and ripped out a handful of ropy intestines. Blood and shit and half-digested donuts spilled out onto the interrogation room floor. Hutch, blinded from Gnick's attack, slipped in the pool of viscera and cracked his head on the concrete floor.

"Marlin! Let's go!" Gnick shouted as he ran toward the door.

Marlin looked at Gnick. He looked at Starsky's guts strewn all over the floor. He looked at Hutch lying in Starsky's guts. He looked for Hutch's eyes, but didn't see them. *Did Gnick eat them?*

Marlin fainted. When he came to, Hutch was standing over him, snapping his fingers in front of his face.

"Earth to Marlin. You in there, buddy?"

"I'm sorry, I, I ... Did I pass out?"

"Yeah." He helped Marlin back up to his seat. "You were smiling, though. What were you thinking about?"

Marlin looked at Gnick, still in the evidence bag. Hutch still had both of his eyes. And Starsky's guts were still contained to his abdominal cavity.

"Nothing," he whispered.

"Marlin, did you just dream that Gnick came to life, killed both of us, and rescued you?" Starsky asked.

Hutch cocked his head and grinned. "You did, didn't you?"

"No."

"Marlin, Marlin, Marlin ... What are we going to do with you?" Starsky checked his notes. "What did you say you do for a living?"

"I work in the widget factory."

"Thank God you're not a writer, because that rescue fantasy would be strike two. And you know what happens at strike three?"

"You kick me in the nuts again?"

"Again?" Starsky laughed. "Were you just fantasizing about me kicking you in the nuts?"

"I wasn't fantasizing about it."

"Yes, you were. You fantasized about me kicking you in the nuts and then Gnick here came to life and killed us, didn't he?"

"How'd he do it?" Hutch asked. "Bash my brains in? Rip my arms off? Burst through my chest?"

Marlin pointed to Hutch. "He poked your eyes out like the Three Stooges." He looked at Starsky. "And he pulled your guts out. And then you," he pointed back to Hutch, "slipped in his guts and cracked your skull open on the floor."

"He did, did he?" Starsky asked. "Did he say, 'Nyuck nyuck nyuck' too?"

"Or maybe it was more 'g-nyuck g-nyuck g-nyuck'?" Hutch laughed.

"Good one," said Starsky. He picked up his legal pad and flipped back to the first page. "Let's recap, Marlin. So far you've given us a killer gnome story—"

"A cursed killer gnome ..." Hutch added.

"Right, a cursed killer gnome to explain your missing son, and a fantasy escape sequence when you realized we weren't buying it. Wanna try one more time?"

"I know it sounds crazy, but Gnick really did kill all those cats."

The speaker crackled back to life. *"And a couple dogs. Don't you dare forget about those sweet, innocent doggos!"*

Marlin sighed. "And a couple of dogs. And I don't know why I kept the collars. I'm sure it made sense at the time, but like I said, I've been under a lot of stress lately—"

"From the double shifts and Marlin Junior's cold?" Hutch interrupted.

"Yes."

"What about the bedroom?" Starsky asked.

"The bedroom?"

"You know, marital relations. Any problems there?"

Marlin's cheeks flushed. "That's none of your business!"

"Marlin, your son is missing, and you want us to believe your garden gnome may have killed him." Starsky set his legal pad on the table, then gave Marlin a cold stare. "Right now, *everything* is our business."

Marlin swallowed. "Okay, yes. Rose has been a bit cold lately."

"You sure about that?"

"Yeah, maybe Rose isn't the problem," said Hutch. "Maybe Gnick hit you with a magic impotence curse."

"Wait, can a cursed item put another curse on someone?" asked Starsky. "Wouldn't the two curses cancel each other out?"

"Like a double negative? That's a good question. What do you think, Marlin?"

"I'm not impotent!" Marlin shouted. He took a deep breath. "Rose is just cold. But even if I were, it has nothing to do with this."

"We'll be the judge of that, Marlin."

"Fine. The point is, I've been under a lot of stress, but I'm not crazy. Gnick really did kill those cats." He looked at the mirror. "And the dogs." He looked back at the detectives. "And now I'm afraid he's done something with Marlin Junior, but instead of looking for him, you're in here badgering me. I wish there were some way I could make you believe me!"

"There is, Marlin," Hutch said.

"There is?"

"Sure. Just push that button." He pointed to the table.

In front of Marlin sat a box with a big red button and a sign that said, "Push Me!" Had it been there the whole time? No, surely he'd have noticed a box like that, wouldn't he? Of course, he had been under a lot of stress lately. "Where'd this come from?" he finally asked.

"It doesn't matter where it came from, Marlin," said Hutch. "All that matters is, once you push it, we'll believe you and we'll start looking for Marlin Junior."

"You will?"

"We will."

"Promise?"

"Promise."

Marlin put his hand on the button. "What about Gnick?"

"What about him?" asked Starsky.

"What will happen to him?"

"What do you care? He's a cat killer."

"*And a dog killer.*"

"And you think he may have killed your son," Hutch added. "I'm surprised you're even worried about him."

Marlin looked at Gnick, flipped him off, and pushed the button.

"Are you ready to go?" he asked the officers.

"Ready to go?" asked Starsky. "We're ready to arrest you."

"But I pushed the button," said Marlin. "You said you'd believe me if I pushed the button! You promised!"

"Button? What button?" asked Hutch.

136

"It was right here!" Marlin said, pointing at the empty tabletop. Where was the button? "You said if I pushed it, you'd believe me and we'd start looking for Marlin Junior. So I pushed it. Can we go now?"

The speaker crackled back to life. *"Deus ex machina, Marlin? Really?"*

Marlin looked at the mirror. "What ex what?"

"It means 'god from the machine,'" said Hutch. "It happens when a writer's written himself into a corner, and rather than figure out a way to solve the problem, he intervenes in his own story and—"

The voice on the speaker interrupted. *"It could be a she. The writer could also be a she."*

Hutch rolled his eyes, then continued. "She intervenes in her own story and introduces a miracle to solve the problem."

"It's a real hack move, Marlin," said Starsky.

Marlin had no idea what they were talking about. "I don't understand," he said.

"You were stuck," said Hutch. "You knew we wouldn't believe your cursed killer gnome story. You'd tried fantasizing your way out of your present predicament, but that didn't work either. So, you imagined a button that would magically make us believe you and everything would turn out okay."

"But everything didn't turn out okay. I pushed it and—"

"And? Did we believe you?"

"No! The button didn't work!"

"That's your *deus*, Marlin. Not ours." Starsky stood up.

"It's also strike three. And do you know what happens at strike three?" He paused. "You're out."

Starsky pulled his gun and shot Marlin in the face.

Marlin sat up in bed. His sheets were soaked. He felt his forehead. No bullet hole. "Thank God it was all just a dream," he sighed.

"Oh, it wasn't *all* a dream, Marlin." Gnick threw Marlin Jr.'s bloody binky at Marlin. It bounced off his forehead and landed on his pillow. From across the hall, Rose screamed.

Larry Hinkle is an advertising copywriter living with his wife and two dogs in Rockville, Maryland. When he's not writing stories that scare people into peeing their pants, he writes ads that scare people into buying adult diapers so they're not caught peeing their pants. His work has appeared in *The Horror Zine*, *Red Room Magazine*, *Another Dimension Anthology*, and *Alternate Hilarities 5: One-Star Reviews of the Afterlife*, among others. Feel free to visit him at larryhinkle.com.

The Writing Retreat
By Angelique Fawns

Lorelai threw her printed manuscript into the bonfire and watched as the pages curled and smoldered. A little smile played on her lips. She warmed her hands over the fire and hoped a stray ember didn't light up her frizzy dry hair. Being a bleached blonde came with a cost. The other writers at the week-long retreat had already gone back inside. Mosquitos gnawed at her bare legs as a June bug dive-bombed her ear.

The four of them had arrived almost a week ago, taking the ferry across Lake Erie from Leamington. Elda, the owner/organizer of the retreat, picked them up in a minivan for the fifteen-minute drive to her lakeside home. The idea was to have very little distractions and plenty of quiet writing time. There was no television, no radio, and no landline phone. The renowned Canadian author Anabel Boucher was also up for the week to lead workshops. Her novels had won multiple awards detailing fictionalized accounts of missing women in Northern Ontario.

At the beginning of May, the small island was almost deserted because cottagers and day trippers didn't start visiting until the long weekend at the end of the month. Being the southern-most point in Ontario, the trees were already in bloom and an Alfred Hitchcock-ian amount of birds squawked and filled the blue sky.

Lorelai watched the flames dying in the fire pit and took a deep breath. Her stomach roiled, thinking about her creative direction and writing career. At the workshop yesterday, the other writers had joked how the worst novels were about definitely zombie stories.

Anabel advised, "No one is looking to publish that sort of story right now. Focus on creating work your readers can connect to. Readers respond to truth."

In fact, this group disparaged any genre literature. Lorelai decided not to share that she'd spent the last year writing a guide on how to survive a zombie apocalypse.

Taking the last swallow of her local Pelee Island Chardonnay, she walked back into the cottage. The décor was rustic and comfortable, lots of heavy wood accenting the interior and a big wood stove warming the rooms. Her fellow writers sat on the couch in the living room with Elda and Anabel. Each had a drink in their hands passionately discussing plot points and levels of vulnerability.

Jennifer was the youngest of the group and pretty in a heroin-chic kind of way. She was working on a fiction book based on the use of psychedelics to treat victims suffering from post-traumatic stress disorder. Jack was an older man with a wide girth and even wider smile. He was writing something called "Swimming in International Waters" about money markets. Tammy was sixty-something, yoga-thin and creating a vegan cookbook. Elda wasn't a writer herself but loved painting pictures of hibernating local species which she sold in the Island gift shop.

Plopping into an antique rocking chair, Lorelai tried to check Facebook—cat memes always cheered her up—but it wouldn't load. Sure enough, there were no bars on her cell phone. The house Wi-Fi wasn't working, either.

"This might be taking 'no distractions' too far. Check your phones, would you? I can't get Wi-Fi or reception," she asked the others.

Jennifer offered Lorelai the joint she was holding with the tips of her long purple nails.

"Smoking a bit of this might make you not care."

Lorelai politely declined.

"The reception is spotty here, but I like the feeling of disconnection," Elda said, heading over to the study. "The green light is on, so the router is working."

Jack and Tammy confirmed their phones weren't picking up.

"If we've lost cell service because of aliens, I want to be the first one to get a tour of the ship. I better get some sleep," yawned Jack.

Before he could maneuver out of the deep couch, the lights went out. A collective gasp.

"One minute everyone, don't panic, darkness is wonderful for discovering our true inner selves," Elda stumbled into the kitchen where multiple drawers slammed open and shut.

"Here we go! My emergency drawer with flashlights. Always be prepared. Now we can discover ourselves without tripping," she said, passing out mini flashlights.

Lorelai walked to the back porch windows where the bonfire was still smoldering. Lake Erie lapped gently. It was a gorgeous clear night. Luckily there was a full moon illuminating the sky and keeping them out of pure darkness.

"There's no storm or even any clouds in the sky. Why would the electricity go out? Odd."

Elda stood behind her, "Everyone has a flashlight, except Anabel. She must have slipped back to her room."

The air was cool and crisp, and Lorelai took a deep breath as she followed Elda down the stone path leading from the cottage to the water's edge.

The guest writing instructor was staying in Elda's small boat house on the shoreline. Luckily it had a pull-out couch, small bathroom, and mini kitchen instead of actual boats in it. Elda knocked on the door. No answer. She knocked again, then pushed open the door and confirmed it was empty.

"She's not in the living room, and she's not in her boathouse. Perhaps she is using this opportunity to meditate and search for inspiration for her next book," Elda said.

Lorelai walked in and pushed open the bathroom door. Also empty.

They walked back into the house where the three other writers were amusing themselves telling ghost stories with flashlights under their chins.

"Has anyone seen Anabel?" Lorelai asked.

"She wasn't at dinner today, I had all the lentil soup to myself; as a fellow vegan, we have been sharing the meatless options," Tammy said.

Jennifer was rolling a marijuana cigarette. "I didn't notice she was missing, but it's not like I'm counting heads."

"Maybe she's hooked up with someone. I don't think she goes for nice older guys like me. I bet she is out with a burly workman helping him with his tools," Jack speculated.

"There is nothing we can do about it right now in the dark with no power or cell service; let's go to bed and Anabel will probably turn up in the morning," Lorelai said, heading up to her bedroom.

She gave her hair a quick brush and splashed her face with cold water. Having a pudgy face and curvy figure made her look younger than her thirty years. The loss of electricity and the missing writing instructor had distracted her from her writing crisis. She shouldn't panic; there was still time to launch her writing career. Tammy hadn't started writing till she was fifty and was on her third book. Maybe she could figure out a serious literary idea for a novel in her sleep.

The sun woke her up, and she could hear her fellow writers in the kitchen downstairs. Pulling a sweater on against the chill in the still powerless house, she navigated the stairs and joined the grumbling group.

"Somebody should get Elda up. There's no coffee!" Jennifer said, her blue hair spikes lying flat and disorganized against her head. Tammy and Jack nodded in miserable agreement.

Lorelai looked over at the wood stove where last night's fire was cold ash. She went back upstairs and knocked on Elda's door.

"Elda, are you in there?"

The hostess was normally the first one up, spryly getting the coffee going and toasting bread. Lorelai opened the door and saw Anabel standing beside the bed with Elda still sleeping under the sheets. The writing instructor's hair was wild, her face blood-streaked, and her eyes vacant.

"Anabel! Are you okay?" Lorelai stuttered.

Anabel didn't answer and picked up Elda's arm and took a bite out of it. When the sheet shifted, it was obvious this wasn't her first nibble. The hostess was dead.

Lorelai clamped a hand over her mouth to prevent a scream. Was she actually witnessing a real-life zombie eating the hostess? Hyperventilating and face flushed from adrenaline, she closed the door quietly. She'd spent a year researching this. Don't panic and don't draw attention to yourself. Remove yourself from the scene. Get help.

In her novel, there were resources for her survivors fighting the undead in the city. This was an almost deserted island, and right now there were no phones. No internet. No power. Plus one zombie cannibal. She didn't like how this equation was adding up. Where did Anabel go last night? Was she a zombie, or just feeling a little low on iron? Either way, Lorelai was not attending the workshop planned for this afternoon. Spending a minute calming herself down, the wisest course seemed not to panic the others. She quickly ran down the stairs and sat at the breakfast table with Jack and Jennifer.

"Looks like Elda wants to sleep in," she said casually.

Could they tell she was in a living nightmare? They were both eating cold bread with Nutella and didn't seem to notice that she was sweaty and trying to act calm.

"Jack, didn't you tell me that your cell phone picked up the American towers when you were hiking on Fish Point?" Lorelai asked.

"Yes, I was furious when I saw the roaming fee warning yesterday." Jack said.

Jennifer sipped some of yesterday's cold coffee, "I checked Anabel's boat house, and she's still gone."

"If she is in the arms of a burly hunk, why would she hurry home?" Jack laughed.

Lorelai wanted to distract them from any discussion about Anabel.

"I've always wanted to visit the southernmost point of Ontario. Let's go see if we can piggyback cell service on the Americans," Lorelai said.

It was best to get everyone out of the house before the writing instructor wandered downstairs, looking for more breakfast.

She didn't want to panic, but obviously finding help and getting off this accursed island was priority number one. This scene was suspiciously like some of the pages she had thrown into the flames. Then she noticed there were only two at the table.

"Where's Tammy?"

"Oh, she went to do her morning walk," Jennifer said.

Lorelai considered waiting for the older lady, but haste was prudent. Grabbing sweaters and hats, they climbed into Elda's minivan. The keys were in the ignition—hard to steal a car on such a small island. Driving down the dirt road, Lorelai saw Tammy sitting by the side of the road. She slowed down to pick her up, but noticed Tammy was chewing on one of the large brown rabbits that hopped everywhere. Keep driving. Luckily Jennifer and Jack were in the back seat hunched over their cell phones still looking for service. Lorelai tried to slow her breathing. Hysterically she thought, how's Tammy going to fit that into her vegan recipe book? Rare Road Kill Rabbit? She just had to think of this as research. Maybe her zombie survival novel hadn't been such a dumb idea. Might even be a Best Seller.

Fish Point National Park wasn't far, and they climbed out of the van. The path was clearly marked with a sign, so they walked into the forest on the wood chips lined with white and red trilliums. There were hundreds of birds chirping in the trees. Red-Winged Black birds, Blue-Winged Teals, and Scarlet Tanagers were just a few of the noise makers.

Finally breaking through the woods onto the long stretch of sandy beach, they pulled out their cell phones. The sand came to a long narrow jut, and thirty some odd seagulls scrambled and splashed into the lake as they walked to the furthest point. After a few minutes they looked at each other in dismay. Nothing. No bars.

"Hey, there is someone further down the beach!" Jennifer said.

"I don't like that weird shambling walk. Stay away from him, Jen," Lorelai cautioned.

"Look, we all have PTSD of some sort. That guy probably just needs a hit of acid and a therapist. Besides he might have a working phone," Jennifer threw over her shoulder, quickly trotting off.

"Jen, No!" Lorelai hollered, but it was too late, Jennifer was on a mission.

Lorelai started after her, but then Jack distracted her. He was leaning on an old willow tree that twisted out over the lake.

"I wonder if I could get American service if I got further out on the water? I can see the US Kelley Island from here," Jack said tucking his cell phone into a back pocket and clambering out on the deadwood.

"I'm not sure that's such a wise idea, Jack! It might not hold your weight," Lorelai warned.

He was several meters out when the branch broke with a loud crack and Jack tumbled into the foam-capped waves.

"I can't swim," he yelled as his bald head bobbed up and under the waves.

Lorelai knew the water was freezing this time of year and she wasn't a strong swimmer. Trying to save Jack would be a suicide mission. Both her writing companions were in jeopardy; this was not how to survive! Stay together, don't do anything dumb. In the last few seconds they had broken both rules. She peered down the beach and saw Tammy fall as the shambling man jumped on her. A high-pitched scream came as Tammy tried to fight, but was quickly silenced as ... Lorelai couldn't watch. She looked around desperately for a branch or something to extend to Jack, but his head had already sunk beneath the water. He didn't come back up again.

Lorelai sobbed, "I can't even," as she desperately tried to dial 911 on her cell.

Of course, no service. Calm down, remember those that panic end up dead, or even worse—undead. She had been preparing for this

144

for a year with every page she wrote. She'd researched every zombie novel. Watched every episode of The Walking Dead.

She staggered back down the path, paying no attention to the remarkable wildlife. Maybe this was just on the island? Maybe whatever virus was causing this could be contained? Time to get the first ferry back to the mainland. But then the fact that there was no American or Canadian cell service made her very nervous. And why was there no power? What if Pelee Island was the last place to be affected?

She hopped back into the minivan and drove to the other side of the island to the ferry dock, but the chain link fence was closed. A sign was tacked to the drive-through window.

"Ferry is cancelled until further notice."

A sinking feeling in her gut. This might mean the worst. She parked her car and looked around for someone. Anyone not shambling with a dead-eye stare, that is. There was one guy, a fisherman floating in his boat a few feet off shore. Lorelai walked out on a tourist sight-seeing dock so she was almost beside him.

"Excuse me sir, why is the ferry cancelled?"

"No idea. But haven't seen one all day, and my neighbors have become not so neighborly," he said out of the corner of his mouth around a cigar, as he wound fishing line.

"Do you have a landline or cell service?"

"Nope."

"Are there any doctors or police on the island?"

"Not yet."

Lorelai looked at him in frustration, "I am desperate, sir. Can you take me to Leamington? I can pay you. My friends are all dead. I need to find out what's going on."

He looked up at her and shifted the cigar to the other side of his mouth. He moved his fishing boat to the dock.

"I figure it's safer on the water than on shore. You don't know what's waiting for you back in the big town, but it may be more of these inhospitable zombie folks. Guess I can't float out here forever. Let's go see if Leamington is still standing."

Lorelai clambered off the dock onto his boat and sat down on one of the seats at the stern. Several cases of water, a bunch of beef jerky, cucumbers and tomatoes were visible in the cabin. He tossed her a big rain jacket, and then turned the boat towards the Canadian mainland.

She patted her pocket where her USB memory stick sat safely. She still had her novel saved digitally. The burning of the paper copy had been symbolic. Her story on how to survive a zombie apocalypse might become very relevant. If there were still a New York Times Best Seller List, it could even hit the top. As the boat bumped up and down on the waves of Lake Erie, Lorelai tried to think positively. If they got to Leamington and everybody was a zombie, she wouldn't have to go back to work. There would be plenty of time to finish her novel.

Angelique Fawns is a writer of speculative fiction and has a day job creating TV Promos in Toronto.

"The Writing Retreat" was inspired by an actual retreat where a few things went wrong on a remote island. All the attendees joked about an apocalypse happening on the mainland, and this tale was born.

You can find her work in *Ellery Queen Mystery Magazine*, *The Corona Book of Ghost Stories*, and several additional horror anthologies.

The Haunting of Mr. Mip
by Alex Azar

"I can't take it. I've got to get out of here!" Mr. Mip screams, but
no one is around to hear his words. He fears this home he moved into
three months ago will become his tomb. He runs from front door to
back, even the exit in the basement, but they're all sealed beyond his
ability to escape. "I'm only here for a job. Please, just let me leave."

Back in July, Ray and his wife moved to North Bergen, New
Jersey, also known as the sixth borough of New York, following Ray's
company moving to the Big Apple. Ray doesn't care where he lives as
long as he's with the love of his life, Kate. Unbeknownst to him, his wife
disagrees with that sentiment, and her lover is growing ever more
frustrated at Ray's ignorance. According to Ray and Kate's prenup
agreement, if she were to initiate the divorce proceedings, she'll receive
nothing. However, if he were to begin the process, she'll be entitled to
her half. The prenup was a surprising move by Ray, one Kate never
expected, but was brought on by his father. At the time, Kate truly
believed they'd always be together; then, she started living with Ray.

Kate's lover, Stieg, has grown tired of waiting. No longer willing
to bide his time and let the marriage dissolve naturally, he uses an old
Swedish curse he learned from his grandmother on Ray. The thinking is,
if Ray is in the looney bin, divorce won't even be necessary.

The curse started simple enough: falling books, creaking boards,
false reflections; then things slowly escalated. Ray would feel a hand on
his shoulder while alone in the house, or hear voices from an empty
room. Ray knew things were getting bad when the twenty-four-ounce
steak he bought for himself on his birthday turned moldy in the time it

took for the grill to heat up. Still, he held strong. "It's only a steak. At least I've still got you, my sweet love."

"Yeah, sure, that's great and all, but don't you wonder why these things are happening?" Kate questions, unable to comprehend her husband's acceptance of these obviously unnatural occurrences. "It's not very manly of you, you know."

Hurt by his wife's accusation, Ray feels the need to defend himself, an act he hasn't employed since assuring his father that Kate really was 'the one' on their wedding day. "Aw, don't say that, my love. As long as you're okay, I don't care what happens to me."

Frustrated at things not going her way, Kate abruptly leaves for an impromptu rendezvous with her paramour. Ray wants to protest her leaving for the night, but lets her go without another word. Although they hadn't been intimate for several months, Ray assumed his birthday would be different, but apparently not.

Days later, things have returned to normal, or about as normal as Ray's world would allow. Kate spends more time away from the house than with him; virtually every light flickers whether Ray turns them on or off, the house has nearly become one giant cold spot, and every football game he records is replaced with a Bollywood movie. Despite not being able to turn on the subtitles, Ray has developed an admiration for the beauty of Indian cinema.

With all clothes that go into the washer coming out tie-dyed, even his black socks, Ray has resorted to purchasing new clothes every day. This almost drives him over the edge, but he opts to not make any rash decisions without caffeine. "Large caramel latte, please."

"Cool shirt, Ray. I like the new look."

"Thanks, felt like it was time for a change." Those eight simple words from a cute-ish barista are enough to convince Ray to endure whatever is happening to him and Kate, oblivious to her complicity in the haunting. He walks out of the café feeling like a new man, until an unseen bird shits on his new favorite shirt.

Late one night as Ray is wrapped in a blanket adorned with his and his wife's faces while watching a particularly enthralling dance sequence, he hears Kate come home. "Welcome home, my love. Let me heat up dinner for you, I made chicken parm." Historically, Ray has never been a particularly good cook, but having to fend for himself these past few months he's learned the basics. That's not to say that he hasn't experienced unexplained setbacks during his self-taught training, such as water catching fire, and cracked eggs birthing live chicks, but he persevered and even had a pet chicken for a few days until it inexplicably died in his hands.

"We already ate." He can't be sure, but Ray believes he heard Kate mumble some obscenity under her breath.

None dismayed, his love abounds for his wife. "That's nice. Did you have a good time with the girls?"

Before answering, Kate enters their marital bedroom, a room she hasn't seen for quite some time. Making sure even her dim-witted, weak willed husband understands her words, she forces eye contact by blocking his view of the colorful dancers on screen. "I wasn't with the girls. I was never out with the girls."

Not giving her shocked husband the chance to ask the obvious question, Stieg walks through the doorway. "She was with me. She was always with me, buddy."

"But ... who ...?" With great difficulty and a heavy heart, Ray finally understands. "Oh Kate, but why? Weren't you happy? Weren't we happy? Why?"

"The only times I was happy were the nights I spent with Stieg. As to why, you'll have plenty of time alone in this godforsaken house to figure it out." Tempering her anger and frustration, Kate saves her breath, wasted on any other words and simply grabs her luggage from the closet. Ray pauses the movie while she packs her clothes.

Ray and Stieg exchange a few glances, but the room remains silent but for the sounds of drawers opening and closing. When all was said and done, not much was said, but plenty had transpired.

Kate and Stieg made their way out of the room, but just beyond the doorway they embraced in a long passionate, erotic kiss meant to anger Ray. They leave him to wallow alone as he watches from his seat on the bed through the window as they pack the luggage paid for by Ray, filled with clothes purchased from his salary. All the while, Ray doesn't plea or beg, he doesn't fight or protest, he doesn't raise his voice, in fact he doesn't use his voice at all, he simply sits on their ... no, his bed now, as his eyes wonder to the colorful garments frozen still on screen, wondering how things came to this.

With all lights flickering frantically, Ray turns to the invisible night imp sitting next to him, "I guess it's just you and me, Mr. Mip."

"I told you that's not my name, maggot."

"You also said I wouldn't be able to pronounce your name, so Mr. Mip it is." Unable to stand up for himself against any human that confronts him, Ray doesn't know why he has the strength with this imp.

"Stop calling me that or I'll rot all your food, starving you to death." The imp jumps around the bed, not allowing Ray to rest comfortably to finish the movie.

Rising to his feet, Ray places his hands on his hips, defying the creature. "No, you won't. You said you were summoned to force me to divorce Kate, and if you kill me before I do, you'll be stuck on earth forever, unable to return home. That's how hauntings go, right?"

Mr. Mip doesn't say anything, confirming Ray's assessment. "Now that she's left, I have no reason to actually divorce her, so you might as well get comfortable."

Seeing the flaw in his plan, Mr. Mip resorts to bargaining with Ray. "How about I fix everything wrong here in the home, and hook you up with that barista you like? Will you file for divorce then?"

"No, I don't think I will. But since you're going to be here for a while, you mind making things comfortable for us? Being from Hell and all, you can't like this cold, right?"

"I'm not a demon, you dolt, I told you, I'm an imp, i.e. not from Hell." Mr. Mip looks around the room, contemplating his current circumstance. "Still, it is a bit nippy in here. Guess I can balance things out for now." With that said, warmth enters the room and Ray sheds the blanket.

"See, isn't that better?" Ray stretches wide, shedding the last of the chill in his bones before returning to his spot on the bed. "Ready to finish the ..." He's cut off by the ringing of his cellphone. Checking the caller ID. "Kate, is that you? I forgive you. Come home please."

"Come home? Don't you understand, you sad sack of shit, that will never be my home." Through the phone, she can practically hear Ray's heart break all over again, which she derives a perverse pleasure from. "I'm only calling to tell you that I don't care if you divorce me anymore; I emptied the bank account like I should have done from the beginning. Have a miserable life, you pussy of a man." With all she had to say finished, she ends the call, leaving Ray as devastated as he's ever been.

"Wow, she is one cold hearted bitch. She'd make a great imp." Despite his purpose in Ray's life, Mr. Mip almost feels bad for him.

Focusing on the only thing he can still control, Ray shouts at Mr. Mip, "Hey, that's my wife you're talking about. Watch yourself."

"Are you serious? You're still calling her your wife, after everything she just put you through tonight alone? Not to mention the months of cheating and lying to you, and the fact that her lover, that

Swedish sex god, Stieg, is the one who cursed you with me?" Truly baffled at Ray's complacency, Mr. Mip sees no means of escape from his situation. Then it dawns on him; his torturing has turned into a curse unto him. "I'm starting to think you actually deserve to be haunted. You might learn something from me."

Unable to process his heart ache any further, Ray focuses on the imp before him instead. "Learn from you? You're just as stuck in this situation as I am, you wanna-be-demon. Just let me sleep for once." With that Ray rolls to his side, trying to ignore any forthcoming rebuttal.

Little does he know, his verbal jab has affected Mr. Mip more than he'd suspect, and the imp decides to leave Ray alone for the night. However, he drops the temperature of the room to a chilly 50 degrees. Little victories, he thinks to himself.

The following night, after making and eating dinner with little difficulty, Ray sits down to finish the movie Kate and Stieg interrupted. "What's going on, Mr. Mip? You weren't a complete dick to me today. Everything okay?"

"How do you do it?" Mr. Mip paces the mattress of the bed, walking u-shapes around Ray, "Last night your wife reveals she's been cheating on you, and leaves you for the guy, the guy, might I remind you, that cursed you with a night imp, and here you are less than twenty-four hours later about to watch a Bollywood movie you don't even understand. How are you still in one piece?"

Sitting up in his bed to be eye level with the imp, Ray answers honestly, "If I love her like I say, shouldn't I want her to be happy? Why force her to stay in a one-sided relationship, you know?"

"No, I don't know. I don't get it. You want her to be happy, very chivalrous of you, but you should be angry, you should be furious, you should absolutely hate her, hate her face, hate the thought of her, hell, you should hate anyone with the same name, until you've processed everything. Then you can start the healing process. Because I've been around humans for centuries, and this isn't healthy." Mr. Mip passionately pleads with Ray, jumping on the bed every few words to accentuate his point.

Ray can only shrug his shoulders, "What good is anger? What will hatred actually achieve for me? Besides, I already know they're never going to last."

"Huh?" Mr. Mip stops his pacing and jumping, "How do you know that?"

"Kate hates the Swedish, she's against the idea of IKEA, and gets sick at the thought of Swedish meatballs. No chance they make it through the year." Ray stands up and walks towards the bedroom door. "When they break up, I'll be here for her like I always promised I'll be."

Mr. Mip follows Ray, floating behind him in the air, "Wow, you're a real piece of work, but you're wrong. End of the day, you need to divorce that bitch. And I don't mean so I can be released from my contract. No, this is for you. You two will never be happy together; she made sure of that. Where are you going?"

Descending the stairs, Ray answers without looking back. "I feel like a beer. You want one?"

"Yeah, but all the ones in the fridge are skunked. Sorry." The imp shrugs his shoulder, showing the extent of his remorse.

Ray stops halfway down the stairs, lowering his head. "You know what? You're a real piece of shit, Mr. Mip."

Alex Azar is an award-winning author bred, born, and raised in New Jersey. He had aspirations beyond his humble beginnings, goals that would take him to the skyscrapers of Metropolis and the alleys of Gotham. Alex was going to be a superhero. Then one tragic day, tragedy tragically struck. He remembered he wasn't an orphan and by law would only be able to become a sidekick. Circumstances preventing him from achieving his dream, Alex's mind fractured and he now spends his nights writing about the darkest horrors that plague the recesses of his twisted mind and black heart. His days are filled being the dutiful sidekick the law requires him to be, until he can one day be the hero the world (or at least New Jersey) needs.

Learn more at http://azarrising.com

Lovecraft vs. The Trash Pandas of the Apocalypse
by Lena Ng

A foul odor has pervaded my sleep. What rotting, sulphuric, decaying stink of the nether realms have tainted my dreams? Such odors sparked nightmarish visions of great ghoulish garbage monsters, fetid horrors from the other dimensions, stalking me in the night. Body shivering and heaving until—crash—the sounds of large trashcans overturned yanked me from my restless slumber.

As I glanced out the window to seek the source of the noise, I noticed an unsettling configuration of the stars. While others may read omens in the paper slips of the fortune cookie, the smudged ink of the newspaper horoscope, or the deep frown on spouse/overseer, I can read warnings in the mincing winking of the stars, in the cartwheel of the comets, in the juggling of the moons.

You may think me mad. I, Plymouth Huxley Lovecraft, descendent cousin to the terribly pretentious over-writer HP Lovecraft. I, who instead of basking in the vainglory as an author, despite my glaring talent, decided not to lead the poverty-stricken, debauched, vape-addicted life of a creative, but rather had taken his father's pragmatic advice and became an accountant. I, whose eyes water under the vapors of India Ink and whose head spins under the weight of ledger mathematics, could not envisage such a ghastly tale.

But besides this horrendous stink and bizarre positioning of the stars, other omens unnerved me. A load of lost socks, a slow-draining sink, a worrying growth on the side of my nose. An expanding of my girth, a squint at my books, a cramp in my hairy big toe.

And this accountant especially enjoys his sleep, not to be disturbed by some vile, stomach-scratching creature rooting around in the garbage. I emerged from my room in my too-short robe, and having made haste to the sliding glass door, squinted mine eyes into the backyardian darkness.

And what evil doth I see, but five pairs of ominously glowing eyes staring back at me? Five pairs of eyes and five pairs of delicately long-clawed paws picking through the remnants of discarded egg salad sandwich and crumbs of stale cruller. Black-masked eyes, ferociously fat grey bodies, thick black rings on tails, red velvet capes cloaked coquettishly over shoulders; what evil do they conjure from the depth of my trashcans?

I would not take such insolence from raccoons, these wicked trash pandas from the pain-in-the-nether dimensions. I had battled such creatures before, with chili flakes and fox urine, with flashing lights, with garden hose, with complicated knots on bungee cord. But now, under the samba-ing stars, they again have congregated before me.

I hailed my weapon: my broomstick, my sturdy brother-in-arms, which had fought with me valiantly in the infamous War on Feral Felines. It had stayed loyal during the intense sweeping of the house; it battled bravely against the infernal cobwebs; it flounced away all the malevolent neighbor's leaves which had infiltrated my porch. Extensive training had I on its use and I had felled many a pesky creature—mouse, cockroach, teenager—with a fierce, unrelenting sweep.

Now was a test of its strength. I slid open the sliding glass door with a menacing creak, holding the straw-tipped weapon before me. The black-masked villains squeak-intoned their curses against me. I lunged at the chief raccoon. It reared up and swatted the broom away like a matchstick. I turned my attentions to the smallest raccoon. It twirled a 360 spin and then executed a perfectly formed double Salchow into the trashcan. The remaining raccoons ran circles around me, gesturing obscene signs of black magic with their middle fingers.

With all my strength, I slammed the petrified blackwood of my sweeping implement deep into the metal can's side. Then I reared a foot back and punted the trashcan with the fury of a thousand fireballs into the rummaging horde.

The velvet-cowled raccoons flew into the air, spread their limbs, piked, tucked, and landed into a furry pyramid, hefty chief raccoon at its pinnacle. The trashcan ricocheted against a tree and bounded back onto the porch with a clanging thud.

A phosphorescent glow arose from the base of the spinning trashcan. Pulsing like an overripe pimple, the light was a sickening, vomitous yellow-green, the color of which I had once plucked from the depth of my nostrils. From this glow—portal—came a purple-tainted tentacle. One tentacle, two, then a gross, squirmy eruption of squidish horror.

From nerveless fingers, I dropped the broom. My feet knew better than my brain, and they legged it down the street. Up and down the slumbering street of the suburb, the neighborhood raccoons emerged, from the trees, from the garages, from their nests in the attic. They assembled into a swarming horde. From this ring-tailed mass, no trashcan was safe. Airborne lids, flapping Styrofoam take-out containers, knotty snotty tissues took to the sky.

I ran, but bumping and clanking, bouncing and clanging, the trashcans fell upon their sides and rolled after me. Some flapped their lids in a threatening manner. Others turned end over end in a somersaulting pursuit, purple tentacles flailing about in an angry thrash. They threw themselves at my fleeing body, but I leapt over each missile until I landed gracefully face-first into a bush.

All this noise had not gone unnoticed. Lights turned on in bungalows and backsplits, front doors opened in cottages and manses alike. Sizely neighbors in barely-covering bathrobes, housewives in curlers, arthritic grandpas in diapered onesies hobbled to the door.

"Prepare yourselves," I screamed. "The time is nigh upon us."

The caped coven of raccoons spewed out their spells and—what gibbering horrors!—the mass of strewn trash reassembled into a towering form. They walked the earth, these hulking garbage monsters, swinging arms of soda bottles and dented cans in the air. With one swat and Mrs. Blewett hung by her ankles from the elm tree. Another swipe and Mr. Jensen clung, howling at the moon, to the chimney.

This rampaging refuse would bring about our total annihilation. Such creatures should never stalk the earth. Only a powerful counterspell could save us.

I raced back to my backyard shed, the plywood painstakingly carved with protective rites. With a loose brick, I broke open the lock on the door. There I broke another lock to the steel trunk, then another lock to the lead container. A few more locks on a few more boxes and I exuded a hellish sweat. Finally, I came upon the Apocalyptica, the evil book of evil, one my great-grandfather had warned me never to read unless it was the end of the world. A thin book, really, so small and slim, it could fit into my back pocket.

Pages and pages of spells were laid out before me. Spells deflecting jealous eyes, spells curing fungating toenails, revenge spells against those stealing one's parking spot. Spells to silence barking Pomeranians, spells to finish projects on deadline, reversal spells for spells which had sorely backfired. I flipped through its defiled pictures, most of which resembled old-timey naughty photographs, until I came across the words in large letters:

STOP! USE ONLY IN CASE OF END-OF-THE-WORLD EMERGENCY

After which came words upon words, and words upon words, words over which my tongue tripped ticklingly, and words around which my tongue twisted terribly.

But my voice had not the adequate power. The peeping raccoons snickered behind their garbage-picking paws. Quickly, I gathered the neighbors. I helped Mrs. Blewett down from the tree. I brought Mr. Jensen a ladder. With my broom, I beat down the tentacles entrapping the newspaper boy.

We all joined hands in a circle. We slowly intoned all the words. Our voices rose over the hideous smell. Like giant junkyard hermit crabs, the tentacled garbage cans scuttled around us.

At the end of our incantation, the earth trembled beneath our feet. The tremble turned into a rumble turned into a tremor turned into a quake. From the south of the city, an enormous mushroom cloud of light blew into the sky. An overpowering smell, stronger and stronger, filled with the stomach-cringing odors of kitty litter and coffee grounds, chicken bones and chop suey came towards us.

Stomp.

Stomp.

Stomp.

A huge shadow came over the neighborhood. A blasting roar sounded overhead with sulphuric death breath fouler than Satan's own wind. Feet bigger than garbage trucks, body shaped by rotting cardboard boxes and plastic bags, large as an irradiated dinosaur with gargantuan legs and stick-thin arms. Standing before us, taller than a skyscraper, was a monstrous Garbagezilla. Emerging from the landfill, it stomped on

Mrs. Thomson's petunias. It batted away the chimney tops and felled several trees, leaving fetid footprints on formerly manicured lawns.

The raccoons scurried over this heaving mass, hurling diaper balls and decaying cabbage heads. After they had finished amusing themselves, they jumped away and began to infest the houses. One insolently peeled a shingle from my roof, squeezing its bottom into my attic.

I thought back and realized the mistake we had made. Instead of saying "Hippopotomonstrosesquippedaliophobia," someone had said "Hippopotomonstrosesquippedaliophilia," which was completely wrong and opposite to our intention. So instead of eradicating the trashcan monsters, we'd released a mega-monster.

Alarms blared in the distance. One hundred men in bright yellow vests came into view, some marching on the street, others in large trucks, others in vehicles with long vacuum hoses. An army of garbagemen armed with big plastic bags, hooks, and steel pincers began the attack. They speared and scooped, and filled bag upon bag, but the sheer volume of trash overwhelmed them.

Finally, the garbagemen gave a secret signal, and from the aluminum cans and yesterday's newspapers, they animated a giant recycle monster to do battle with Garbagezilla. The nose-splitting fumes of the clashing monsters rattled my brain.

Other men in uniforms arrived with nets and traps for the raccoons. They chased these wily creatures, but all were too canny to be caught. To aid them, I returned to the pages of the Apocalyptica until a picture of a raccoon with glowing eyes stopped me. The Book of Revelation, Bestiary Edition, explained an alternate apocalypse, one not seen in any holy book or Bible. The conditions of the beastpocalypse must be met for mankind to be dethroned and the animals to rule the earth.

A disturbing alignment of stars. Check.

A raccoon pyramid. Check.

Tentacled deities through garbage pail portals. Check.

Rampaging garbage monsters from the depths of the earth. Check.

One last condition. Massive hurricane called forth from the sky.

I glanced around and saw the velvet-caped raccoons in a colossal formation, bigger than a marching band at the Superbowl half-time show. They squeak-chanted an enchantment. I realized that the power for the fall of man originated in the raccoons. I must remove their magic before they caused the hurricane to drop.

I sought another spell, but a forceful gale snatched the Apocalyptica from my hands. I watched with deflating heart as the book was blown into the sky. Instead of an approaching dawn, the skies darkened. The winds raged around us, stinging red my ears. Mighty elm trees snapped like twigs. Shingles flew from the roofs and I dodged their asphalt anger.

I was caught in the hurricane's fury. Around and around I spun, feet off the ground, higher and higher into the sky. In this spinning vortex, chanting raccoons, barking Pomeranians, Mrs. Blewett, Mr. Jensen, the newspaper boy, yellow-vested men, Garbagezilla in a sleeper hold by Recyclemaw, all were swirling in a reverse drain into space. In the blackness of the cosmos, I felt a Zen-like peace. I floated and thought the end of the world wasn't so bad. But somehow gravity caught me, and I was thrown back to this crazy little place called Earth.

A delicious odor has perfumed my sleep. It seeped me into consciousness, this heavenly aroma of eggshells and orange peels, chicken bones and moldy cat food. I awoke upon a cedar deck. I followed my nose to the fragrance's source. The tempting smells were trapped inside a metal can, bound by an elastic rope. Greedily, I picked at the knots when—

Whap!

A straw-tipped implement hit me full-force upon my head, wielded by a velvet-caped, black-masked beast. As I scurried into the trees, a purple tentacle waved to me from beneath the trashcan's lid.

Lena Ng is from Toronto, Ontario. She has short stories in over two dozen publications including *Amazing Stories*. Her 2019 publications include *Hinnom, Gallows Hill, The Literary Hatchet*, and the anthologies *We Shall Be Monsters, Colp, Beer-Battered Shrimp*, and *The Little Book of Fairy Tales. Under an Autumn Moon is her short story collection*. She is currently seeking a publisher for her novel, *Darkness Beckons*, a Gothic romance.

https://www.amazon.com/Under-Autumn-Moon-Tales-Imagination-ebook/dp/B00O1FMWZ6/

https://www.amazon.com/dp/B082VC26MN

https://zooscape-zine.com/toads-grand-birthday/

Of Blood and Blubber
by Carlton Herzog

I thought I had seen every weird and crazy thing the world had to offer. I once saw a nun stab a priest on Easter. Then there was the blind guy who bit the police horse, the hooker who ate her own shoe, and those two midgets giving each other tattoos. But the wackiest thing I ever did see was that fat old vampire stuck in the motel swimming pool.

I came upon him by accident. I was working on a story about mysterious disappearances in Tulsa, Oklahoma. One day they were there, the next day they weren't, and nobody had a clue as to where they had gone.

I was staying at the Renfield Motel. It was round about midnight. I decided to take a dip in the pool to cool off, the room's air-conditioner being less than up to the task of alleviating the heat and humidity.

As I came around the corner, I saw what appeared to be a giant quivering blob of blubber sitting on the pool's edge. When I came closer, I saw that it was a makeshift man, a hulking gelatinous distortion of humanity rippling with folds and creases and dimples of shiny fat. A small white planet with arms and legs and head perched on the pool edge contemplating I know not what.

The next moment it slid off the patio and into the water, like a baby hippo sliding out of its mother's uterus. It created a mini tsunami that caused the water on the other side of the pool to splash out.

I laughed. It heard me and turned. It had a bloated man's face with a twisted aquiline nose and lips redder than a Kansas City hooker's. It hissed. It bared two long yellow fangs that book-ended double-rows of jagged teeth.

It said, "Come closer and let me get a look at you."

My animal me said, "Keep your distance." But the cerebral me, and the journalistic ambitious me, wanted a closer look at this diabolical oddity. I was like Buridan's ass, not knowing whether to go forward or backward, so I stayed put and just stared.

It smelled of dead fish and open graves.

I could hear it talking again, not into my ears, but into my mind. I was helpless to resist its siren call and walked toward it.

I reached the pool's edge. It lunged and missed. It bounced back and as it did, I saw the shock waves ripple up its blubbery mass.

It lunged again, only this time it tried to drag its massive bulk out of the pool. But those flabby sausage fingers couldn't grip the slick stone. Again, it recoiled into the water, creating yet another tsunami.

I forgot my fear and asked, "How did you get so fat?"

"Every time I fucked your wife, she made me a sandwich."

"My aren't we the clever blood-sucker. Never in my wildest dreams did I think I would run into an actual vampire, let alone one too fat to get out of a pool by himself. You've got more chins than a Chinese phonebook. Should I order you a blubber sandwich with extra butter? When's the last time you looked down and saw your own feet?"

It said, "It's been a while. Even longer for my dick."

I asked, "Why not use your gypsy tricks to do an end run around the blubber and turn into fog or better yet, a bat?"

This time it said, "I'd be too fat to fly; conservation of mass, you know."

The sudden bit of real science puzzled me. I asked, "I always thought the supernatural didn't conform to laws of physics."

It said, "Yes and no. Supernatural is a kind of twisted physics and warped chemistry, and exotic cause and effect that overlap in places with those of the natural world."

"Why did you jump in the pool in first place?"

"I was sweating my ass off. I prefer the ocean, but the last time I went to the beach a walrus tried to do me."

"Makes sense. He saw the fat; he saw the fangs. He must have thought 'close enough.'"

"Don't get cocky. If I ever get out of this pool, I'm going to rip off your arms and beat you to death with the wet ends."

"Step off, Tubby, or I'll ram a stake into your heart."

"The stake hasn't been made that can pierce this swamp of flesh. As for sunlight, I'll sizzle and crackle like bacon, but that's about it. No bursting into flames and then gone in a puff of smoke. Just a low-level grease fire. The downside is all the things living in the folds of my skin. I'm like the Cloverfield monster. Critters are jumping out of me all the time. There goes one now. I can never find Renfield when I need him."

"But seriously, how did you get so fat?"

"Isn't it obvious? No? Nowadays, everybody eats fast food. If I drink the blood of fatties, then I get all the fat and calories, salt, and sugar they do. It's gotten hard to find anybody with a healthy weight. So, between the blood of an obese public and my own candy addiction, I'm doomed."

"Candy addiction?"

"I love sugar more than blood. When the other vampires have their annual virgin slaughter, I can be found cruising the candy aisle at Wal-Mart. Two hundred Snickers bars is just an appetizer."

"If you're too fat to hunt, then how do you catch your prey?"

"The same way I drew you closer: the power of the mind. There are plenty of weak minds addicted to everything from food to sex to social media for me to seduce. You just got lucky in that I need help getting back on dry land. I don't suppose you could call a tow truck?"

"Maybe, but first tell me how you became a vampire."

"Have you heard of Vlad the Impaler?"

"Who hasn't? So, you're Dracula?"

"No. I'm his cousin Freddy, or as I was known back then, Frederick the Staker. Vlad didn't like me because I copied his whole kill 'em and put their head on a stake. So, he impaled me with his spear and my soul went straight to Hell."

"What was that like?"

"The Devil met me at the gate. He said, 'You did good work up there, so I'm going to cut you a break. See those three doors over there? Behind them are three different hells. You get to pick the one you like best.'

"So, we go over and I open Door Number One. There's a mass of people all standing on their heads. It's a wooden floor. I passed. I wanted to see my other options. So, I open Door Number Two. It's the same deal, only the floor is made of concrete. I passed on that one as well."

"We get to Door Number Three. I opened it expecting the worst. But it wasn't half bad. People were milling around drinking coffee and smoking cigarettes. The only problem was that they were standing knee dip in shit."

"Nevertheless, Door Number Three seemed like the best option. So, I stepped inside, closed the door behind me, and got a cup of coffee. I was chatting up a young mountain girl with the most beautiful set of load-bearing hips this side of Transylvania when the devil stuck his head back in and said, 'Okay—break's over. Everybody back on your heads.'"

"So how did you break out of hell?"

"Vlad felt bad about the way he treated me. By now he was a vampire. He put in a good word for me, and I was sent back as a vampire. The Devil has big plans for me."

"If I help you out of the pool, then what's in it for me?"

"You have two choices: become a vampire, my protégé as it were, or be my familiar. Either way, you'll be rich. Remember—I've been around many years and have amassed incredible wealth. The dividends from but a portion of my portfolio would make you wealthy. I could even make a good faith down payment tonight to secure the deal. How does $50,000 dollars sound?"

"You have that kind of cash just lying around your motel room?"

"Even more since I can't bank in daylight. Besides, cold harsh cash greases palms so much more immediately and effectively than the promise of future rewards. I'm in A13. There's a suitcase on the bed with $50,000 in 100-dollar bills. Feel free to count it and when you're done, go find me a ladder."

I didn't need to think it over. I walked over to A13 and pushed open the unlocked door. I walked over to the suitcase, unzipped it, and began fondling he money. I heard a thick German accent coming from inside a closed box: "What do you think you're doing pal? Does Freddy know you're up in his business?"

I put down the cash. I leaned close to the box. The voice spoke again: "Open this contraption up so I can get a good look at you.'"

I opened the door and found myself face to face with Hitler's head—its eyes wide open and staring right at me.

"What's the matter, dipstick? Never seen a disembodied head before?"

"First time for everything. Why is what's left of Adolph Hitler in a box?"

"Long story. Reader's Digest version is that Freddy needed a sidekick. But he wanted one that couldn't run away. So here I am. Why are you in Freddy's room?"

"Freddy can't get out the pool without help, so he's paying me fifty grand to fetch him a ladder."

"I told that fat bastard not to go for a swim! 'Take a cold shower,' I said. But did that lardbelly listen? Of course not."

"Well, you are just a head. I'm sure it's nothing personal. I don't think he's a headist. Got any ideas about where I might find a ladder?"

"A few. I'll show you if you take me with you to look. I've got cabin fever on top of head box fever. This shit would make a monkey crazy."

So, we headed toward the maintenance room. As we passed the pool, Hitler yelled out to Freddy: "Hey Fatback, you're looking a little shriveled. Should we throw you a fish? Would you like that, Seaworld?"

Freddy glared at him from the waterline because the rest of him was submerged like a great lard iceberg.

We went around the corner and ran smack into the hotel manager, Ed Renfield. He looked at me as if he were going to say something, then his eyes met Hitler's. The sound that came of his mouth as he choked on his words was somewhere between a gasp and a belch. He stood there, just staring.

Adolph broke the ocular stalemate. "I'm a talking head, dipshit. Now you have something to tell your kids and grandkids about besides running this fleabag motel. Now get lost before I bite your nose."

Adolph's teeth chattered. Renfield did an about face and without saying a word, walked away in silence.

We found a large extendable ladder. I put Hitler on the pavement. When I began dragging the ladder, Hitler levitated alongside me.

"If you could do that all along, why did you let me carry you?"

"You like to help people, so I let you."

"For a disembodied head, you're a real asshole."

"I wish."

I dragged the ladder to the pool, slid it in, then braced it with my body as Hitler hovered nearby. Fatback tried to climb out, but every time he did, he slid back into the water.

"You should probably get behind him and push."

"Not gonna happen."

This circus act went on for over an hour. During that time, the other motel guests came to watch. Some recorded it on their phones.

Tired of waiting, Hitler said, "there's an easier way to do this."

"What's that?"

"Just leave him in there and sunrise will do the rest."

"That won't do it. Between his blubber and the water around him, he's protected from the sun's rays delivering a mortal blow."

Hitler said, "Then we need to make the water work for rather than against us."

"How?"

"We give Tubby our best one-two punch. First, we turn the pool water into holy water. Second, we make sure he can't get out of the pool when the sun rises. Bang zoom. Our corpulent friend is liquified before our very eyes. After he's out of the way, I give you access to all his cash. The only condition is, you take me with you."

"Fine, but how do we make pool water holy?"

"Easy; our friend here keeps a copy of the ritual with him so he can do to another vampire what we're planning to do to him. It's in the little drawer on the backside of this box."

I opened the drawer and pulled out the paper. I stood beside the pool as two red eyes glared at me from the water line. I recited the short incantation: "O Lord, bless and cleanse this substance that it may be the living water of our salvation. Let it renew our spirit and destroy the armies of hell."

No sooner had I said the magic words, than the pool water began to bubble and froth around Freddy.

Freddy for his part was cursing a blue streak:" I'm gonna get you, Hitler. When I get out of here, I'm gonna have a witch graft your head to a donkey's body."

When the sun finally rose in the east, the pool went from slow cooker to deep fryer, the water rising to a full boil. Freddy went berserk screaming and flailing his arms. He reminded me of a lobster being boiled alive.

We watched as his skin blistered and cracked, then liquified. In less than ten minutes, Freddy had been reduced to a pungent yellow film that steamed on the water's surface. We went to his room, grabbed his valuables, and hit the road.

It's been ten years since that fateful day. Hitler is long gone. I hooked him up with a witch who promised him a new body along with help to kickstart the Fourth Reich. I haven't seen him since. But there do seem to be more hate groups of late.

As for me, I'm living the dream: hookers, coke, the best cars and hotels. Forget hard work, the stock market and the lottery. The road to wealth, for me at least, is paved with blood and blubber.

Carlton Herzog: USAF Veteran; B.A. Rutgers magna cum laude; J.D. Rutgers Law School; Articles Editor, Rutgers Law Review. He publishes non-fiction (see Google Scholar) and fiction—horror, sci fi, fantasy and thriller—see Amazon and Lulu. He is a self-taught artist whose sculptures have graced the cover of *Schlock Webzine* and art shows.

Fun but Not Fatal
by Sylvia Son

"Explain to me this again, why you are doing this?" Stella asked for the fifth time as they sat in the diner waiting for Death.

"We have to start here," Said George.

"Why?" That part still confused Stella.

"It's part of the rules."

"Rules? There are rules? Death needs rules?"

"His name is Roger."

"I don't care. Why are you following his rules?"

George was somehow able to roll his eyes and drink his coffee at the same time.

"It's complicated."

"Complicated? You're in a game with the Grim Reaper; how is that not weird?"

Two hours ago, Stella had gone to George's apartment. She wanted it to be a quiet birthday with George, but the moment she'd pressed the buzzer to his apartment door, it got weird. A bald man dressed in a yellow tracksuit and a black cape threw open the door and pushed past her. Stella had to shield her cake with her arms.

The cloaked man stopped halfway to the elevators and spun around to the door and aimed a finger.

"And don't you forget it!"

George appeared and leaned against the doorway, completely indifferent by the strange man's outburst. "Yeah, yeah."

After his declaration, the man turned back and stomped toward the elevators.

"Hey, Stella," George said casually.

Stella was still speechless.

George pointed at the box. "Is that cake?"

Stella didn't wait for George to invite her in. She drove past him and into the apartment.

"You okay?"

Stella placed the box on the table. "What was that?"

He briefly glanced back. "That? Nothing to concern yourself about." George closed the door behind them.

Before she could even answer, the door swung open and the tracksuit stranger stormed back in, and this time he was actually embarrassed.

"Sorry," he excused himself and swiped at something on the coffee table. "Left my keys." George didn't respond. He just ate his cake. The suit guy stopped and saw Stella standing and staring at him. "I recognize you." He held out his hand. Stella took a step back.

He shrugged, not offended. He eyed George eating cake. "You're eating cake? Oh, you're so going down."

George was nonplussed. "Are you sure about that?"

"The streak ends tonight."

"You say that every year."

Then the stranger did a deep knee lunge. "See that? I wasn't able to do that but this time, I'm more limber and in shape."

George carelessly waved at him. "Yeah, yeah." He took another bite. "Want some?"

The stranger was taken aback by what George did. "Are you nuts? Are you aware of the amount of fat and calories are in that?"

"Uh huh." And to prove something to him, he reached for a slice of pizza and jammed half of it into his mouth.

The stranger shook his head. "You're hopeless. The least you could do is take this seriously. I guess not. For me this will be my year, so I'll see you at the usual spot."

And he just left without a second glance. George didn't react. Stella waited thirty seconds for George to explain himself. After thirty-one seconds, she just exploded.

"What was that?" She pointed at the door.

"That?" George started to do jumping jacks. "Oh, that's nothing. That was just Death." He said it without sarcasm or humor. He was quite serious that that person was Death. Stella just stared and wondered if he was insane because of celebrating his birthday alone.

"What? Are you serious?" George didn't break or laugh. "Did you say Death? As in the scary guy in a cloak and sickle who comes around and takes you when you die?"

"Something like that."

This was worse than she thought. All that isolation from family and friends had made him so delusional that he actually wanted Death in his life. She knew she had to handle this tactfully, or just get straight to the point and use that first-year psych class in university.

She played along. "Why is Death visiting you?"

George shrugged, all nonchalant. "It's nothing really."

Stella wanted to strangle him. "No, I want to know."

"Oh," George was surprised by her insistence. Probably this was the first person to play along with his delusion. "Well, seven years ago on my birthday, I was alone and a little depressed. There was a knock on the door, and there was he was. Death. He came to collect my soul. At first I didn't believe him until he did this trick with my fish which you had to be there to see, and that convinced me. And at that moment I realized I wasn't ready to go, and tried to reason with Death. Appeal to his generous, more compassionate side, and then I realized something."

"What is it?"

George said quite bluntly. "He doesn't have one. He was an unrelenting hardass. I never met a 'man' more inflexible in my whole life, and I worked with Brandon in Supplies."

Stella pinched the bridge of her nose. A headache was flaring up through her eyes. This LARPing was getting out of hand. How was she supposed to deal with this?

"Fortunately, I was able to convince him."

"Really? How?"

"I have my ways."

It was a good thing for George that Stella hadn't been there to see for herself how he had clung to Death's leg, refusing to let go until George could "negotiate." And Death had a hard time shaking him off, which resulted with him shambling down the hall, dragging his leg with George attached to it like a remora.

However, Stella sensed something missing in the story. "You begged, didn't you?"

"No no no. It wasn't like that at all." Stella just stared. "Well. Okay. He may be inflexible, but he does have a weakness for a wager. He seemed bored, so I offered a deal."

"Bored?"

George stopped himself. "Death can get bored."

This LARPing was setting a little thick, but she played along. "So, what was the deal?"

"We race. If he wins I'd go with him, but if I win, he'd let me live."

"A race? That's it? That doesn't sound hard." There had to be a catch.

"Just race? From where? Here to—I don't know, the main floor? Queen Street?"

George shook his head. "It's not like that. It's a 12-hour race that starts at 8:00 a.m. here and finishes at 6:00 p.m. at the Sunset Park, followed by a celebratory steak dinner at the Firkin."

Stella was still confused, especially by the math. "How is it possible to race for ten hours? Won't you get exhausted?"

That's when George paused to respond. "Okay, racing was a little bit of an exaggeration."

"So, you don't race."

"There is racing."

"For ten hours?"

"Can you let me explain?" Not that she really cared, but okay.

"There is racing; well, just the last few minutes where the finish line is placed at the park. The rest of the nine-plus hours is also a game of evading Death before the deadline. During that time frame throughout the city, I have to make sure Death doesn't catch me."

That didn't sound like a marathon race, more like ... "So it's like hide and seek meets tag."

"No it's not." George was offended by the implication. "It's a race."

"Yes it is. It's exactly like hide and seek."

"It's a race."

"Hide and seek."

"Race."

"Whatever," Stella said. This back and forth could go on all day, but she didn't have the energy for it and she assumed he didn't have much time, since she'd checked her watch and it said 7:50 a.m. "So you won. Then why is he still here?"

George scratched his head and smiled weakly. "What can I say? He was sort of a sore loser and he was really pissed off that he lost and forced to honor his end of the deal. It got awkward, especially when it

170

looked like he was going to trash the city. We negotiated something that didn't kill the city."

"So, what happened?"

"I would do this every year on my birthday until he beats me at this, and then takes my soul." Stella just stared.

"Are you following this?"

"No. Honestly I think you and 'Death' ..." she trailed off. She made air quotes with her fingers. "Are you okay with this?"

George shrugged. "It's no biggie. Oddly enough, this is something I am actually good at."

"You are taking this LARPing way too seriously."

George rolled his eyes and went to the fridge and took out two eggs. "You think this is LARPing?"

"No, of course not," she said drily. "You and 'Death' are on the race of a lifetime for the fate of the world and etcetera and whatever."

George cracked the eggs into the glass. "Well, not the world but yeah, it's true." He was quite emphatic.

"Then you and he are both delusional and in serious need of help."

"Really?" He gulped down the glass of eggs down and grimaced. "Ugh, that's nasty. If I was crazy or faking, could I do this?" And he pulled out a large kitchen knife from the lower drawers.

Stella held a hand up and took a step back. "Uh, George, what are you doing?" She panicked; this was the part of the horror movie when he turned the knife on her. She pulled out her pepper spray just as George drove the knife into his neck. "Shit! Oh my God!" She ran to grab the knife and stopped. Not only was George still standing and alive, but no blood was shooting from his neck where the knife was still embedded.

"Pretty cool, huh?"

Stella didn't think so. A knife embedded in George's neck, and all he could do was smile. She wanted to kill him if he wasn't already dying from the knife wound.

"Pull it out!"

George pointed at his neck. "This bothering you?"

"Yes!"

"Oh." He was surprised by her reaction. Then, he casually pulled the knife out and tossed it onto the table. "There. Happy now?"

Happy? Stella wasn't happy; she was freaked out of her skull. "You had a knife in your neck. Why aren't you bleeding all over the floor or dead?"

"I told you."

"You said you're playing hide and seek with Death."

"A race."

"Well that doesn't explain," she waved her hands at the knife and his neck. "That."

"It's my birthday gift from Roger."

"Roger? Death's name is Roger?"

George shrugged. "For one day only, nothing can harm me."

And it hit like a wet slap on the back. That crazy man was really Death, and George was really racing for his life and he was eating cake. She felt like she was going to throw up.

"This is real? Death. A race for your life."

"Yup. You thought I was making it up?"

"Can you blame me?" She examined his neck. There were no marks or even bloodstains. It was as if it never happened.

This was a lot to process. All she'd wanted to do was bring a cake and maybe convince him to go to some pub for lunch, the TK. But this. She wasn't expecting this.

"Hey," he said casually, taking another bite of his cake. "If you're not too busy, you can stick around at the finish and watch me win." He paused and looked at her expectantly. "If you're not too busy; I mean whatever, okay?"

Considering what she had planned, why not? "Sure. Although ..."

"What?"

"What kind of training regimen do you do? Roger looked really prepared."

"Huh?" was George's only response.

"You know. Weights. Aerobics. Yoga. What do you use?"

George shrugged, his face completely blank.

Stella was getting worried. "You are aware that Death came to your place to show you how prepared he was." She couldn't believe she was saying it out loud and to George.

George waved it off. "You're worrying over nothing."

"And you're not taking this seriously at all."

George waved carelessly. "I've been doing this for seven years; you only found out about an hour ago. Watch this." And he bent over to touch his toes. It took a couple of minutes of reaching and grunting, but finally the tip of his index fingers touched the top of his sneakers. "See that?" he bragged. He was quite proud of himself.

"You're doing it wrong. If you're doing this for the first time, you should bend your legs."

"Right," he said quite smugly, then grimaced.

Stella leaned down. "What's wrong?"

"I'm stuck."

"What?"

"I'm stuck! I'm stuck! A little help here."

Stella rushed behind George, grabbed him at the waist and heaved him upright.

"Whoo!" George said.

"Told you."

"Yeah, yeah."

"Aren't you a little bit concerned?" Granted, hubris like that usually deserved a little taking down, but she honestly didn't want George to die like that.

"If I were, do you think I'd let Roger know?"

George explained it as a mental game as well as a physical one. "He gets you here," he poked at Stella's forehead. "And no amount of training will help if you don't believe you can do it. And after seven years I've seen every psychological tactic he's pulled. And this is the first time he's actually getting in shape. I'm impressed."

Then he regaled his greatest hits against Roger—like the year they raced through the elementary school playground. Thirty meters from the finish line, George took a detour through the monkey bars and lucked out. Roger ended up twisted in the bars and tapped out in defeat just so George could untangle his legs.

And then there was the year when Death collapsed from heatstroke halfway thru the race because of an early spring thaw. In the fifth year, Roger was caught in a wave from a snowplow and got buried.

"... And then there was the year he got lost in the subway and he—" he burst into laughter.

Stella shook her head. "You're enjoying this."

George shrugged. "Sure, why not? I race. I win. I get another year to live, and then a free steak dinner. Everyone wins."

It felt awkward just standing there watching George do calisthenics. "I guess I'm sort of keeping you from your training."

George did knee bends. "Naw, and besides, I think you want to see how it ends."

"No, I don't." Yes, she did. Okay, because it was Death. She was curious.

There was a knock on the door, but it opened before George reached the doorknob. Stella almost made a squeak as Roger's head popped up behind the door. "Uh," he said sheepishly. "If you want to bring your girlfriend to watch me win, tell her to bring something to drink and binoculars." He slammed the door before Stella could respond.

Ten seconds of stunned silence later, Stella finally found a proper response to that.

"I'm not his girlfriend!" Not a great response, but better than nothing.

And that was how they ended up in a diner on George's birthday. This was not what Stella expected. She thought it would begin in a football field, or maybe the park across the street. But not this. When George asked her if she wanted to be at the starting line, she thought, why not? Sitting in a booth was not what she expected. Sort of anticlimactic.

"Does that answer your question?" George explained again.

"No, but it's your birthday so if this is what makes you happy ..." She trailed off slightly as if she should remember something important. "Although, if you lose ..."

"Whose side are you on?"

"Yours, of course. But, shouldn't you be off doing your race thing? I have this image of a really pissed-off Death because you made him wait."

"Oh," he said and took another sip as if he was reminded of something mundane. "Don't worry about that. It started twenty-five minutes ago."

Stella jumped from her seat. "What? Why didn't you mention that?" She looked around to see if Death was behind them.

George grabbed her hand and tried to pull her back down to her seat. "You're causing a scene."

She sat down. "Isn't it dangerous to do it so publicly?" George's blank reaction forced her to elaborate. "You know, at a park or gym or something, I don't know, somewhere less public. Why are you acting so casual?"

From behind, the waiter approached with their bill. Stella looked up at the man as he reached over with a slip of paper and to touch George's shoulder. Before she could speak George, without even turning his head, grabbed the man's wrist and deftly judo-flipped him onto his stomach while still holding his arm into a vice lock. George stared down at the man with a smirk.

"George!"

"Hah!" George said. "Thought you could sneak up on me again?" He peeled off the piece of skin along the jaw line.

Stella realized it was a rubber mask, and underneath it was Roger glaring up at them.

"It was worth a try," Roger said.

"Only by that much." George shot back and pinched his finger, then released Roger. "Gotta go. Can you deal with the bill, Stella?" And he ran off before she could even agree.

Death struggled to his feet and followed in the same direction George went. Stella was about to follow, but the real waiter blocked the door, holding the bill up.

Stella promised to remind herself that when she got the chance, she was going to kick George's ass for leaving her to pay.

She had a good mind to ditch those two idiots and wait until Monday to find out the result. She was two steps towards her apartment when she stopped. Part of her couldn't let it go. She wanted to know how it would end. No, she needed to know. She was owed that much. A frustrated growl: "I'm such a schmuck." She turned around and headed for the shopping center to get a gift for that idiot.

Finding a gift for George was harder than Stella thought as she entered her fourth store. This time, a men's clothing store. She riffled through a rack of shirts before it occurred to her that she didn't know his shirt size or color preference. She thought about getting him a CD or movie at the HMV but honestly, she didn't know what he liked. She didn't really know him that well. This was harder than she thought; she should have just gotten a gift card. That's a sad thing, she thought; she wasn't as good a friend as she thought she was.

She walked past a table of ties and Death petting a large black horse and wondered if a tie was an appropriate gift, or would it be too intimate?

She stopped two steps. Hold on. Was that Death and a horse? She rushed back to the table and there he was, standing there with a real live horse.

"Hello?"

She wasn't sure what to say. Death, or Roger, stopped brushing and briefly glanced at her. "Oh, it's you," he said and resumed brushing.

"Yeah, it's me. I thought you were on a race?"

"I was, but I forgot to put my horse in a secure place until it's all over. And I thought this was good enough," he waved at the animal.

Stella doubted a horse wandering about the mall would be safe, hygienic or inconspicuous. "I don't think they'd let you just dump a horse in the middle of menswear."

"Don't worry, Boris here is invisible. Hey, do you know where George is?"

"What? No. If I knew, why would I tell you where he is? You plan to kill him."

Death leaned into her face. "So, you don't know where he is?"

"No."

Roger rolled his eyes and grumbled. "Boy, George was right; you really are no fun."

"What? He said that?"

Roger had the decency to be embarrassed. "Ah, I wasn't supposed to say that." He held up his bare wrist. "Oh, look at the time, I have to go and hunt down the birthday boy; see ya."

With just a 'see ya' and a wave, he jogged out of the front entrance and into the main mall area. Stella looked up at Boris. Boris just snorted back at her.

Next to a rack of dress shirts came a hissing noise.

"Psst."

She looked to her left, and then to her right. There wasn't anything around to make such a noise.

"Psst. Hey Stella."

She heard it again. The source of the sounds seemed to emanate behind a row of jackets. Her hand reached out and parted a navy blue suit jacket and she stared face to face with George.

"Ah! Shit! What the—?"

"Shh." George slapped a hand over her mouth, and she responded by biting it. "Ow!"

Stella spat a couple of times. Yuck. Sweaty palms. "What are you doing here?"

"Hiding, duh." He made a brief glance around the area. Stella smacked him on the shoulder. "Ow! What?"

"Have you been telling stuff about me?"

"Why?"

"Roger said you said I was a killjoy."

"When did he say that?" He ducked under a display table.

"A few seconds ago, right after he left me with horse-sitting duty."

"Where did he go?"

"Does it matter?"

"It does."

"First, I want to know why you told him I was a killjoy."

"It wasn't like that." A glare from Stella showed she wasn't convinced. "Okay, something like that. I may have mentioned that you were a little sort of intense. Can we discuss this later?"

Stella looked over her left shoulder. "He's coming this way."

"Shit!" He ran out of the entrance.

"Sucker," she smirked. Boris rumbled behind her, and she thought he was actually laughing.

With George's gift bought and wrapped up, she decided to wander out to the main area and upstairs to the third level bookstore. So far, Boris remained inconspicuous to everyone as they entered. No one even reacted to the tall black horse standing next to her.

She was flipping through a magazine when Boris gently clamped onto her coat collar with his teeth and pulled her away from the magazine stand.

"Whoa! Wait! Heel! What is it?" To everyone in the store Stella looked like she was lurching dramatically across the floor. He stopped in front of a table of artisan candies. Stella snorted in her head. What kind of bookstore sells candy?

"This?" She pointed at the boxes. "This is what you wanted me to see?"

The horse nodded.

Stella wasn't so sure. Wasn't chocolate bad for a horse? Or was it just dogs who couldn't eat that stuff?

"I'm not sure I should buy this. You might get sick and then I'd have to explain to Death why I almost killed his horse."

Boris snorted and shook his head. Stella thought she was crazy, but she got the feeling that Boris didn't want it for himself.

"Does Roger like this?"

Boris answered with a nod.

"Are you sure?"

Boris nodded again.

She checked the price and almost had a stroke. People pay that much for that? Stella sighed and shook her head. She didn't want to, but she did promise. He'd better appreciate it, she thought miserably. She grabbed the box and went to the cashier.

Satisfied by what she did, Boris rumbled and nuzzled against her back.

Her stomach growled and she checked her watch. 12:30. No wonder she felt hungry. She decided to take a lunch break at the food court downstairs. Two steps out of the bookstore, she collided with Roger and crashed to the floor.

"Jesus! What the hell?" Stella struggled to sit up. "Are you trying to kill me?" She checked that her packages were not dented or crushed.

Roger rubbed the side of his face that Stella's head hit. "I doubt it. It's not May 11, 2042."

"What?"

Death pursed his lips. "Never mind." He pulled himself up to his feet and headed for the exit.

"No wait!" She grabbed onto arm. "You said ..."

"Just drop it!" He sped up his walking.

"But."

"Aht! I'm on the clock, okay?"

"Fine, but after—"

"Yeah, yeah."

Roger stopped and ducked behind a large plant stand. Stella rolled her eyes. Roger briefly popped up a couple of times and then quickly dropped down.

"What—"

Roger poked his head out petulantly "Shh!" he hissed.

Stella shook her head. "He's not here."

"How do I know you're not covering for him?"

"Really?" She grabbed onto his arm and pulled him to his feet and pointed at what Roger was hiding from. "See that? That's just the janitor emptying the garbage."

"Are you sure that's a janitor?"

Stella was surprised by his lack of observation. "Not unless George gained thirty pounds and aged thirty years."

Roger stared. "Oh yeah." Instead of acknowledging Stella was right, his stomach growled.

"Hungry?" Can Death get hungry? What does Death eat? "I'm going to the food court downstairs. Wanna join me?"

Death crossed his arms, looking huffy.

"My treat."

And what a surprise! Roger was standing next to her on the escalators. Stella preferred him to be more subtle and less conspicuous as he craned his head up and down. Finally, he leaned over the escalator railing so deeply he nearly toppled over, and Stella had to yank him back. He was a lot heavier than he looked.

"Would you relax?" Pulling him had almost dragged her over the edge. "And if you keep doing this, you'll attract security."

"So?" Roger said.

"So? They'll drag you into mall jail and I thought you wanted to win."

"Why do you care if I win or lose?"

"I don't, but with my luck I'll get dragged in with you." She dragged him forcefully by the arm and pushed him not so gently onto a nearby chair. "Now you sit here. Aht!" She held out a hand into his face as soon as he tried to move up.

"Sit! Heel! Stay! Good boy." She mentally cringed when she realized she'd just ordered Death as if he were a dog. But since Roger didn't seem overly offended, he sat there quite obediently. "Now I'll get us both a pizza slice. You like pizza?"

"I guess," he said noncommittedly.

"Good, I'll be back. Don't move."

It was quicker than she thought when she returned with a tray of two cheese pizza slices and two cans of Pepsi. She stopped two feet from the table to see a man talking to Death about something, and holding out a pamphlet. She couldn't hear, but as soon as he held out an empty box, she realized he was asking for a donation. Roger responded by reaching up and poking him on the forehead and the man collapsed on the ground.

"What did you do that for? Is he dead?"

Roger shrugged. "Only for a couple of hours; after that he'll wake up."

"You can't kill him."

"Why not?"

"Not in front of witnesses."

"What witnesses?" Stella looked around. Everyone in the food court, from diners to food court workers, were all on the ground. Possibly dead.

"This better wear off."

"It will. I'm not a monster."

She didn't want to argue about this. She dropped the tray on the table. Roger didn't wait for Stella to sit. He immediately grabbed his slice and wolfed it down in two minutes. He grabbed his can and popped it open with one finger and guzzled it in four gulps. "I'm done!" he said. He slammed the can down. He got up from his seat.

"Wait! You can't run soon after eating. You'll develop cramps."

"I think that's for swimming."

"Whatever." Roger looked at the gift-wrapped box on the floor. "What's that?"

"This? Oh, a shirt for George if he makes it to the end. Wait. Before you leave, explain to me why you have to do this. Not that I want to see George dead, but all this seems ..."

"Dark? Weird? Bizarre?"

"No," Stella added. "Stupid."

"You wouldn't understand," he said.

"Try me."

"It's a man thing."

"Try again."

Roger sighed. "It's not easy to explain. Eight years ago, George was moody and depressed, and I was bored and needed a change. Then, after George's ridiculous begging, I came up with the game."

"I thought—never mind. Just like that?"

"Sure. Why not?"

"Doesn't sound like fun."

"Are you kidding? This is the highlight of my year."

Stella cell phone went off in her purse, and she checked the display and saw she had a text message. "Hold on," she said to Roger. "I got a text from George." She pressed a couple of buttons and read the message and rolled her eyes. "That doesn't sound so lyrical."

"What?"

"Roses are red. Violets are pink. It's taking you this long. You sure do stink. Oh, and are you enjoying your pizza?"

Death leapt to his feet and looked around the food court. So far, everyone was dead on the ground. "Where is he?" A whistle; he looked up, and George was on the second floor of the mall waving at him.

"Excuse me, gotta go." Roger ran off.

As he disappeared up the escalators, Stella heard a groan and a man on the floor next to her table sat up.

"Did something happen?"

Stella didn't bother to justify that response.

5:55 pm. Sunset Park.

Stella felt like an idiot sitting on a picnic table all by herself with the shirt and chocolate by her leg, and it was freezing. She checked her watch for the twentieth time. Shouldn't they be here by now? This was not worth freezing her butt off. She looked at Boris. If she left right now, was she supposed to take the horse with her?

"Is this supposed to take this long?'

Boris rooted around the snow.

"That's not helpful."

It was faint at first, but growing and coming from behind her. She turned around and saw the two of them running, and she could have sworn there was screaming or roaring. Stella held up her binoculars. She could see George was ahead, running and straining himself, while Death seemed to be catching up. No no no no. This was not good at all. George was going to lose and be taken by Death!

"Come on George!" she screamed. She looked through the binoculars again. Death was now less than five meters away from George. Then three. Now two. Roger's hand was reaching out at the back of George's shirt. His fingers were inches away when he fell. George kept on running and crossed the finish line, which was a garbage can with a flag taped to the side.

"I win!" George gasped. "The streak lives on."

"No fair. I demand a redo. The ground was bumpy."

"No way. I won fair and square. I get to live for another year and have a steak dinner." He ran up to Stella. "Well?"

Stella turned to Roger. "By the way, can he still feel pain?"

Roger shrugged. "My birthday gift covers life-threatening injuries."

"Oh good." Then Stella hit George in the back of his head.

"Ow! That hurts!"

Stella didn't stop. She unleashed a flurry of smacks hitting him on the head and shoulder.

"Quit it!" George said.

181

"No! That's for dragging me into something so stupid and wasting my time. And this is for nearly scaring me to death. No offense," she said to Roger.

"None taken," Roger said. Actually, he seemed to enjoy watching George get what he deserved.

"Will you stop hitting me?"

"No. I was worried you were not going to finish at all."

"Thanks for having such faith in me."

"You're welcome, and happy birthday. No, seriously. Those last few meters you were struggling."

"Whatever," he said.

"You should consider proper marathon training next time."

"I won; that's got to count."

"You were lucky."

"Luck. Skill. It's all the same. So, steak dinner?" he said directly to Roger.

"Sure."

"Don't forget, Roger. You're paying."

It was kind of weird for Stella to sit at a table at the Fox and the Firkin with George at one end of the table eating a steak and Death on the other side working on his salmon, as if the last several hours hadn't happened. George and Roger catching up since the last time they met. It was very surreal.

"Oh, I almost forgot." Stella bent down and pulled out of her bag and held out the chocolates to Roger. She rolled her eyes at her blank expression. "It's not poison."

Roger looked into the bag. "This is my favorite."

"Boris helped."

"I don't know what to say." Roger almost looked touched by the gesture.

"How about 'Thank you'?"

"Thanks."

George snorted. "Wow this is getting a little too sappy for me." He got up from his seat and excused himself to go to the bathroom.

As soon as George walked through the bathroom doors, Stella spoke first. "I saw you."

Roger had been inches away from touching George. And just as Roger was that close to tagging George, he had performed the worst stage fall ever.

"You tripped on purpose."

"Yup." He delicately placed a small forkful of meat into his mouth. He didn't even bother to act flustered or deny it.

"Why?"

"I could have won the last three times. But to answer your question—why? And let all this end?"

In a weird way, that made sense. Two lonely people found an odd way to bond over competitive hide and seek.

"Couldn't you have attended a baseball game like normal people?"

"Where would be the fun in that? Anyways, it's a bro thing. You wouldn't understand."

Stella would have gagged right there, but that would have been a waste of the chicken she was eating. Roger looked out the window. "I better to check to see if Boris is all right."

"Hey." George had somehow timed it just right. As soon he sat down, Roger was getting up. "Where's Roger going?"

"He went out to check on Boris."

George shrugged and continued eating.

"Are you still going to make Roger pay for this?"

George shrugged.

"You should be nicer to Roger. He let you win."

George didn't stop eating but paused slightly without looking up at her. "I know."

Sylvia Son's fiction has appeared in magazines like *ELEMENTS* and *Green's Magazine* and online with *Defenestration* and *Polar Borealis* and a novella about a man being haunted by a ghost cat until he hosts a cat funeral that made the shortlist for the Ken Klonsky 2014 Novella Contest for Quattro Books.

Dating For Deities
by Diane Arrelle

Baobab stared at the computer screen for about half an hour, which was about five weeks in human time. She just couldn't take her eyes off the large words that had popped up.

LONELY?

Sick and Tired of being sick and tired? Want to fill some of those empty decades with something rewarding and meaningful? Want to get it on with a sexy and compatible deity?

Then this is your lucky day!

Just press the subscribe button below to get started.

She stared some more. "I am feeling a little lonely," she muttered. "And I'd love to finally meet up with someone different." Then she laughed. She never ever ended up with someone different. Whatever name, Mixcoatl, Lenus, or Horus, he always managed to get back into her good graces.

"Well, not this time!" she said with feeling. "I'm going to meet me a new god!" She quickly clicked the button on the bottom of her screen, and then religiously answered all two thousand questions. After what felt like an eternity, except it wasn't, because Baobab really knew what an eternity was, she clicked 'send' and leaned back to wait.

She daydreamed about who she could possibly meet that was new. There were so many gods and goddesses around here because the Earth had once been the be all-end all for immortals looking for some meaning in their existence. Seriously, she couldn't have met everyone yet, could she?

Sure, she realized that their numbers had diminished in the last two thousand years as many of the immortals, having lost followers, moved on to other worlds, other galaxies, other dimensions. But the ones that stayed, well, they stayed because they liked it here. After all, there had been so many gods in the beginning, so many primitives looking to pray to the sun, the stars, the weather, the trees, even the air. The immortal's choices had seemed endless. When a religion slowly died off, it was replaced by a new one and the immortals would just switch it up and become another deity. It had been such fun when the world celebrated animism and polytheism. Like oops, your worshipers became extinct one day, oh well, move on. Be an African god one millennium, an Egyptian god another, then dabble with the other continents. Yes, life had been good in the old days.

She frowned and shifted in her seat. The memories she had tucked away awoke, and she remembered how she always ended up with him. He was like her poison, and she his. Every time they saw each other they would hook up. Man, she really loved him when he was Thor; oh, that long blond hair and that perfect six pack, not to mention the violent thunderstorms when they made love. She smiled despite herself. He had been just so cool!

She recalled one of her all-time favorite affairs with him. It had been so much fun. She was Persephone, and he'd kidnapped her. Oh, she'd been really pissed because she had sworn off ever seeing him again. She'd been sure she wouldn't have to anymore, what with him being condemned to the underworld. But he kidnapped her, and she had to spend all the time that remained to the Greek gods living part-time in the underworld. The fact that he was Hades was just the icing on the cake. He gave new meaning to the phrase hot as Hell. They'd set off quite a few volcanos and earthquakes during that era.

Baobab's computer dinged and she pushed memories of him out of her mind. She was going after something much different this time. She wanted an immortal who was fun in as well as out of the bed, without the help of the endless vineyards like when he was Bacchus. She wanted romance, and maybe even a little male worship.

She read the pages of fine print, and finally clicked to the page with her list of prospective dates and sighed. The list she'd been given was short, and she knew four of the five. They were okay, but no one to worship. The fifth, well that was a different story. She knew he had to be a deity to be on the list, and not anyone from the mortal realm, but his name was Bob. What kind of god called themselves Bob?

She drank some of her stash of nectar and picked at a bowl of ambrosia until she finally decided she was procrastinating. She typed: Hi Bob. I'm Baobab. I am amazed we have never met, but this dating service seems to feel that we should.

She hardly waited a minute when she got an answer. Hi, back at you, Baobab. Guess you were once an African Tree Goddess, huh. Still being worshiped?

A rush like a soft electric current started at her head and travel through her entire body until it hit her toes. Baobab suddenly felt like a teenager. No matter how long she lived, she still loved that tingle whenever she was faced with possible love. She didn't even think; she just started typing, saying the words out loud as she pressed the keys. "No not at the moment, but I certainly can use a little adoration in my life about now. As I'm sure you know, down times are tough on the ego. So tell me about yourself; why are you calling yourself Bob?"

Well, like you said, down times are tough after you spend millions of years being worshiped. I hesitate to add, and I hope you won't think less of me, but I haven't been in a meaningful relationship for well over a hundred years. I'm lonely and I lost my one true love over a silly squabble. As far as being known as Bob, and this is really scraping bottom here, some humans saw a portable toilet glowing one night and decided it was a divine message. They've been worshipping it for about a year now. They keep waiting for it to glow again, but it won't because back a year ago a bunch of kids dropped about 50 glow sticks down the opening. So, since I was bored and feeling sorry for myself ... well you know ... it was a job. They have two hundred members in the Church Of Bob and although it is a shitty gig, it is kind of satisfying.

She started laughing. Golden tears trailed down her cheeks, and she was shaking so hard she couldn't write back. Wow, she thought. I haven't laughed like this since I was with him.

A message popped up. Hey, Baobab, you still there? TMI?

Still laughing, Baobab started typing, giggling out the words. "Yeah, I'm still here. Sorry, I just started laughing. Thanks, I needed that. Well, at least you're working; I've been out of steady work for a couple hundred years. Every time I found some work, like being a tree goddess, missionaries came and ruined the whole thing. Say, this has been fun and it's been almost a hundred and fifty years since my last date. Don't think me too bold, but do you want to meet?"

Sure do! Today? How about we meet on the mortal plane and see if we can find each other? That's always a fun game. Then we can grab something to eat among the humans. Philadelphia, historic district, in an hour?

She watched the words crawl on the screen and smiled. Hide and seek was always her favorite game.

An hour later, Baobab was walking around Independence Hall. She was a teen-aged boy, tattooed and pierced, with a guitar slung across his back. She even added a scattering of acne, just for authenticity. She watched the crowd. They all looked so mortal. Humans rushing around living out their lives, having no idea that the gods walked among them for fun. After her third rotation around the building, the Liberty Bell, and the park, she sighed with exasperation. Bob was nowhere in sight and she wondered if he were coming at all, or if it was some cruel joke.

"Once more around the blocks and then back home," she muttered and started to walk forward. She felt a tap on her shoulder and spun around. She gasped in shock.

"Found you first," he laughed. "But then, I always did."

"You...? You're Bob?" she asked, trying to decide whether to be furious, disappointed or surprisingly happy. "Well, then, you were cheating! You knew who I was and what to look for. You know my aura."

He laughed and she drank in the sound, realizing how very much she had missed him. "Well now, I guess I did cheat a little, but how else was I going to get you in a place where you won't have a temper tantrum and cause a tsunami?"

She stamped her foot and the wind suddenly whipped up into a frenzy, then immediately died down as she smiled back at him. "I guess this is unavoidable, isn't it? There is no one else for us but us?"

"Yeah, and seriously, I think these little breaks give us a big break from each other. Forever is just such a long time to be with the one you love."

She nodded, knowing he was right. The last fight they'd had, and it was a blow out, caused fires and earthquakes all over the world. The only good that came out of that fiasco was that the more primitive humans who were affected by the climate disruptions started praying to the old gods again, which made a lot of the immortals happy. She shrugged off that memory, but she knew there were so many memories like that. Their first lovers' battle had caused Vesuvius to erupt and destroyed Pompeii. They hadn't spoken for almost two hundred years that time. She started grinning and she saw him staring at her with a puzzled expression. Oh, but the three centuries we spent making up were divine, she thought, but said nothing to him.

"Let's get a coffee," she said, and started walking. "You know, pretend we are humans."

"Only if you change out of that awful disguise," he said and reached to take her hand.

The tingle was even better this time; she clasped his hand and they walked. "Ever wonder why we have such an effect on this world when we break up?" she asked. "Do the others cause this much damage?"

"I know the stronger couples do. I know we are one of the strongest couplings. That's why no one dates us when we are apart."

"Hmmmm... I have an idea," she said. "Why don't we call a meeting of the remaining immortals and I'll tell you about it? But I gotta ask, is the Bob worship real?"

He squeezed her hand and nodded yes.

Baobab stood before her fellow immortals and said, "I know this world is getting boring; not much need for us. Look at Bob over there; he is a porta-potty deity! This race, these humans, who used to need us, don't need anyone anymore, not even each other. This place is crawling with hate, with pollution, and they are killing their world. I think that as their gods, we owe it to them to hasten the ultimate demise of their societies, to end their destruction of the air, the earth and the seas. If they continue this way there will be no one left, no living world left, and we will all have to move on."

A question rang out, "What do you suggest?"

Bob stood next to her and said, "An end of the world as we know it. Kill the modern age and bring back the simple life to humans. The physical Earth will be saved, and we will all be needed again."

Murmurs echoed throughout the chamber. "And how will we do this?" someone called out.

Another voice: "We are their gods; we can't purposely wipe out most of the human race, even if they are killing the world. What are you proposing?"

"Really?" another deity called. "As I recall, human annihilation was always good sport."

Bob and Baobab held hands and smiled at their fellow immortals.

"I say we all have a prolonged getaway on the mortal plane and make love like only gods can. That should take care of all the problems, work those fault lines, reshape the earth, and we all get to know each other again," Bob called out.

The old Greek and Roman gods perked up. "An orgy!"

Cheers resounded and everyone left to prepare.

Bob and Baobab stayed behind. They were a bit tired because they had already tested their theory, and California had finally fallen into the ocean. "This is a genius idea, darling," he said. "I'm all for loving our problems away and we always do better together when we are both working. Besides, it's time for me to find another gig; I really don't enjoy being the toilet god at all."

She nodded, "Well, then, let's go get ready to screw this old world back into shape. The humans will thank us. They always do."

Dina Leacock, writing under the name **Diane Arrelle**, has sold more than 250 short stories and has three published books including *Just A Drop In The Cup*, a collection of short-short stories, and a collection of horror stories, *Seasons On The Dark Side*.

She is proud to be one of the founding members as well as past president of The Garden State Horror Writers and is also past president of the Philadelphia Writers' Conference as well as a current board member.

Retired from being director of a municipal senior citizen center, she is now co-owner of a small publishing company, Jersey Pines Ink LLC. She recently edited the horror anthology *Crypt Gnats* for Jersey Pines Ink. The book was released in October 2019.

She resides with her husband and her new cat on the edge of the New Jersey Pine Barrens (home of the Jersey Devil).

www.arrellewrites.com Facebook: Diane Arrelle

Four Fab Physicists
by Henry Herz

"Nothing's gonna change my world," the song ended.

"Ladies and gentleman, that was the Fab Four!" Polite applause broke out. The band members bowed from the waist, waved, and exited the stage. John and George slung their Gibson guitars over their backs. Paul hefted his Höfner bass. Andy carried only his sticks, since the drum set belonged to the drummer of the next band.

The four sauntered out of the building, joined by John's girlfriend, Yoko, as they crossed Abbey Road. The flickering neon sign of the not-so-subliminal Don't Pass Me By pub beckoned; a silent siren's song for the sober.

The five squeezed into a small wooden booth, worn by use. Several types of smoke swirled. "First round's on me, mates," John offered. "We're getting better, don't you think?"

"Aye," replied Paul. "Many thanks, Andy, for filling in on drums on such short notice."

"Any time, mate. How Pete managed to shock himself on a soundboard is beyond me."

"Five pints of Bass, luv," John told the barmaid.

"Man, I'm knackered," said Paul.

"Me too," agreed George. "We've been burning the candle at both ends, working at the Uni and playing gigs at night."

"Working? Physicists just sit around on their bums thinking," joked Andy. "Only engineers actually work."

"Oh, go bugger off," John replied with a grin.

The barmaid arrived with five mugs balanced on a round tray. She expertly distributed the ale and glided to the next booth after winking at Paul.

"You guys have to choose," said Yoko. "You can't be scientists and musicians."

"We've been over this before, luv," replied John. "Music's in our souls. It's gives our lives meaning. But there isn't a steady paycheck in it. And we studied long to earn our doctorates. We don't want that to all go to waste. If our current experiment's successful, we'll earn tenure. We'd finally have financial stability."

Paul chuckled.

"Why's that funny?"

"Not that. Do you think anyone will ever figure out that 'Fab Four' refers to our Fusion Acoustic Barrier experiment?"

"Doubtful," George replied. "Most people aren't familiar with how fusion reactors work. They don't know that inertial confinement isn't efficient, or that magnetic confinement is more promising. And they'll certainly not have heard of our Wall of Sound device. No one else uses hyper-focused sound waves to compress and heat reactor fuel."

Yoko scowled. "Maybe you should focus more on getting your experiment to work."

She's gonna' break up the band, thought George. "Next round's on me," he offered to lighten the mood.

The following morning, the Fab Four, hung over and sleep-deprived, calibrated their acoustic equipment in the University's fusion lab. "Wall of Sound, Test 27," called John. "Starting in three, two, one, mark!"

Sensors monitored the sound waves' ability to focus the miniature fusion reaction so it wouldn't sputter or rage out of control. "Results tracking normal," reported George.

Yoko strolled into the lab. "I brought tea and scones."

John smiled. "I was gagging for a cuppa, luv. You're an angel."

Paul scowled, but not at John's lovesick language. "Look at this. We've got anomalous readings. Signal strength's bouncing all over the place. It read nominal until Yoko walked in."

"Surely you're not suggesting she's causing the spiking," John replied.

Paul shrugged. Andy checked the equipment. "The settings and wiring are correct."

"Humor me," said Paul. Yoko gave an exaggerated sigh, but left the room and walked down the hallway. "The signal's normal again. George, do us a favor and go fetch Yoko."

The two returned. "Bloody hell!" said Paul. "Shut it down, Andy. Then meet us when you're done in Conference Room 2B."

Paul, George, and Yoko sat at the oval conference table. John paced. On the verge of tears, Yoko asked, "What's wrong with me?"

George scratched his head. "I wish I knew."

"This could have severe health implications," said John, putting an arm around her shoulders. "We need to figure out what's causing this straight away."

"Yes, yes, of course," replied George. "But we lack the proper diagnostic equipment. Unfortunately, it's quite pricey and we've no budget left."

Paul added, "We're also running out of time. Either we complete our FAB experiments within a fortnight, or we lose this chance for tenure. Our years of hard work will be for naught. I'm so tired of pinching pennies."

John glared at Paul. George stared at the floor. No one made eye contact with Yoko.

George's face brightened. "Let me try something." He dialed the conference room phone. "Hello, Mrs. Rigby. This is Dr. Harrison." After dispensing with the social pleasantries required to lubricate the wheels of academia, he requested an appointment with the physics department chair.

George smiled, thanked the ever-efficient Mrs. Rigby, and hung up. "Good news. Dr. Koschmider has an opening right now. While I'm off, someone ask Andy how quickly he could configure the diagnostic equipment."

"I'll do it," volunteered Yoko.

George entered the conference room wearing a sour expression. "No luck?" asked Paul.

"None. The parsimonious prick wouldn't part with a penny, nor even agree to us borrowing the equipment from the computer science department."

The conference room phone rang. Paul answered it. The blood drained from his face. "Quick, follow me!" Paul sprinted to the lab with John and George on his heels.

Andy lay unconscious behind a control console. Yoko knelt beside him. "I called emergency services. I think he may have been shocked while disconnecting the wiring. But at least he's stable, poor dear."

"Yoko, please go with him to the hospital," said John. "George, Paul, come with me."

The three strode down the checkerboard linoleum hallways toward their office. "John, I know you were keeping up a brave front for Yoko's sake," said George. "But we desperately need to earn tenure. Paul's about to lose his flat, and the only reason I'm not is that I'm living with my parents. Even so, I'm thousands in debt. And I don't see how we can help Yoko in time without the proper equipment."

"Or without an engineer," Paul added. "We have to choose, John. I can't earn a living based solely on my charm and good looks."

"It's not a choice for me," replied John. "Yoko's my muse. And it's her health, maybe even her life, at stake! I'll leave the band if that's what it takes to save her."

George and Paul exchanged a long look and sighed. "Well, you have been a more prolific song writer with Yoko around," admitted George.

"And who needs a steady paycheck anyway?" Paul asked rhetorically.

"Yeah. All you need is love, man," George agreed.

"Thanks, mates. Let's put our heads together. We could try to earn some quick cash playing extra gigs."

"Without a drummer?" Paul asked.

"I've got friends in the engineering department," said George. "Maybe one of them's a drummer too. I'll make enquiries immediately."

John shook his head and leaned against an oscilloscope. "Ah, George, I've always said you're a dreamer. On another note, what if we borrowed the diagnostic equipment from the computer science lads?"

"Ooh, I like it. We'd be physicist pirates!" said Paul. "We could nick ... er, borrow it late tonight. Then we'd unborrow it when we're done."

"Gentlemen, we have a plan."

"How's Andy doing?" John asked Yoko over dinner in his flat.

"As well as can be expected. But the doctor said he must stay in bed for a week. What's my prognosis? I had my first migraine ever today."

Damn! thought John. But he said, "I'm optimistic. We're gonna get the equipment we need tonight. You're cordially invited to the lab at 11 am tomorrow for some delightful diagnostics. And George hit the jackpot with the engineering department. He found not one but two chaps who're amenable. And they both play drums! Apparently that's common among engineers. Anyway, their names are Jimmy and Ringo. We've asked Jimmy to configure the new equipment first thing in the morning."

"Ringo? That's an unusual name."

"Yes it is, but his last name is Starr. Now that's a cracking stage name!"

"Well, you're my star, John. I can't tell you how grateful I am that you're sacrificing tenure to save me."

"How could I not? You're the love of my life."

Yoko arrived at the physics lab promptly at 11 am. She kissed John. "How are my heroes doing?"

"Last night's extracurricular activities went well," replied Paul with a wink.

"Fantastic." Yoko turned to the new man. "You must be Jimmy."

"Pleased to meet you," replied Jimmy. "We're all set. Would you sit over here?"

"Wall of Sound, Test 28," called John. "Starting in three, two, one, mark!"

"Jesus! Look at that," said Jimmy.

"Wait, it gets more bizarre," replied John. "Yoko, would you please walk out of the lab and then come back." The acoustic signature returned to normal, then spiked when Yoko returned.

"I've never seen anything like it!" exclaimed Jimmy.

"Exactly," John replied. "Let's fire up the diagnostics and figure out what's cocking up the signal."

Three hours and three pots of Assam black tea later, Jimmy pushed his chair back from the display console and stretched. "Are you seeing what I'm seeing?"

"Bloody hell," said Paul.

"Will somebody please tell me what those odd images mean?" Yoko asked.

Jimmy glanced at John, who nodded. "These things that look like tiny silver beetles seem to be, for lack of a better label, microscopic demons circulating in your bloodstream. They emit a powerful signal in the same frequency as our experiment. That's what's mucking up the Wall of Sound."

"Demons! How is that possible? Are they affecting me?"

"They seem to be interacting with your nervous system, but we can't yet tell to what extent. We don't know how immediate the health threat is, nor how easily they might infect other people."

"You lads need to get those demons out of me!"

George pointed at the blackboard. "Well, there's good news and bad news. The good news is that if we modify the Wall of Sound to generate harmonic oscillation in the demons, we can neutralize the little buggers. The bad news is that our 500-watt tube amplifier is far too weak. Our calculations indicate that we'd need at least a 25-kilowatt amp. And the Uni doesn't have anything that powerful."

"Hold me tight."

John hugged Yoko. Her shoulders quivered. "We'll think of something, luv."

George picked up the lab phone. "Maybe if Koschmider sees this for himself, he'll free up a few quid." George called Mrs. Rigby and worked his silver-tongued magic. He hung up the phone and smiled. "Koschmider's on his way down now."

Bruno Koschmider stood with his mouth agape. Eventually, he regained composure and control of his jaw. "I wouldn't have believed it if I hadn't seen it for myself."

"Yoko, would you please excuse us," asked John. "Uni business and all that."

"Understood. I'll wait in your office."

George pointed at the blackboard. "So you see, Dr. Koschmider, in order to cure Yoko, and anyone else who might be similarly affected, we need at least a 25-kilowatt amplifier. This is a medical emergency! Can you release some funding?"

Koschmider nodded. "I'll go check the budget right now."

As Jimmy escorted the department chair out of the lab, his gaze fell on the signal monitor. His brow furrowed. "Thank you for your time, Dr. Koschmider."

Jimmy closed the door. "Did any of you notice the signal levels?"

George nodded. "They were the same as yesterday."

"Yes," replied Andy. "Even after Yoko left the room. But they're nominal now. Therefore..."

"Koschmider's infected too!"

"Bloody hell."

Jimmy sighed and stood. "I'll go get Yoko."

John, Paul, and George disconnected the diagnostic equipment, loaded it on a cart, and covered it with a tarp. They rolled the cart down the hallway to the creaky old elevator, which descended to the second floor. Approaching their office, they overheard heard Yoko conversing with Jimmy. Just as they entered the room, a blue-white bolt shot from Yoko's outstretched arm, striking Jimmy. He flew backward and crumpled to the floor.

"What in God's name ..."

Yoko turned to face the newcomers. "Oh, hi guys."

"What did you do to Jimmy?"

"We were just chatting. Why?"

"Look!"

Yoko turned back. "Oh, no! He must have been shocked by the wiring."

"Just like Andy, eh?" Paul rushed to Jimmy's side. George called Emergency Services.

"What's Paul talking about?" asked Yoko. John stared into her eyes. They betrayed no sense of guilt or deception. The faint smell of ozone lingered in the air.

"Umm, nothing, luv. Would you do me a big favor? I left my briefcase at home with some important calculations in it. Could you fetch it while we take care of Jimmy?" Yoko nodded and headed down the hallway.

John rushed to Jimmy's side. "How's he doing?"

"About the same as Andy. Why'd you have her leave?"

"I know her as well as I know myself. I sensed no lie in her denial."

"But we all saw what happened!"

A polite knock interrupted John's response. "Oh, please come in Mrs. Rigby."

"Dr. Harrison. Dr. McCartney. Dr. Lennon. I'm afraid I'm the bearer of bad news. Dr. Koschmider said that this year's budget has been fully allocated. He won't have more funds for months."

"I see," said John through tight lips. "Thank you for letting us know." Mrs. Rigby departed.

John turned. "It's all too much coincidence. I think the demons control their host's behavior without the host's knowledge. Yoko shocked Jimmy, and probably Andy and Pete now that I consider it. Yet she credibly denies the evidence of my own eyes. Koschmider's also infected and he hasn't helped us."

"But he's always been a wanker," Paul replied.

"The demons must recognize that our Wall of Sound represents a threat," said John. "So, they've undermined our progress at every turn. They've disabled our engineer three times and blocked our access to the proper equipment twice. I have no idea what they're doing to Yoko or what their intentions are. That scares the shite out of me."

George and Paul rocked back in their chairs. "And we still need to get our hands on a 25-kilowatt amp."

John paced. Then his gaze fell on an advertising flyer pinned to the office cork board. His mouth formed the beginning of a grin. "Perhaps we should pursue musical rather than academic careers after all."

"What?"

John pointed at the flyer. "There's a battle of the bands tomorrow night—at the Liverpool Philharmonic Hall. That's a posh venue, so they'll have world-class amps! But we'll need to modify the Wall of Sound design to accommodate the higher power level."

"Right." George fired up the teapot. Paul erased the blackboard.

Two hours later, John stretched his arms over his head. "Well, I think that's it. I double-checked Paul's math, and the calculations look correct."

Paul snorted. "Of course they're right."

"Hang on. Aren't you forgetting something?" asked George. "How can we play in a battle of the bands when we never signed up?"

"Good point," replied John. "An obvious and apparently insuperable obstacle." He pushed his long hair out of his face and sighed.

"I'm feeling peckish," said Paul. "Let's go to the cafeteria for a bite and to clear our heads."

What the University cafeteria lacked in quality, it made up for in proximity. George picked at his alleged chana masala. Demonstrating gustatory bravery bordering on the reckless, John and Paul raced to wolf down their fish and chips. "Slow down, you two," George urged.

Paul eyed his dessert with suspicion. He tasted a forkful of his bread pudding and grimaced. "Hello, who's that?" he asked, pointing over John's shoulder. When John turned to look, Paul swapped his bread pudding for John's apple pie and took a bite. "Mmmm. Scrummy."

"You're a cheeky one, aren't you? Reminds me of Yoko. If we get different flavor scones, she always eats half of hers and then swaps with me. It drives me mad. But her idiosyncrasies also make her so endearing." He smiled. She really is the love of my life, he thought. We've got to save her. Wait a minute. Swap? "That's it!"

"What's it?"

"We swap with one of the other bands. The flyer listed the contestants. I read that Johnny and the Moondogs will be there. Remember attending secondary school with them? They always used Johnny's rusty old van to transport their instruments to gigs. What if right before the concert their van inexplicably suffered four flat tires?"

"You're a bad boy."

"We'll buy him new tires afterward."

"Clever, if dodgy," said Paul. "But you're forgetting that we need an engineer to configure the new design. We'll also need a drummer if we do manage to get on stage."

"Well, we know someone who fills both requirements. And he's a real Starr," said George.

"Have you heard him play?" asked Paul. "He's not exactly best drummer in Liverpool."

"He won't even be the best drummer in the Fab Four," joked John. "But necessity is the mother of invention."

It's certainly a mother, thought George.

Ringo spent all day modifying the Wall of Sound to meet the new specifications. "Our equipment and instruments are too bulky for us to drive my car," John noted.

"Well, then you'll borrow a Uni flatbed lorry," replied Paul.

The final incarnation of the Fab Four loaded the flatbed. It rumbled down Blue Jay Way. Five minutes later, John turned left at Blackbird Street, and parked a hundred meters from the home of the lead singer for Johnny and the Moondogs.

"Okay, Ringo. You're up," said Paul.

"Keep the engine running," said Ringo. "I'll be back." He hopped out and hurried down the street with a knit cap pulled far down on his head and both hands stuffed in his coat pockets.

George sat in the cab with John and Paul. "Christ! This boy is sweating like a pig."

Ringo approached the Moondogs' van. He peered into the rear window to confirm their instruments were already loaded. He checked the street for traffic. Hustling around the van's perimeter, he squirted fast-setting glue into each keyhole.

"I told him to do that," said Paul. "Less obvious than four flat tires. And they won't be able to transfer their instruments to another vehicle."

His sabotage completed, Ringo sprinted to the flatbed and jumped in. "Go! Go! Go!" John sped down the street.

The Fab Four picked up Yoko at her flat on Penny Lane and drove to the Philharmonic. "Let them know the Moondogs are here, John," Paul said. "We'll unload."

Paul, Yoko, George, and Ringo untied their musical instruments, mixer, monitors, and Wall of Sound equipment. The last item proved the heaviest. "If we lift all together now, we can carry that weight," Paul directed. They heaved the Wall of Sound onto a dolly and rolled it backstage.

When the previous act finished, Ringo connected the Wall of Sound to the hall's infrastructure. George peeked through the curtains at an audience many times larger and far more nicely dressed than was typical for the Fab Four.

The evening rushed by in a blur. Johnny and the Moondogs played Hey Jude and While My Guitar Gently Weeps. The crowd roared with enthusiasm, completely unaware of the harmonic oscillations created by the Wall of Sound.

To their astonishment, at the end of the battle, "Johnny and the Moondogs" won first place and a £5,000 prize. As the gobsmacked physicists hurried to load their lorry and depart before the real Moondogs arrived, a middle-aged man in a suit and tie introduced himself as Brian Epstein. Epstein explained that he ran a music shop and offered to manage the group. "And I know a producer at EMI I'm confident would want to work with you lads." Needless to say, the evening ended in a blurry mixture of celebration and inebriation.

The next morning, after the hangovers wore off and the caffeine kicked in, the Fab Four brought Yoko to their lab. Ringo set up the diagnostic machine. Within minutes, a big grin spread across his face. "Tell me what you see," he said. The others hunched over the display.

"No sign of demons!"

"Do you know what else we achieved last night?" asked John. "We don't need tenure. We can follow our dream of being full-time musicians!" He hugged Yoko.

"Though we do need a new band name," replied Paul. "How about The Beatles?" he asked with a grin. "After all, we never would've won the prize without those little silver beetles."

"Clever," replied George. "We've gotta invite Koschmider to our next concert. And we still don't know who else may have demons in their blood. So we should go on tour to cure as many people as possible."

"Agreed. I guess our world's changed quite a bit after all," John noted.

And indeed, the world of music was never the same.

Author's Note

The musician names in this story are supplemented by the following Beatles Easter eggs, listed in order of appearance.

1. "Nothing's gonna change my world" is a line from the Beatles song, "Across the Universe."
2. The Beatles were known as the Fab Four, although "Fab" was short for "fabulous", not Fusion Acoustic Barrier.
3. Like the fictional band, Spinal Tap, the Beatles went through a succession of drummers, including Pete Best, Andy White, and Jimmy Nicol, before finally settling on Ringo Starr. Unlike Spinal Tap, drummers for the Beatles didn't explode.
4. Abbey Road is the name of a Beatles album.
5. "Don't Pass Me By" is the name of a Beatles song.
6. "Getting Better" is the name of a Beatles song.
7. She's gonna' break up the band—Many Beatles fans believe Yoko played a role in the eventual dissolution of the band.
8. The Wall of Sound was Beatles producer Phil Spector's name for a music production approach.
9. "I Feel Fine" is the name of a Beatles song.
10. "Something" is the name of a Beatles song.
11. "Eleanor Rigby" is the name of a Beatles song.
12. I've always said you're a dreamer— "You may say I'm a dreamer" is a lyric from John Lennon's song, "Imagine."

13. We'd be physicist pirates!" said Paul—Paul McCartney played a pirate in the movie Pirates of the Caribbean: Dead Men Tell No Tales.
14. "Yes It Is" is the name of a Beatles song.
15. "I Will" is the name of a Beatles song.
16. "Wait" is the name of a Beatles song.
17. Silver Beetles was one of the Beatles' prior band names.
18. "Hold Me Tight" is the name of a Beatles song.
19. "I've Got a Feeling" is the name of a Beatles song.
20. Bruno Koschmider was a Hamburg music club owner with whom the Beatles had a contentious relationship.
21. "Help" is the name of a Beatles song.
22. "And I Love Her" is the name of a Beatles song.
23. "All You Need Is Love" is the name of a Beatles song.
24. "I'm So Tired" is the name of a Beatles song.
25. "It's All Too Much" is the name of a Beatles song.
26. "Ask Me Why" is the name of a Beatles song.
27. "Slow Down" is the name of a Beatles song.
28. Johnny and the Moondogs was one of the Beatles' prior band names.
29. "Bad Boy" is the name of a Beatles song.
30. He won't even be the best drummer in the Fab Four— "Ringo isn't the best drummer in the world. He isn't even the best drummer in the Beatles," is a line famously if inaccurately attributed to John Lennon.
31. "Drive My Car" is the name of a Beatles song.
32. "Blue Jay Way" is the name of a Beatles song.
33. "Blackbird" is the name of a Beatles song.
34. "I'll Be Back" is the name of a Beatles song.
35. "This Boy" is the name of a Beatles song.
36. "Penny Lane" is the name of a Beatles song.
37. "All Together Now" is the name of a Beatles song.
38. "Carry That Weight" is the name of a Beatles song.
39. Brian Epstein was the Beatles' band manager.
40. "Tell Me What You See" is the name of a Beatles song.

Henry Herz edited the dark fantasy anthology *Beyond the Pale,* featuring short stories by award-winning and *New York Times* bestselling authors Saladin Ahmed, Peter S. Beagle, Heather Brewer, Jim Butcher, Rachel Caine, Kami Garcia, Nancy Holder, Gillian Philip & Jane Yolen.

He participates in literature panels at a variety of conventions, including San Diego Comic-Con and WonderCon.

Henry also writes fiction and creative nonfiction for children. His most recent books are *The Magic Spatula* (with Sam Zien, Month9Books, 2020) and *I am Smoke* (Tilbury House, 2021).

www.ingramcontent.com/pod-product-compliance
Lightning Source LLC
Chambersburg PA
CBHW070502260626
47161CB00004B/1418